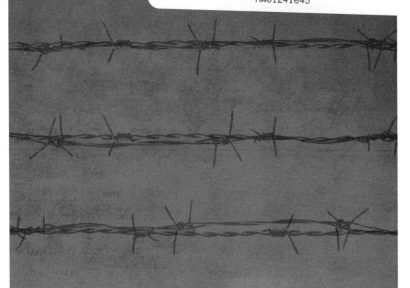

MY ENEMY
MY LOVE

A NOVEL

DAVID FIEDLER

My Enemy, My Love
A novel by David Fiedler

First printing 2011

Fiedler, David W. 1971-
My Enemy, My Love
First edition

ISBN 978-0-9830225-1-0

Published in the United States of America by D. W. Fiedler LLC
Printed by Sheridan Books, Inc. Ann Arbor, Michigan

Cover design and layout by Kate Huffman

For Norma Jacob -
Thanks for your continued
support and interest in
the POW story. Getting to
know you through your
connection to the Enemy
Among us and the
Eckingarten camp was a
true highlight for me.
Best to you always -
David Fredh
(2/20...

MY ENEMY

MY LOVE

My Enemy, My Love

Chapter 1

"So can I stay longer? It'd just be another three weeks."

It was August 1940 and Stefan Biermann's final trip to the States was coming rapidly to a close. He had been there to study the pricing strategy of grain futures on the Chicago Board of Trade. This research exchange was a nifty perk arranged between the University of Chicago and Germany's Heidelberg Universität, where he was a professor. Not only had the program paid for his travel, meals and lodging in the States, but also continued his professor's salary the whole time.

"I want to make the most of this last trip to America," Stefan told Dr. Hutchins, shifting nervously from one foot to the other as he stood in front of the man's desk late one afternoon earlier in the week. Hutchins was the faculty sponsor for the research program, responsible for coordinating details of his visa.

Over the last five years, Stefan had made several such visits to the United States. But this would be the last, he knew. The American government had already announced the end of the program, thanks to Germany's invasion of Poland the previous fall.

Hutchins said nothing, just remained hunched over his desk, peering at a large blotter full of notes to be used in his next lecture. Finally he glanced up.

"Three weeks, eh? What the hell for?"

"Drive to Los Angeles," said Stefan, looking at his shoes. He ground his toe back and forth on one spot on the floor as he spoke. "Route 66 the whole way."

At the mention of Route 66, Hutchins's head snapped up from his work. His eyes focused on Stefan and he chewed on his pencil. The road had been paved end-to-end just two years before, the first direct route across the United States.

"I've always wanted to do that," proclaimed Hutchins, displaying a previously unseen burst of enthusiasm and emotion. He turned and looked out the window as his voice trailed off, pencil now turning slowly in his fingers. Then, he looked back at Biermann.

"Of course you can go," he said. "Sounds fantastic." Hutchins paused. "But what are you going to do for a car? Maybe I can help you there too."

Stefan couldn't have been more surprised at this than if Hutchins had declared that FDR and Bing Crosby would be riding along, too.

"What's the matter?" snapped Hutchins, seeing the surprised look on Stefan's face. "You better say yes before I change my mind. If my wife and my work allowed such adventures, I'd do it in a second. But that shouldn't stop you. Just send me a postcard now and then along the way."

And so here sat Stefan on a park bench, Hutchins's loaner Chevy tucked against the curb behind him, waiting to carry him away. The sun finally peeking over the horizon told him it was time to go. So with little more than a map, his battered suitcase, and a carton of smokes, Stefan climbed into the car and set off.

※

Stefan made pretty good time those first couple of days, stopping only when he wanted to stretch his legs or look around. Once he got past St. Louis and its plodding drivers clogging the streets, Stefan figured he'd have smooth sailing all the way to Tulsa and Oklahoma City.

He was far out in the country, over a hundred miles past St. Louis, when suddenly the number of vehicles on the highway grew. He had been zipping along on the open road, only an occasional car to meet or pass, when without warning the traffic grew thick and he found himself clogged in a jam that stretched as far as he could see.

"Verdammt," Stefan muttered. He raised himself higher in his seat and peered over the windshield of the convertible, trying to figure out what was going on. It made no sense. It was noon on a Thursday and here he was, out in the middle of nowhere, surrounded by cars and trucks crawling along on the choked two-lane highway.

"Was zum Teufel?" He scowled and beat his thumbs impatiently on the wheel. He was befuddled by the traffic and already tired of breathing other people's exhaust. At this rate, he would be late getting in to Oklahoma City tonight, if he made it at all.

"I'm stopping," Stefan said to no one in particular. He needed gas and something to eat and hoped that the clog on the road might loosen in the meantime.

Soon a gravel parking lot presented itself on the right. It was attached to a diner slumped at the edge of a small town. A faded wooden sign with peeling white paint stood in some weeds beside the highway. "Welcome to Waynesville. Home of the Future."

Stefan eased in, turning past rows of dusty cars whose drivers apparently had the same idea. He climbed out of the car and ambled around the front of the restaurant. Opening the door, he found to his dismay that the diner was just as jammed as the highway.

"Damn," muttered Stefan again. He was about to turn and go, when an old farmer perched on a stool by the door wiped his mouth and stood. Stefan slid in quick to grab the man's seat at the counter.

"Get ya something?" asked the waitress, smacking her gum, already pouring him a coffee. She slid him a menu and started reciting the day's specials.

"I'll need a few minutes," said Stefan. As the waitress disappeared to help other customers, he frowned thoughtfully at the menu, finally settling on an open-faced roast beef sandwich.

"Know what ya want?" she asked, back again.

"Roast beef. What's with all the people?"

She laughed at little in response. His question, and the accent that still lingered at the edges of his words, told her that Stefan was an outsider.

"Well, the government's puttin' up a big new army post right down the road," she said, wiping the stray crumbs off the counter in front of Stefan. "Forty thousand acres. Got things all kinds of crazy. Used to be real quiet here, but now it's like someone done drug us off the porch and set our underpants on fire."

Ah, the war, thought Stefan. Even out here you still couldn't get away from the effects of the damned thing. It was coming, sure as a dark storm looming on the horizon on a hot summer night.

"Don't know if they've got a name for it yet, but it's gonna be a big place," said the waitress.

"Fort Leonard Wood," said a woman sitting on the next stool drinking a cup of coffee. She had paused mid-sip, and Stefan couldn't believe he hadn't noticed her earlier. Perhaps in her mid-twenties, she was strikingly beautiful with dark hair and dark eyes. An empty plate sat in front of her. "That's what they're calling it."

"Leonard Wood?" said the waitress, frowning. "What kind of name is that?"

"He was a general in the war, a Harvard doctor," she replied, sipping her coffee delicately. "Served as chief of staff for the army."

"How 'bout that," declared the waitress. She had no more helpful commentary to add.

"It's going to be a training post for new recruits," said the dark-haired woman, turning to look at Stefan. "Opens in the fall. They're putting up roads and buildings as fast as they can. That clog on the road is due to the project. It's construction workers, government men, job seekers and your garden-variety rubberneckers."

Stefan laughed. "It sounds like you know something about it."

"Not much more than what's been in the papers." She looked at him and smiled. "What's your name?"

"Biermann. Stefan Biermann."

She held out her hand in greeting. Her grip was soft yet firm.

"Nice to meet you, Stefan Biermann. I'm Katherine." She was direct, self-assured. "I hear an accent. Where are you from?"

"Germany. How about you?"

She smiled, shrugged.

"No place exciting like that. I'm pretty much from here," replied the woman, though her manner and appearance made it obvious that she had not just stumbled out of the woods. "What brings you all the way to Waynesville?"

"Just passing through. On my way to Los Angeles."

"California? Oh, wow. What takes you there?"

"Nothing particular," replied Stefan. "Just the opportunity to travel and I wanted to take advantage of it while I still could."

She smiled again and stood.

"Sounds like a smart idea," she said. Both knew that war between their countries was a very real possibility. She fished in her purse for a couple of bucks and paid her bill.

"Have a wonderful trip," she said, turning to him once more as she tucked her pocketbook under her arm. "Maybe I'll see you again."

"Hope so," replied Stefan. He paused to take a sip of coffee but before he knew it she was out the door, the stool beside him empty. A man in denim work clothes who smelled like sawdust came and took the woman's place. Stefan closed his eyes and tried to capture her lovely face. He hadn't seen beauty like that in a long time.

"The name Lorberg probably doesn't mean anything to you, does it?" said the waitress.

"Pardon?" said Stefan, eyes flapping open again.

"That woman you were talking to. Lorberg is her name. Katherine Lorberg. Her daddy is Walt Lorberg. He's the reason this big army post is being put in here."

"Are you talking about Walter Lorberg, the senator?"

"Who else?" She paused, frowning at the German. "You've heard of him?"

"Sure. He's the reason I was able to come to the United States," explained Stefan, amazed at the coincidence. "I'm a professor, and Senator Lorberg sponsored the academic exchange program that brought me over."

"A professor?" the waitress seemed impressed. She eyed him up and down. "What do you teach?"

"I'm an agricultural economist."

"Hmm," said the waitress, trying futilely to come up with something thoughtful in response. She raised her eyebrows, gave up and retreated to the familiar. "More coffee?"

Stefan smiled, shook his head wistfully. He wished he had known the woman's story. She might have enjoyed hearing the connection they shared.

Ten minutes later, he had finished lunch. He plunked down a couple of bucks and, still thinking about Katherine Lorberg, gave the waitress a wave and headed for the car, ready to continue his trip to Oklahoma and beyond. Sliding in behind the seat of the roadster, he fired up the engine and eased slowly into the still-heavy traffic without a backward glance.

Chapter 2

Lorberg Farms and Orchards in Augusta, Missouri, carried an unpretentious name, one that hardly reflected the size and scope of the operation. Even its faded old logo—sunrise over a hill, broad yellow beams falling on green fields dotted with chickens and cattle—wasn't going to impress anyone not already familiar with it.

Walter Lorberg was barely 20 when he started farming in 1906 with one old mule, a falling down barn and 40 acres of rich Missouri River bottomland inherited from his granddad. Thirty years later, through a combination of hard work and good luck, the farm now spread over 8,000 acres. There Lorberg and his family cultivated corn, tobacco, apples, watermelon, sorghum and livestock, including several hundred hogs and a thousand head of cattle.

"Hello, Mr. Wade," said Walter, greeting his neighbor down at the Dandy Donut one morning in early 1940. "How are things with you and Stella?"

"Thank you, Walter. We're doing great," replied his neighbor. He sat at the counter, wearing faded overalls and old work boots adorned with dried manure. The waitress refilled his cup with steaming hot coffee, and he blew on it before taking another sip.

"What kind of tinkering are you doing these days?" asked the elderly man. His farm sat on rich ground adjacent to the Lorberg's place and he was always interested in what Walter had going.

"You know, lately I've been reading a bit about soybeans in some of the ag journals. No one around here has ever done much with them, but they're saying you can get all sorts of things from them—oil, poultry feed, a bunch of stuff."

"Well," said Mr. Wade, "I'll be danged." Walter always seemed to have his

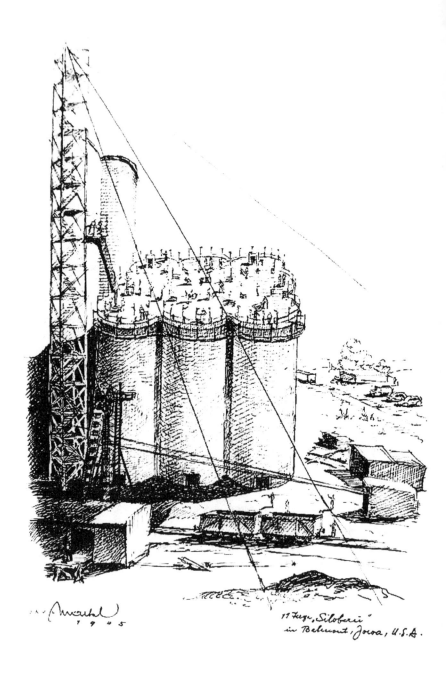

finger on the pulse of agricultural advances, and Stanford Wade knew that he was probably on to something here, too.

"Yep, they say from a 60-pound bushel of soybeans, you can get 48 pounds of protein-rich meal and 11 pounds of oil. It's the most interesting thing," he said. "I'm going to give it a whirl on those 40 acres next to you. You want to try it too, all you'll have to pay for is the seed. The equipment will be there, and I'll be glad to put it in for you."

"I'll think about it," said Mr. Wade. "Sounds interesting for sure."

Another man might want to keep this sort of golden goose for himself, to hold the secret and squeeze as much money out of it as possible before anyone else had the chance to jump in. Walt Lorberg was just the opposite. He gladly shared what he saw, telling his neighbors all about it, encouraging them to benefit from his research if they thought it sounded good.

That philosophy had proven itself again and again. Not only did it make the farm very profitable, but it also produced an enormous reservoir of goodwill in the grateful and admiring people around him. This ultimately paid off in Walt's election to the legislature, where he served 20 years as a state representative in Jefferson City plus three terms in D.C.

But it wasn't really honest to call Walt Lorberg a true farmer any more. Now in his sixties, political work precluded much involvement in the day-to-day operations of the farm. It was really run by Walt's three kids—John, Michael and Katherine. John, age 30, was the oldest. Michael and Katherine followed him each two years apart. All college graduates, together they managed the business and financials of the massive enterprise.

Over time Walt's focus had become more external, for his strength was in his salesmanship. These days, he was far more effective making the rounds in the capitol in Jefferson City and in Washington, D.C. than he was trying to run a tractor or overseeing the farmhands.

Occasionally one of Walt's can't-miss schemes backfired, but the winners far outpaced the duds. And soybeans would turn out to be one of those successes, punctuated by a moment in 1940 when Henry Ford took an ax handle to a car trunk made with soybean plastic to demonstrate its durability. The publicity increased the public's awareness of uses for soybeans and drove a tenfold increase in demand, making a lot of money for farmers such as Stanford Wade who had listened to Walt Lorberg. Sometimes, though, this generosity seemed excessive to his kids.

"Dad, why'd you say we'd plant soybeans for the Wades?" John asked his father one day after dinner. He paced back and forth on the front porch of the big white house, watching the last few farmhands drift in from the fields.

Their house sat on one edge of a large courtyard, a space as big as a football field that marked the heart of the property. Massive barns loomed three and four stories on the opposite side, while the tower of a grain elevator vaulted even higher, standing proudly above the half-dozen silos clustered around it. Several sprawling machine sheds ringed the perimeter, parked full with enough equipment to humble just about any implement dealer in the state.

"Not only is this going to mean a bunch of extra work for us," John continued, "but why do you have to be so quick to tell everyone all about it? This promised to be our biggest money maker for the next five years, at least."

"Think about it over the long run," said Walt. The older man was enjoying a fat cigar and a glass of bourbon as the twilight set in. "Stanford Wade's never gonna be in a position to compete with us or produce enough to drive down the price."

He puffed on the cigar, sending a cloud of blue smoke up toward the ceiling fan that turned lazily overhead.

"Here's what's going to happen. He'll grow some beans, but not enough to make it worth hauling to St. Louis or Kansas City. So he'll sell them to us and take in a little money. Then we'll roll it in with ours and make a few bucks off it too."

He took a sip of the whiskey and looked at John over the edge of his glass.

"But you know how this is really going to help us? Old Stanford Wade will only be farming for another couple, three years at most. Then he'll be looking to sell most of his land, including those 240 acres on the northwest corner of our ground. And do you know who he'll come talk to first?"

John didn't need to answer that question. He watched as Gus Davis, the main farmhand, came in from the fields with the last few men. He gave them a wave from the other side of the huge courtyard, then disappeared into the office from which he oversaw the workers.

Davis had worked for the Lorbergs as long as anyone could remember. He was probably close to 70, though no one, Gus included, really knew for sure. He had been hired on by Walter's granddad at age 12 and had been with them ever since.

"That's right. Ol' Stanford'll come to us," Walter continued. "That's good land and we'll pay him a fair price. Be able to add a bit more to our ground without getting into a bidding war."

John nodded. He knew his father was right. He looked inside to where his wife, Susan, helped wash the dinner dishes. Little Ellen, their 18-month-old daughter, sat in her wooden high chair joyfully banging a spoon on the tray.

"Need help with the dishes?" John stood quickly and started for the kitchen before his father could resume his soliloquy. He knew his dad was right, but still wished that he'd have kept their project to himself, just for once.

𝕏

Katherine Lorberg thought of all that was waiting for her back home as she returned from Fort Leonard Wood, her black Ford sedan chasing the curves of the narrow two-lane blacktop that led to the farm. She was the youngest of the three Lorberg children raised by Walter and Caroline, and the only girl. Like her brothers, she had worked in support of the farm's operation her whole life. She discovered her aptitude for math in high school and went to the University of Missouri to study accounting. Now she was back home, doing the books, keeping track of the financials for the farm, calculating taxes, doing payroll, handling the insurance. She enjoyed the work, felt happy to be with her family, but . . .

Gray clouds gathered to the west. With only a half-hour to go, it looked like it might rain. Maybe she could still get home before the storm. She drummed her fingers on the steering wheel and fiddled impatiently with the radio dial. Her mind drifted back to that day's visit to Fort Leonard Wood.

She had gone there to nail down the final details of a contract for Lorberg Farms to provide over a million board feet of lumber that the government would use in its push to put up over 6,000 new buildings on the new post. Once again, Walt Lorberg's connections had allowed them to be in a position to provide competitive bids on several aspects of the project.

Her mind drifted back to the young captain she had sat across from that afternoon. He was responsible for procuring material for the work. It was the second time she had met him, a Texan named Magee who spoke with a slow, soft drawl. He was about her age, and they had laughed and talked easily as she outlined what Lorberg Farms would deliver under the terms of the contract. He had brown hair and soft brown eyes and—what she noticed for the first time today as he inked his name on the contract—a wedding ring, the smooth gold of the spaghetti-thin band blending in nicely with his tanned skin. An unexpected lump climbed in her throat as she signed her name below his, smelled his soft cologne lingering in the air.

She liked the trips to Fort Leonard Wood, knew they offered the farm unequaled opportunities for new business. But seeing the young officers like Magee busy around the post in their crisp tan uniforms reminded her—much as she wanted to deny it—that she was alone.

"Thank you for coming, Miss Lorberg," Magee had said, standing to shake her hand as she rose from her seat. His gaze held her steady, his hands warm and strong around hers.

"It's been my pleasure," said Katherine. She tried to swallow as she gathered her papers and turned quickly for the door so he couldn't wonder about the slight trembling of her chin.

There had been nothing between them at all but the normal business and pleasantries. But still, in moments like when he released his hands from hers and finally took his eyes away, she wasn't so strong. She ached for attention, something to reassure her that a man might still find her desirable.

Katherine wasn't even certain if she'd remember how to act if a man actually did show some interest. Sure she had dated before—even had a steady during her senior year of college. But that had ended when Arthur returned to St. Louis after they graduated. He had to be an insurance man, working for his father's big firm downtown, and Katherine just couldn't see herself living in the city. And so it ended, just like that. Katherine still thought of him from time to time, but when his Christmas cards began to arrive with "Mr. and Mrs. Arthur Christiansen" on the return address, she had given up the notion of maybe trying to contact him again.

She hadn't really gone out with anyone since. The boys that lived around her in the country were just that—boys. They were hard-working and sincere, but immature and none too bright, certainly not her equal in any regard.

So Katherine figured that at the ripe old age of 26 her time may well have passed. Finding somebody to marry and settle down with probably just wasn't in the cards. She thought she was at peace with that. She could usually set that longing aside by wrapping herself up in the hustle needed to keep up with an operation like Lorberg Farms. But not always. Sometimes she just couldn't make that ache go away, no matter how hard she tried.

She thought about all this as she covered the last few miles and the rain clouds converged, throwing heavy drops on her windshield. The wipers went on, squeaking back and forth across the glass.

Chapter 3

Grudgingly Stefan had returned home at the conclusion of his cross-country jaunt through America the previous September. But soon enough, he found himself again immersed in the details of a new semester, and the war seemed far away. His days were filled with teaching, nights spent compiling the data from the research trip into a grand project that would hopefully crown him with tenure when it was all done.

He thought back to the path that had brought him this far. His grandparents, now in their eighties and still going strong, were the keepers of a large vineyard in the hills above the Rhein. Stefan and his brother, Michael, four years his junior, often stayed with them during school breaks, helping out where they could. As Stefan grew, so did his understanding of grape-growing, and in time they trusted him fully with each aspect of the planting, the pruning and harvest.

Even as a boy, Stefan understood that there was also a business aspect to the farm, that planting grapes was not an end in itself. He remembered his grandfather sitting at the table in the evenings as Stefan and Michael played on the floor nearby. Pencil in hand, the man's eyes turned to the ceiling as he calculated what he had spent in the vineyard against the return he expected when he'd sell his product, either in fresh grapes or finished wine.

From this, agricultural economics was a natural fit. It was the perfect pairing of those summers spent on his grandparents' farm and Stefan's fascination with numbers and analysis. He loved those perfectly rational symbols that were neither arbitrary nor changing in their worth or meaning.

Stefan's work was his passion, and with the long hours devoted to his research, he had little time or interest for romance. He figured that his career at the university came first, and that he'd meet someone in due time if it was meant to be. Or so he said.

"Okay, Biermann, better start thinking about a date. Know any girl who is going to feel sorry enough for you to say yes if you ask her out?"

Stefan looked up from his desk. Dr. Wilhelm Goetz, his boss and the head of the economics department leaned through the doorway to his office at the university. His eyes twinkled as he flipped an invitation to Stefan for the coming faculty party, a festive affair in July to celebrate the end of the academic year.

"Last year you skipped this thing. I'm not going to allow it to happen again. It's not helpful for your career. Plus, it'll be good for you to get away from your papers for once and out with a member of the opposite sex."

"But Dr. Goetz—"

"Find a date, Biermann." The man winked at him, but he wasn't kidding.

That's how Stefan came to find himself down the hall that evening, standing with his knuckles aloft, poised to knock on the door to Maria's apartment. They lived in the same building, and she seemed nice enough the few times he had passed her on the stairs.

Stefan hadn't mustered the courage yet to actually bang on the door, just stood there frozen with a dry mouth and pounding heart. He was just about to turn and run when she opened the door first.

"Umm," she smiled sweetly at him, surprised but still friendly. She had a handbag beneath her arm like she was heading out somewhere. "Can I help you with anything?"

"Are you doing anything Saturday?" he squeaked. "I'd like to ask you out for the evening."

Sure, she'd go with him, she said. Maria was a teacher too, though she tended to kindergarteners rather than college students. She was just his age and single as well. She'd noticed him also, spotting him coming and going. With his leather satchel and clean hands she had already pegged him as an accountant or attorney, a member of some well-paying profession.

Stefan worried the days away until it was time for the event. He changed his tie three times getting ready, finally settling on the one he had tried on first. With a bouquet of flowers clutched in his fist, he presented himself once again at her door, this time mustering the courage to actually knock.

He drew his breath sharply as she opened the door to him.

"Hello, Stefan," she said. Suddenly he found himself drawn to her, and it was like a new day had dawned. Instead of wasting another night at some stuffy academic affair, he saw Goetz had been right. He was captivated by Maria's dark, sparkling eyes and dark hair, the sound of her laughter, the way his hand felt on the small of her back as he guided her around the room introducing her to colleagues.

He was smitten by her and the others could see it, too. They nodded knowingly at each other as he laughed too loudly and too long at her comments, and fumbled at helping her with doors and chairs.

The warm, summer night passed quickly as they drank and danced in an open courtyard under the stars. Laughing together, they stumbled back over Heidelberg's cobblestone streets, Maria clutching his arm tightly. She passed by her own door to come to his small apartment, where the wine and kisses overwhelmed them. Soon, they were joined together in his bed.

Stefan remembered how she looked when he awoke the next morning. He had opened his eyes to see her nude body, pale and delicate next to his. She still slept, and he watched the slight rise of her breasts with each breath she took. He looked closely at her face. My God, she is beautiful, he thought. She was the first woman he had known, and he believed himself the luckiest man on Earth.

As he watched, Maria turned on her side to face away from him. She sighed once and kept her eyes tightly closed, pretending to still be asleep. She wondered how long she'd have to lie there before she could go.

✕

"Hey Stefan," Michael called to his brother from the street below early one evening. He stood with arms outstretched, a bottle of wine in each hand. "Want to get some fresh air? It would do you good to get away from that typewriter."

Growing up, Stefan had always been the conservative one who obeyed the rules and looked to please his parents. But Michael had an independent streak that pushed him down another path. He had fallen in with a community of free-thinkers, artists and writers who sought for themselves a meaning that standard society did not offer. But it was becoming a dangerous time to stand out.

Stefan took the stairs two at a time to meet his brother. The two hiked the hills that ringed the city, climbing high above the steep-roofed buildings that lined the narrow streets of Heidelberg's Altstadt. A bench high in the woods was one of their favorite spots because its vista spanned the whole valley. As night began to fall, they could see lights twinkling in windows all across the city, with the black line of the Neckar snaking across and cutting it in two.

They first chatted a bit about the day-to-day details of their lives. But then for a long time they just sat quietly, no need to say anything, simply happy to be together.

"It's good to see you," said Michael, looking over at Stefan as they sat in the growing darkness. "I want to ask you something."

Michael was a poet, and in the past year, his work had increasingly turned to subtle and sometimes more direct criticism of the government. His words had been appropriated by the resistance and they flowed along the underground current, an inspiration to those in the movement.

"Are you bothered at all by what's been happening?"

"Like what?"

"You know the rumors that go around. The secret police. The camps. People disappearing in the night," said Michael softly.

"Sure," said Stefan. "But what's a person to do?"

"Enough people find out the truth, these bastards that have taken over get ousted. But they've got to know."

They sat in silence until Stefan voiced the question about the resistance he had been afraid to ask.

"Michael, are you involved?"

His brother said nothing, just looked out over the lights of the city. He shifted on the bench and took another deep swallow from the bottle. Their eyes met, and Stefan knew.

"Do you want to help?" Michael asked.

Stefan frowned. He was just starting at the university and was eager to get established in his career. He had worked for years just for a shot at a teaching position and was afraid to blow it now. He could not afford to do anything that might jeopardize his dream.

Now, it was his turn to look away from his brother and out over the city. He shook his head almost imperceptibly.

"I can't," he replied.

The pair sat there in the darkness for a while longer until the bottle was empty. They did not talk about it again.

Had Stefan been as good at reading Maria as he was at analyzing statistics, he might have given their developing relationship a little more scrutiny. But he was blinded by love, and especially by sex. It was good, sure, but for a man who hadn't sat at the table before, it was like Christmas and all his birthdays had come at once.

One afternoon as they lay together, the warm breeze drifted through the bedroom window and flowed over their naked bodies. They were silent, Stefan tracing idly along the line of her collarbone with his finger.

"Maria, do you love me?" asked Stefan. She was next to him, looking at the lace curtains on the balcony fluttering gently in the breeze.

"Mmmm, I don't know. I've never really given it much thought."

Stefan's eyes flashed angry and hurt for a moment, but then his face became calm again. "I know that I love you," he said. "It's been two months that we've been together and I think we ought to talk about being married. Wouldn't that be lovely?"

"Why, I guess it might, if that would make you happy," replied Maria, wondering what kind of salary a junior faculty member at the university earned. "We should talk about it a bit more. Perhaps in six months."

Stefan wanted to hear her say more, she knew, something meaningful, but she had nothing else to add. Besides, she was getting hungry and wanted to think about dinner.

"Come, dear," she said. "Let's get dressed and go to the café down the street."

⋊

Outside of that one conversation with his brother, Stefan felt the war's intrusion in just one other way of any consequence, through the regular visits to the draft board. Every six months, he'd check in, just like all other men between 16 and 35. His position at the university made him exempt, so this was just a formality, a minor chore, one that he certainly didn't mind. It reminded him each time that he was safe, that life was good, that he could spend his time working on his research and making love to Maria.

Stefan always saved the task for a day when the weather was good. It got him out of the office and gave him an excuse to walk. Sometimes, he'd even stop at a café on the way back, ducking in for a glass of wine or pastry, a small celebration for the good fortune that had smiled upon him in planting him at the university.

But the last time he'd been in, just six weeks before, Stefan noticed that things were different. He was quite familiar with the elderly ladies who manned the office, knew them well from his visits there over the past three years. In fact, one of them, Mrs. Eschelbach, was his neighbor. She was a pleasant lady in her seventies, and she always joked with him when he came in.

"Ach, there's the professor," she'd say. "When are you going to come by the house for coffee?"

But on this last visit, there was no joking, none of the earlier chit-chat. As he entered, Stefan felt a heaviness in the air, though sunlight streamed through the tall windows that fronted the street. Another man was already there when Stefan arrived, and he watched the people passing on the sidewalk as he waited his turn.

"Done," said the man in front of him, marking the completion of his paperwork and signing the last form with a flourish. He nodded to Stefan as he picked up his hat and headed for the door.

"Good morning, Mrs. Eschelbach," Stefan said, stepping to the desk. Noise from the street wafted in as the other man left, honking horns, truck motors, a snatch of conversation. Then the door was closed again and the office was quiet.

The woman looked up from the desk and gave him a smile.

"Good morning, Dr. Biermann. And how are you today?"

"Thank you, quite well," said Stefan. "I noticed the other evening that the flowers in your garden are especially lovely right now."

Mrs. Eschelbach smiled. "Thank you, Dr. Biermann. It's a pleasure to see you, as always. And how are things at the university?"

"Ah, fine. The usual fun with students and classes. It seems like they know more about less every year." Stefan winked at her. "I assume all is in order with my academic exemption?"

Her eyes came up briefly to meet his, but then she looked away quickly, turning back to the papers on her desk.

"All is in order," she said. "However . . ." The woman flipped through the forms spread in front of her. She checked a box on his registration papers then looked back at him.

"Dr. Biermann," she whispered, leaning toward him with a sad smile. "The army is calling more and more men each week, even those who weren't on the list before. Older men. Managers from the factories. Those you think would be safe."

"They're not taking teachers yet, are they? Don't the recruits already know their ABCs?" he joked. "I'm still okay, right?"

"They're already taking teachers from the high schools," said Mrs. Eschelbach. "They've called a half-dozen from this neighborhood already.

Right now your academic exemption is still good. But I don't know for how much longer." She leaned forward to him, whispering now. "I keep pushing your name down the list, but I've almost run out of others to send."

The office door opened, and the noise from the street came to them again. Stefan stood with a frozen smile.

"Well, I'm sure it's nothing to be concerned about," said Mrs. Eschelbach in her normal voice. She smiled warmly again. "I do thank you for coming in again, Dr. Biermann. The Führer appreciates your willingness to serve your country."

※

Sometimes when he was out, Stefan saw Maria in the schoolyard, her charges clumped around her. One particular afternoon Stefan waited in the hallway outside her classroom, watching and listening as she taught. He had been out walking during the noon hour and his path took him past her school. He knew she had a break coming, and so he waited, looking forward to talking with her for a minute when the opportunity allowed.

Two children painted at a table while the others played. He could see the little heads bent over their papers, working intently at their artwork. Maria talked about her children frequently, and he recognized the girl, Claudia, with her blonde hair pulled back in a ponytail, and the boy, Thomas, a slender boy with thick brown hair that fell down over his forehead. His tongue poked from the corner of his mouth as he concentrated on his drawing. A deep dish of bright blue paint sat by his elbow at the edge of the table, and the only interruption to his work was when he paused to dip his brush in it.

"How are we doing here?" Maria asked the painters as she circled the table. Her back was toward Stefan and she was unaware of his presence. "Are you finishing up? Just a minute or two left."

"Look," said Claudia, and she proudly pushed her paper toward Maria. A blue boat sailed on a blue sea and blue m-shaped birds flew beneath a blue sun. "Look," she said again.

"Claudia, that is lovely." She smiled. "And you, Thomas?"

Thomas made no response. A row of houses stood on his paper. Some were big, some little, but one by one he had made them all blue, carefully painting around windows, doors, and chimneys. Only a single house remained unpainted.

"Thomas, we need to finish our work. Painting time is almost done." She tapped him on the shoulder. He looked up, hearing her for the first time, blinking at the intrusion.

"Time to stop," she said.

Thomas was puzzled. His project was not done.

"I have one more house left," he said.

"Thomas. Time to stop painting." The smile was gone.

"Just one more," he pleaded. "Please. Just one more to do."

"No." Maria reached for his paper. She was getting angry. "Give me that."

Thomas tried to shield his drawing with his arms, but she grabbed a corner and yanked it away from him. As she jerked the paper, he pulled the other way, tearing it in two and knocking the bowl of paint from the desk. In slow motion it flipped in the air, end over end, sending a splatter of bright blue paint across the floor, across the desk, across Maria and across little Claudia.

There was a second of stunned silence. Then Claudia began to wail and a fearful rage broke loose in Maria.

"You!" she screamed. "Look what you've done." Her face was red and twisted with anger. She leaned toward him over the table and slapped him fast and hard across the face. Stefan couldn't see the blow, but the proof of her fury was evident in the blue smears on Thomas' face, streaked now with tears that ran over the red outline where her hand had found its mark.

His cries joined with Claudia's, the only sounds in the otherwise silent classroom. The rest of the children huddled together, wide-eyed and frozen in a corner of the classroom as Maria said nothing more. She stood, fiercely grabbed the halves of Thomas' paper and crumpled them in both hands. She stalked to the trash can, pitched in the wadded and ruined artwork and began to mop at the spilled paint on the floor with a rag from under the sink.

After the children left the classroom, Stefan went in. Maria was on her hands and knees, scrubbing at the last bit of paint on the floor. She looked at him and smiled sweetly.

"Hello, dear. Just finishing a bit of cleanup."

"Why'd you hit that boy like that?"

She stopped smiling and looked back at the floor. A frown slowly crept across her forehead, its little lines wrinkling her smooth skin. Maria focused on the rag and kept rubbing and rubbing at the same last spot of paint.

"Stefan, he had it coming. That boy had been an absolute devil all day."

"But, Maria. All he wanted to do was finish the pic—"

She looked at him quickly, angry again. He saw the fury coming back. She rose on her knees and pointed at him with the rag clenched in her fist.

"Don't you 'But, Maria' me, Stefan. You haven't been here all day. So don't you dare just show up and start criticizing me when you don't know what the hell you're talking about."

Silence. She glared at him, daring him to speak, to contradict her. Stefan looked at his feet, remaining quiet as long as he could bear it. He could feel her narrow angry eyes still burning on him.

"You're right," he said at last, trying to push the image of the crying boy from his mind. "You're right. I'm sure he's a real handful."

Chapter 4

As the early morning light began to creep through the windows, John Lorberg stood in his bedroom on the second floor of the large house. He carefully folded the last few items of clothing, placing them into a suitcase. His wife sat on the edge of the bed, still in her nightgown. Her legs were folded underneath her, and her hands lay in her lap. She had been crying.

"I wish you didn't have to go," she said.

John paused, looked up from the socks and underwear laid neatly in the suitcase and tried to smile, his own eyes welling with tears.

"Susan, you know I have no choice. Either I go this route, or they take me eventually as a draftee."

"But we'll be apart for such a long time."

"Everyone is facing this, hon. It's not like we're the only ones. Besides, if I end up stateside after officer school, you and Ellen can join me. We can still be a family."

She looked unconvinced and sighed deeply. For a long time she had been preparing herself for this day. Now it was time to be strong. For herself and for Ellen, their two-year-old still sleeping in the room next to them.

A light tapping came from the door.

"You ready, John?" asked his brother from the hallway.

"Almost," said John. He tossed in the last two items then closed the lid of the suitcase and snapped shut the latches. "You can come in."

Michael opened the door slowly. He was already wearing his overcoat and carrying a suitcase of his own. He nodded to Susan.

The two brothers descended the stairs together. Susan followed a couple of steps behind, carrying sleepy Ellen. It was almost time to say goodbye. Entering the kitchen, they saw Caroline standing by the stove. She covered her hand with her mouth at the sight of her sons together ready to leave for the war. Gus Davis waited with her, drinking coffee as the car warmed up outside. Great clouds of exhaust blew from the tailpipe on the frosty January morning, quickly whisked away by the brisk north wind.

At the front door, Susan pressed herself into her husband, crying now without restraint. Caroline cried, too, as she embraced first one son, then the other.

It was time. Gus cleared his throat, and the two men began to unwrap themselves from the women who clung to them.

"We need to get going if we're going to have time to see Walt," Gus said. He was driving John and Michael to Jefferson City, where their father was already a couple of days into the new legislative session. The two would have just a few minutes with him for a last round of farewells before boarding a train at noon that would carry them away.

"Be a good girl," John said, bending to give one more kiss to Ellen. The tiny girl waved bye-bye to her father and then padded back to her room as the three men turned and headed for the door.

Susan stood at the front door, her face pressed against the cold window. She watched as the men left, John's gloved hand giving her a final wave from the passenger's window as the car rolled slowly down the long lane.

Chapter 5

"Herr Doktor Biermann?" called out the fresh-faced student in a lecture back in April. It was a sunny Tuesday morning and the rows of wooden tables that filled the large lecture hall were half-full. Stefan stood at a podium at the bottom and front of the hall. The kid who asked the question was probably 20 or 22, not long out of high school, one of the few males in the classroom. It was a wonder that he hadn't been called into the army.

"The Reich's market directives have resulted in higher productivity than ever before," said the student. "The past three years have set records for industrial and agricultural output. What do you think is the key to this success?"

A routine question. But Stefan was thinking of Michael. He waited and waited to answer the question. Then the words came and he was unable to stop them.

"Forced labor," said Biermann, his voice bitter. "That's your answer. Germany's increasing productivity comes from the growing use of forced labor from prisoners."

The classroom lost its usual background buzz and fell into stunned silence.

"Sir?" asked the boy, raising a withered hand that had been lying in his lap. "I'm sorry? I don't understand . . ."

When he saw the hand, Stefan recognized the boy. His name was Heinrich. He and Maria had grown up in the same neighborhood, though he was four or five years younger than she, and it was the disability that kept him from the army.

"Are you deaf? I said forced labor," snapped Biermann. He himself was shocked by his answer and his boldness in repeating it. "The labor ministry is using prisoners for much of the work previously done by paid workers. Costs go down, productivity goes up. Highly efficient, no?" He thought of Michael and smiled bitterly.

An uncomfortable murmur grew, retreated.

"Sir? . . . " said Heinrich. Stefan stared at him. Maria's and Heinrich's father both participated in Party activities at the local level, and their wives moved in the same circles.

"Surely you know about the internment camps that have been created?" said Stefan, his voice rising. "The ones that imprison those the Nazis consider enemies of the state? We're talking about artists and writers for God's sake."

The class sat in silence again. The boy shifted uncomfortably in his seat, fiddled with the Hitler Youth pin riding in his collar. He lived down the street from Maria and his route to the university took him by the school where Maria taught. They walked together sometimes when their paths intersected.

"Or how about the other camps? The ones set up for Jews and gypsies, the undesirables?" Stefan continued. He was nearly shouting now, and couldn't stop the torrent of words. "These men and women are being forced to work for us. The high productivity rates you view with such pride? They are being built on their backs and paid for with their blood and sweat."

"But sir? . . ." stammered the boy. "Isn't it true that these people have put themselves in the camps simply by being who they are?"

Michael had been taken away, seized on the street corner by Gestapo men who jumped from a waiting sedan. Stefan learned later that Michael had been taken to the infamous camp at Dachau. Michael was a poet, a peaceful non-conformist who loved Germany but disliked those who had hijacked his country. That was enough for the Nazis to take him away.

"The majority of these people have done nothing wrong," said Stefan. This time, the gasps of his students were audible. "They are patriots who speak their minds. And the others – who can choose their place of birth or their religion? God help us for what we are doing to these men and women."

Michael had spent the first week of his interment in solitary confinement, his only human contact the daily beatings administered by the SS men who ran the camp. First his body was broken, and then his spirit. When he was released after a week, he staggered out of his cell, shielding his blackened and swollen eyes from the blinding sun. He worked meekly after that, week-in and week-out for ten months, picking potatoes from the field until his exhausted and malnourished body collapsed there, falling face-first into the warm, dry soil somewhere in between the rows.

The buzz turned angry now. Stefan closed his notes, trying with trembling hands to shove the papers back into his leather satchel.

"The lecture is over," he said. "You are dismissed."

Stefan turned and left the classroom by the exit door at the front, hearing the disturbed murmuring of the students continue behind him as he ran for the sanctuary of his office.

My Enemy, My Love

Chapter 6

When John Lorberg left for the war, neither he nor Susan knew about the seed growing inside her, planted there during their last night together. But this realization came quickly, of course, and the house was full of excitement over this blessing. While the first pregnancy with Ellen had gone smoothly however, this was not the same.

They had summoned the doctor early on when it was apparent there was reason for concern. Before long he came each day to monitor her status.

"This is getting rough," said the doctor, a soft-spoken young man during his third visit that week. He stood over Susan's bed, shaking the mercury back down the thermometer. Her temperature was high; so was her blood pressure. "She's been having contractions all morning."

Susan moaned softly and clutched her belly.

"Do you know how to contact John?" he asked, looking at Katherine through his round glasses. "It's too early for this."

"Oh God," thought Katherine. John was in Georgia training for the military police corps. "I don't know if I can reach him."

"You better try. He needs to get back as quick as he can," said the doctor, turning back to Susan. Her eyes were closed, and he bent to listen to her labored, shallow breathing.

Katherine ran for the phone. The long distance tolls would cost them a fortune but she didn't care. Again and again, the local operator tried to connect to the post, but the calls kept getting dropped.

"What unit is he with?" asked the operator politely when they finally got through.

"I don't know," stammered Katherine. She closed her eyes for a moment and shook her head with frustration. "He's at officer school there. Isn't that enough?"

"No ma'am," came the voice from far away over the wire, a soft twang caressing the words. "I'm sorry. There are over a thousand men here right now at that school. Let me try to patch you through to one of the company offices. They might be able to help."

There was a click and Katherine waited expectantly for someone to pick up. Instead, all she heard was silence, minute after minute. The line was dead.

"Damn it," she said, her eyes filling with tears. She slammed down the phone, then just as quickly picked it up, trying to summon the operator again.

"I don't know what happened," came the same voice over the wire after they were finally reconnected. "Let me try again."

This time the transfer took and Katherine felt her pulse rise as the phone on the other end started to ring. She held her breath and twirled the cord around and around her finger. She waited, as the phone rang on and on for minutes without being answered.

Finally she took the phone from her ear, trying to contain her disappointment as she limply returned it to the cradle. Just as she was about to set it down, Katherine heard a voice crackle over the wire.

"Chaplain here. . . . Hello? . . . Hello?"

"Hello! Hello!" she shouted. "I'm here."

She could hear a chuckle and some heavy breathing.

"Hold on a second while I catch my breath," said the man. "This is the chaplain. We were outside in formation and I had to run to get the phone. What can I do for you?"

"My name is Katherine Lorberg. I'm calling from Missouri. My brother, John Lorberg, is at officer school there. His wife is desperately sick and he needs to come home."

"Well now, Miss Lorberg," said the Chaplain. "I don't know your brother, but let me see what I can do. He's not a member of this company but I bet we can track him down. Let me take your information. Hold on just a sec."

He clunked down the phone and Katherine held the line while he scrounged around the office for a nub of pencil and some paper. She could hear him muttering and the sound of drawers opening and closing.

"Okay," he said, picking up the phone again. "Go ahead."

She glanced at the doctor as he returned and began replacing his instruments in the black leather bag that sat on the kitchen table. He looked grim.

"I promise I'll do my best to get this to them," said the chaplain, pulling Katherine back to the conversation. "But it may take some time."

"Thank you for doing whatever you can," Katherine said to the chaplain, voice trailing off as she met the doctor's eyes.

"You're welcome, Miss Lorberg. God be with you and your family." There was a distant click and the chaplain was gone.

X

Susan held on for two more days, but died just hours before John's return. Katherine watched as her brother burst into the house, ran down the hallway, still in his overcoat, and threw himself on his wife's body, weeping without restraint.

Some hours later, she went to the room. It was getting late and dinner had long since passed. John made no sound as she opened the door. He lay still on the bed next to his wife's body, staring at the ceiling.

"John," she said.

He didn't respond. Not even a blink.

"John," she said again, and touched him gently on the shoulder as she sat on the narrow edge of the bed. He turned to look at her.

"She was everything to me," he said.

"I know. I'm so sorry."

X

They buried Susan the following Monday, laying her body to rest in a deep hole beneath one of the elms that filled the sky in the cemetery. Rows of weathered white tombstones stood silent like sentries while the pastor led the rite committing her body to the earth.

"Ashes to ashes, dust to dust . . . "

Katherine stood next to her father with John on the other side. He held little Ellen in his arms, soaking the neck of her new dress with his tears as they lowered his wife's body into the damp earth. Caroline and Walter stood there too, watching their daughter being buried. Only Michael was missing. He was somewhere in the Pacific, and would not know until the mail finally caught up with him in the fall.

John left his family the next morning to return to the war. Gus Davis waited outside with the idling sedan to drive him to the train station like before.

Chapter 7

The following Monday, the note was waiting for him when he arrived. Stefan's hands shook as he picked it up.

"See me this afternoon, 4 p.m." It was signed by Dr. Goetz, chairman of the department.

He was in deep trouble for what had happened in the lecture hall, he knew. Certainly fired, but much worse, reported to the Party. Soon would come a knock on the door in the middle of the night from the Gestapo.

The hallway was cool and dark, quiet with the departure of the students at the end of the day. As he approached the large wooden door at the end of the hall, light came softly through the frosted glass panes in the door enough to show the nameplate it carried, *Herr Doktor Wilhelm Goetz.* Classical music played quietly inside.

Stefan stood before the door. He had dreaded this meeting, but knew it was inevitable. Hesitatingly, the knocked.

"Come in!" sounded a gruff voice. Stefan grasped the metal doorknob, thin and cold, turning it, pushing the door inward. Dr. Goetz stood with his back to Stefan, looking out the window into the courtyard, framed by the afternoon sunlight.

Turning now to face him, Goetz gestured toward a straight-backed wooded chair. Stefan sat uneasily as Goetz parked himself unceremoniously on his own chair behind the desk, leaning back slightly, hands clasped atop his head. He peered closely at Stefan over the wire-rimmed glasses perched precariously on the end of his long and carrot-skinny nose.

"Good grief, man," said Goetz, frowning at the bags under Stefan's eyes and the way that his clothes hung on him like a scarecrow. "You look terrible. What's happened to you?"

Stefan said nothing. Since his outburst a week ago, he had not slept, ate little and looked gaunt and haggard.

"This whole business is eating you alive, isn't it?" asked Dr. Goetz cheerfully.

Stefan nodded.

"Well, don't beat yourself up about it," he said reassuringly. "It's been fixed. You're not getting fired and no one is coming to take you away."

Stefan raised his eyebrows, shook his head. He couldn't comprehend what he was hearing. It was as if he had been redeemed from the pit.

"Listen," said Goetz. "I know about your brother. What they did to him. I can only imagine how that has affected you. When those little goons from the party came here the next day to ask about your outburst, I simply took care of it with them."

"I don't understand . . ."

"They wanted to know if I had ever had any problems with you before. Any questions about your loyalty to the Party. I told them, no, certainly not, that this whole thing had been just an unfortunate misunderstanding. You had this idea, see, to test the students' comprehension and adherence to party doctrine by throwing out contrary ideas for them to consider and deconstruct."

Goetz smiled and continued.

"I told them that you had just botched the lesson, and said that like many junior faculty members, you sometimes didn't think things through. Your experiment went differently than you had planned."

Stefan could hardly believe what he was hearing.

"Yes, I basically made you look like a fool," smiled Goetz, crossing his arms happily across his chest. "But it worked."

"Why would you do this for me?"

Goetz' face took a serious cast and he leaned closer to Stefan.

"What I am going to tell you cannot leave this room," he whispered. "If you mention it later to anyone, I will deny it and you will be quite sorry that you ever brought it up." Goetz smiled, but wasn't joking. He sat up straighter.

"Our country is on the wrong path," whispered Goetz simply, directly. "What happened to your brother has happened to countless others. It troubles me deeply."

He paused and looked toward the door, a reflexive move, checking that no one was outside listening.

"There is a group here at the university opposed to the regime. It's mostly comprised of our colleagues on the faculty, but there are a handful of students involved who are trustworthy beyond a doubt."

Stefan's eyes grew wide with surprise and admiration.

"It's not much yet," said Goetz, reading his expression. "So far, we have only been planning. Getting organized. Talking about the best way to take back our country from these thugs."

Stefan's mind reeled at the concept of active resistance against the government by his colleagues were involved. What Goetz had just said was an immediate ticket to prison should anyone find out.

"I've watched you, Stefan," continued Goetz. "You could be a part of us. You're smart, principled. You know what they are doing is wrong."

Stefan nodded, taking it all in.

"Now, I'm not asking you to make up your mind today. But think about it and let me know."

Dr. Goetz stood up, signaling the meeting was over. The men shook hands and Goetz turned again to gaze silently out the window at the courtyard, leaving Stefan to show himself out.

Farm in Iowa U.S.A.

Chapter 8

"Dad, what are we going to do? We've lost all our help."

Katherine looked out the kitchen window, seeing corn stalks heavy with ears that couldn't wait much longer to be harvested. In other parts of the farm, several hundred acres of soybeans waited to be brought in along with a half-dozen other crops due to be taken.

One-by-one, the draft had taken every one of the farmhands who ordinarily would have put in twelve-hour days this time of year to bring in the crops. What had once been an ample supply of workers had now dwindled to nothing.

"Well," said Walter, cautiously glancing up from his breakfast and the newspaper, "I hear they're starting to let German and Italian prisoners work on farms."

"But dad," she frowned, her reaction to the suggestion exactly what he thought it would be. She turned to look at him as she sipped her coffee. "Do we really want those people here? It'd be awfully dangerous, don't you think?"

"Did you see John's latest letter? It came on Thursday." Walter went to the side desk and fished an envelope from one of the pigeonholes. He handed it to Katherine, who extracted the folded papers and started to read.

"For the past six weeks, we've been down here in Mississippi," wrote John. "The cotton came in about a month early, and so we've been working like the dickens to help bring it in, moving from county to county so that no group of farmers falls too far behind."

She turned the page, following his neat script along the lined paper.

"People in these little towns have been hesitant at first, sometimes downright hostile to the Germans. I tell you what though, when the folks see them work, they sure feel different about things."

Katherine was still skeptical but read on.

"Sure there's been the occasional incident, but for the most part, we haven't had a bit of problem. These men have lost a lot of their starch since being captured. Most are just glad to be out of the war, and happy to have something productive to do."

Katherine set down the letter and looked at her father.

"I don't know…," she said, her voice trailing off.

"Suit yourself," shrugged Walter. "You're in charge around here. I just don't see where you're going to find any workers."

Katherine turned to look out the window again, where the ears hung heavy on the stalks.

※

Three weeks later the first group of POWs arrived at the farm. There were sixty of them, accompanied by three guards and an officer named Bray. They would stay just a couple weeks until the crops were brought it, and then move on.

Katherine watched as the arriving Germans climbed from the army trucks. They wore blue denim coveralls with POW across the back in white stencil letters. And though they mostly looked like any other farm laborers as they began to work their way through the fields, she couldn't forget that somewhere over in Europe, her brother was engaged in a life-and-death fight against their comrades.

And she carried that inner conflict with her all of those days, though much of her initial concern vanished not long after the men set to work, buzzing around the farm, busy harvesting crops that she previously feared would be lost to November's cold rains.

"You were right about the work habits of these men," Katherine wrote to John. "Having them here has been a godsend to the farm. All went smoothly enough, though we too had one of those 'incidents' you mentioned."

She paused, thinking of the disturbance. She didn't know if she could call it a full-blown riot, but it had come mighty close.

It happened one afternoon about ten days after their arrival. Gus Davis guided the POW work crews, and was putting some of them to work on the winter vegetable beds.

The old foreman found that as a group, the prisoners mostly worked well enough. But he noticed with some irritation that one POW constantly paused in his work chopping weeds from the fields of broccoli, peas and cauliflower. He would straighten himself over the hoe to stand and scan the horizon, and then after a few moments, return again to his work. Finally, Gus, who spoke pretty good German himself, asked the guy about it.

"What the hell do you keep looking for all the time?" growled Gus. "I know there are no weeds up there!"

"Aircraft, Herr Davis, German aircraft," smiled the POW, leaning on his hoe. "It won't be long before our men will be coming through to set us free."

"Keep looking," he said, chuckling a bit at this foolishness, "you're not going to spot anything soon."

"I will be kind to you, sir, when you are no longer the captor," said the German, all seriousness now. "But I will not forget this mocking."

"Okay," said Davis. "Whatever you say, Fritz. In the meantime, just keep hoeing."

Later that day, Davis showed the man a copy of the *St. Louis Globe-Democrat* from the day before. News of war was splashed all over the main page. Allied advances in Europe and the Pacific. German cities destroyed by bombing. Davis held the newspaper at arm's length, spreading the pages wide so they could both get a good look.

"Nein!" said the man. He could speak enough English to grasp the headlines and main thrust of the articles. He shook his head as he stared at it in disbelief. *"Nein!"*

He frowned fiercely as Gus pushed it further, pointing out front-page accounts of Allied advances through Europe, gleefully translating the key parts for him.

"Look here," he crowed. "Patton pushing toward the Rhine!" Gus pointed to another section. "All kinds of stuff getting torn up in the Ruhr Valley. Bombed into nothing! How 'bout that?!"

Other prisoners began to gather around, angry men who also believed their liberation was close at hand, their visions of rejoining their *Kameraden* to march unhindered through the United States openly scoffed at by this American farmhand.

"Propaganda! Propaganda!" they began to shout. They jostled closer to Davis, pressing in on him with clenched fists and angry faces. One of the men tore the newspaper from Davis' hands, ripping it to shreds, and stomping the torn paper into the ground. Seeing the intensity of the growing disturbance, a guard rushed in to separate the foreman from the prisoner mob.

The men left not long after that, but Gus didn't forget the incident.

"I tell you what, I never turned my back on that sumbitch again," Davis told Katherine after the men departed, eyebrows working furiously over his ice-blue eyes. "I'm sure if he ever got the chance to take a whack at me with his hoe, he'd have done it."

X

The only other negative about having the prisoners at the farm didn't involve the POWs at all. Rather, the problem came in one of GIs who accompanied them there.

"Hello," he said the morning they met. It was still early, after breakfast, and the sun sparkled like a million dazzling diamonds off the dewy grass. She was on her way to the farm's office. He was leaning against a truck and leaped out to block her path. "I'm Robert Whitcomb." He took a deep bow, sweeping his arm with a flourish that nearly brushed the ground and tilted his head to her as he turned his eyes downward.

"Good God," she thought. "What's wrong with this guy?" He stayed bent over for an interminably long time. She started to wonder if he was stuck there.

"Um, hello?" she said, waiting for him to stand again.

He looked up at her, revealing a poorly fitted glass eye, and then smiled broadly through a mouthful of crooked, tobacco-stained teeth.

"And where are you off to this fine morning?"

"I'm working," she said, brushing him off. "Excuse me, please."

"And does the lady have a boyfriend or husband?" he asked, stepping aside slightly to let her pass.

Katherine didn't say anything, just smiled at the audacity of this clown as she walked by him without looking back. It was a mistake for sure; he took her smile for encouragement and her silence for affirmation.

The next morning he waited for her again.

"And good morning, my dear Katherine," he said, greeting her with another bow. He had learned her name from a farm hand.

"Good morning," she replied, curt but not rude as she strode past.

"I have a question you may be able to help me with."

She was too polite to ignore him. So she paused, turning in place to look at him with raised eyebrows.

"I'll have a pass to go into town on Saturday night. Is there a restaurant you'd recommend?"

She saw no harm in replying. He was only asking her opinion.

"Sutton's. They have good steaks."

"Great," he said. "Would you go there with me?"

"Um, no thanks," she stammered. She should have seen that one coming. She felt her face turning red.

"You must be busy then?"

"Yes," she said, relieved at this way out. "Yes."

"Well, that's fine. 'Cause Lieutenant Bray says we can switch our passes around if we got somebody to trade with. So we can go another time. How 'bout next weekend instead?"

"Um, I...I... I just don't know."

"Well, you just check your calendar for an open date. I'm gonna keep asking till we find a time that works."

And he did, pestering her persistently about a chance to see her. He was charming, flattering, pressing her again and again until finally she gave in.

"Really, I've got no reason to say no," thought Katherine as she looked at herself in the mirror over the dresser in her bedroom, squinting at the tiny wrinkles forming around her mouth and at the corners of her eyes, invisible to everyone but her.

Lately she had been thinking that she might try a little harder to find some romance. It had been a long time since things had ended with Arthur. Almost eight years had passed since he had gone back to St. Louis to be an insurance man. And she had to start again somewhere. Maybe going out with this soon-to-depart stranger would make the possibilities she had around here seem a bit more appealing.

"Great," was all he said when she finally told him she would go. He held his hat in his hand and smiled broadly at her. "Great. This is going to be great."

Chapter 9

Stefan left Dr. Goetz's office, still amazed by what he had heard, still unsure of what Goetz wanted him to do.

Dr. Goetz was a part of an underground resistance group!

He walked down Heidelberg's *Hauptstraße*, hands jammed in his pockets, head buzzing as he stalked the city's main street. The old buildings towered above the busy sidewalks and Stefan was glad to lose himself in the crowd as he drifted toward the market plaza and the old bridge.

"Let me know," was the last thing Goetz had said to him.

Let him know what? If Stefan wanted to risk his career? If he wanted to lose Maria? Her father was a party official and to even hint at such involvement was dangerous.

Stefan walked and walked, until he found himself on a corner by the university library and St. Peter's Church.

"Let me know."

Let him know if he wanted to be killed by the Gestapo? That's what would happen if it ever became known that he was a part of their little group. Yeah, he knew what he was going to tell Goetz. Thanks, but no thanks.

Suddenly Stefan heard the heavy bells of the ancient clock tolling six o'clock from the tower high above the town's central square. He stopped abruptly in front of the church, and the thought of his brother struck him like a lightning bolt.

Stefan looked up to the spires of St. Peter's, framed like daggers against the clear blue sky and stood as the far-away memory of Michael's christening washed over him. The service was over and four-year-old Stefan ran down the center aisle of the church after the service, leading the family out of the sanctuary. His mom and dad followed along behind, the baby in his mother's arms and a train of happy relatives in their wake. Stefan stood just head high to the pews, and his little feet flashed between the rows as he ran toward the open door and the dazzling sunlight outside.

Then the memory was gone, and anger and bile rose in his throat. Stefan turned abruptly from where he had stopped. He was going back to Dr. Goetz' office. Damn the risks. He knew now what his decision would be.

Evening was coming quickly as Stefan hurried back to the university. The streets were emptier now as shopkeepers began to close up for the day, Stefan's footsteps grew quicker, his long stride lengthening to match the urgency he felt, and by the time he reached the economics building, he was nearly jogging.

The heavy wooden door leading into the building creaked on its hinges as Stefan pulled it open, and the long hallway was empty again. Goetz's office was now dark but Stefan rapped on the door twice just to be sure, his breath coming heavily as he leaned against the door frame. He had been too late.

Pulling a pen from his pocket, Stefan tore a flyer off the bulletin board two steps away from the office door. He ripped the paper in half, pitching the bottom part into a nearby wastebasket. The flyer had been for the National Socialist Students' group on campus, advertising their Nazi rally the following week.

"Hah! To hell with them," he thought, pulling out his pen. Stefan knew Goetz would appreciate the irony. "Count me in," he wrote, then added his initials. Folding the piece of paper in half, then half again, he slid it under Dr. Goetz's door.

Leaving the building, Stefan knew that his action would put him in danger, but his heart was at peace. It was the right decision, for Michael's sake if nothing else. Though he'd have to keep this from Maria for the moment. Someday, when all was right again with Germany, he would tell her. Just not now.

It was fully dark when Stefan finally reached his apartment again. The postman had been by, and turning on the little light by the door, Stefan saw a single envelope waiting for him. After he set down his satchel and took off his coat, he picked it up. The return address was from the army draft board. Stefan tore open the envelope.

"Herr Stefan Biermann: You are hereby ordered to report in one week for service to the Fatherland . . ."

The lines of text blurred before his eyes. The day he had thought would never come had now, in fact, arrived. With his legs growing weak beneath him, Stefan slumped against the wall and slid slowly to the floor in the nearly-dark apartment. Crumpling the draft notice into a tight ball, he flung it impotently across the room. The paper bounced off the far wall and rolled back toward him.

Stefan squeezed his eyes tightly shut, sinking even lower until he was curled up in a ball on the floor. Fists clenched tightly against his face, he shook his head back and forth, again and again, and then started to cry, deep sobs racking his body in the darkness.

Chapter 10

Saturday night came too quickly, and Katherine paced as she waited for Robert Whitcomb to arrive. Saying yes to him had given her some short-lived peace, squelched his persistent presence, but the date still loomed all week like a storm cloud on the horizon.

Caroline stood in the doorway, arms crossed, watching her daughter. Katherine had never talked about having a date, only vaguely mentioned "plans" for Saturday. But Caroline knew. She had watched Whitcomb wait for her daughter each morning in the courtyard, and followed their brief exchanges from the window.

A dusty old truck pulled in the circular driveway in front of the house.

"He's here," said Katherine.

"You'll have a good time," she said.

Katherine gathered her sweater, gave her mother a quick peck on the cheek and pulled open the door. Suddenly, Whitcomb blew a long blast on the truck horn. She stopped short, frozen at this brashness.

"Oh my," muttered Katherine. "Honked at."

She yanked the front door shut behind her and smiled grimly. Katherine marched across the yard to the truck, where Whitcomb stayed in the cab, fiddling with the radio. She circled around to the passenger side and waited by the door for him to open it.

"Hop in!" he hooted out the open window.

"Criminy," said Katherine, trying to steel herself. This was over the top. Normally had something like this happened, she would have turned right around and gone back inside. But she felt her mother's eyes on her from the front window, felt the muscles in her own neck growing tense.

"Well? You comin'?"

She grabbed the handle of the truck door and turned it slowly. Katherine knew her mother wondered about her love life. Caroline never asked her directly, but tried to hint at young men in town or bachelor farmers that she thought Katherine might like. She gabbed about it incessantly on the phone with her friends, worrying about her daughter becoming a dried-up old maid, bitter and alone.

"Alrighty!" said Whitcomb, grinning wildly as she pulled the door open slowly, still hesitating. "Let's go!"

Katherine wanted very much to simply turn around and go back inside. But she couldn't. No way. Her mother had shown remarkable restraint in not asking about her date with Whitcomb, even though her curiosity was about to kill her. But if Katherine were to back out now, her mother would never be able to let it go. She'd badger her about what happened until every bit of information had been extracted. Katherine would sooner have her fingernails pulled out. She clenched her teeth, slid onto the seat and pulled the door shut.

"So, you ready for this?" Whitcomb slurred a bit as he leered at her, head cocked sideways, blood-shot eyes going up and down her slender body.

"Oh, God," she thought, spotting a silver flask tucked under the dashboard. She wanted to jump out and run inside the house, back to where Caroline frowned from the front window. But this time, even if her pride would have let her, he was too quick. Whitcomb stomped on the accelerator, spinning tires and slinging gravel and dust behind him as he fish-tailed down the driveway and onto the county road.

"Hey, how are ya?" he asked as they careened along the rutted gravel road.

"Fine." She managed a weak smile.

"C'mon, why don't you move a little closer?" He patted the seat between them.

"I'm fine here," she said, sliding away from his hand on the seat.

Neither said anything more. Whitcomb fiddled for some tunes on the radio, and other than his off-key humming to the music, the trip to town passed in silence. As they drove, she felt him looking at her again, felt his eyes on her body. Katherine kept staring straight ahead through the windshield, frozen smile on her face.

Soon enough the houses grew closer together and they entered the Augusta city limits. Katherine slunk down in the seat, hoping they didn't see anyone she knew. He looked over again.

"What's the matter?" There was a touch of irritation in his voice. "You embarrassed to be out with me?"

"Oh, no," said Katherine, straightening herself. She sat upright the final few minutes, praying silently that the night would turn out alright.

Chapter 11

The next day, Stefan went back to see Dr. Goetz. It was the same as before. The quiet, dark hallway. Classical music wafting from behind the frosted glass of the heavy wooden door of the office. Stefan knocked softly and the door swung open.

"Come in," said Goetz. He gestured to the chairs and the men sat as they had before. Goetz was surprised and a bit puzzled to see him again so soon. "I got your note," he said. "You're not reconsidering already, are you?"

Stefan shook his head. Pulling the draft notice from the breast pocket of his jacket, he unfolded the papers and handed them to Dr. Goetz. The man read them silently and then looked at Stefan over his glasses.

"You've got to go," he said. He folded the letter and handed it back to him. "There is no other choice."

"Can't I appeal this?"

"Appeal? Hah! There's no such thing. Besides, you were lucky to have avoided it for this long."

Stefan thought of Mrs. Eschelbach.

"But Stefan," continued Dr. Goetz. "Think about it. If you still want to help, this will offer you opportunities to do just that and in ways that would not have been possible here."

Stefan sat quietly for a moment.

"So Thursday is when you report," Goetz continued. "Will you be ready?"

Stefan nodded. He had a lump in his throat.

"You'll be ready," said Dr. Goetz. "I'm sure of it."

They heard footsteps approaching in the hall. Both men stood.

"You must go now," said Dr. Goetz. He stuck out his hand, then pulled Stefan close when he accepted the handshake.

"Though you will not be here, you will have your own chance to do what is right," he whispered. "So be strong and have courage."

He released Stefan's hand from his grip.

"Good bye, Stefan," he said, striding over to the door. He paused a moment before throwing it open. "And God bless you."

Stefan walked past him out the door, leaving the office with his head spinning. He stumbled down the hall and into the dazzling sunshine of the university courtyard, never noticing the young man with the withered hand who lurked outside Dr. Goetz's office.

Chapter 12

The square was busy on Saturday night and they had to make two circles around the courthouse before a spot came open on the street just down from Sutton's corner location. The western-themed restaurant had been around forever. It was popular by default, literally the only place to eat in town.

As they approached in the twilight, the restaurant's red neon sign buzzed loudly and cast its glow on the sidewalk as they passed beneath it. "UTTON"S," it read. The "S" had been broken out as long as Katherine could remember, but Mr. Sutton apparently saw no need to have it repaired. The big windows that fronted the street showed that every table inside was full; even the bar area had diners waiting to be seated. Busboys hustled to clear and reset tables, hefting heavy tubs of dirty dishes as they maneuvered through the crowded dining room.

Approaching the front door, Whitcomb hurried the last little bit, speeding his unsteady steps so that he could grandly throw open the door, holding it wide for her to enter. Katherine had no choice but to follow this dramatic flourish, and as she climbed the three steps that led into the restaurant, she felt all eyes on her.

"Well, hello Katherine," smiled the lady who met them at the door. She wore a red and white checkered apron, and her white hair was pulled in a tight bun. "What a pleasure to have you join us tonight."

"Hi," smiled Katherine, blinking and smiling blankly. Just when it seemed things couldn't get any worse, along came another surprise. It was Stella Wade, her neighbor, who sometimes pitched in on busy weekends, especially if they were short staffed. Having Mrs. Wade see her out with a man was as good as putting it in the paper. Spreading gossip was first-rate entertainment in a little town like Augusta, and Katherine had just provided enough material for the next six months.

"And who's your friend?" asked Mrs. Wade, pursing her lips and leaning toward Whitcomb. She sized him up through her thick glasses, ready to grab this chance for some juicy information. "I don't believe I've seen him before."

"Name's Whitcomb, ma'am. Robert Whitcomb," he jumped in. He stuck out his hand and pumped hers up and down in a fierce shake. "I'm one of the soldiers staying with the prisoners out at the Lorberg's farm."

"Yes," said Mrs. Wade. "I've seen those men out there. Germans, aren't they? It must be exciting work guarding those men."

"Yes, ma'am, it is," said Whitcomb. "Very dangerous. We soldiers have to be extremely vigilant at all times."

Katherine looked at him sharply. Whitcomb and the other two guards spent most of their time either playing cards in the barracks or sleeping under a shade tree while the prisoners worked in an adjacent field. Vigilant was not exactly the word that came to mind.

"Well, thank you for the service you are giving our country," said Mrs. Wade. "It's boys like you who really make us proud."

"Yes, ma'am. Thank you. It's an honor to serve wherever Uncle Sam puts me."

Katherine rolled her eyes.

"It'll be just a couple of minutes more. Care to be seated at the bar?" asked Mrs. Wade. "Perhaps you'd like a cocktail until your table is ready."

"No thanks." Katherine said. "We'll just . . . "

"Great!" he said, grabbing Katherine by the elbow, pulling her toward the two empty stools. She jerked her arm away from him as they sat.

"I'll be right back," said Mrs. Wade, smiling at Robert and Katherine. She returned to her post at the front door where other diners waited.

"Don't touch me like that again!" she hissed at him as the woman left. He was leaned forward, elbows on the bar, scoping out the bottles lined against the back mirror.

A bartender came. "What can I get you?"

Katherine shook her head, "Nothing."

"Two beers and a shot of bourbon," said Whitcomb. He twirled on the barstool to face her. He smiled. "She's a nice old gal."

"Didn't you hear me?" Katherine demanded, but was interrupted again. Mrs. Wade came back and stood behind them, putting her hand on Robert Whitcomb's shoulder.

"Mr. Whitcomb, any time you want to come by for dinner, you are welcome at our house." She patted his cheek gently. "God bless you boys!"

"Thank you, ma'am, and thank you for your kind offer. That would be nice."

The bartender set two glasses of beer in front of Robert and Katherine and poured the whiskey into a heavy tumbler in front of him.

"I didn't order this," said Katherine.

"It's not for you. Cheers." Whitcomb lifted the shot glass, toasted Katherine and downed the whiskey. Grimacing, he clanked down the heavy glass down then picked up one of the beers and gulped about half for a chaser.

"Yep, seems like a nice old gal. You know her?" Whitcomb asked. "She must live out by us, huh?"

"She lives out by *me*," said Katherine.

Whitcomb finished the remaining half glass of beer and wiped his mouth with the back of his hand. He switched the empty glass with the full one in front of Katherine. When the bartender came back to retrieve the empty glasses, he held up the tumbler.

"Another?"

Whitcomb gave what he thought was a subtle nod, a sideways tilt of the head and a wink, and the bartender soon returned with a second glass of the brown liquid.

"You've been drinking already," said Katherine. "I don't think it's a good idea to have any more."

"Nonsense," said Whitcomb. "I'm pacing myself. Besides, what's an evening out at a fine restaurant without a drink or a bottle of wine?"

Katherine looked at herself in the mirror behind the bar and tried to figure out what to do. She couldn't just walk out and leave. That would only provide more fodder for the local rumor mill. She would have to play along, eat dinner and endure the evening. Make it as brief as possible, then try to get the keys when it was time to drive home.

"Your table is ready." Mrs. Wade was again at their shoulders.

"Thank you, ma'am." Whitcomb smiled warmly at her.

"Please," she chirped at him. "Call me Stella."

"Thank you," he lingered on the syllables, caressing them like he was whispering his lover's name, "Stella."

Katherine thought the woman was going to swoon.

"Christ," she muttered. "I can't believe this."

They followed Mrs. Wade to a booth in the back corner of the main dining room. Katherine moved fast and kept her head down, hoping she didn't see anyone else that she knew. She slid into the booth as Whitcomb did the same on the opposite side. Soon the waitress was there and they both looked up as she stood over them holding menus. She was blond, with a tight blouse and a tight face. Her ample cleavage strained against the buttons in the front of her Sutton's uniform.

"Hi y'all. I'm Loretta," she said, note pad in hand. "Can I get you something to drink?"

Katherine frowned, her eyes narrowing. Whitcomb's eyes grew big. His glass eye wiggled like it was going to plop out in his lap. Katherine knew this Loretta but hadn't seen her for years. They had been in the same class in high school. She had been pregnant at eighteen. Twice married. Now she had three kids under age seven and was divorced again.

"You bet!" said Whitcomb, smiling and leering at the waitress. He gave her a big wink. Katherine couldn't decide if she should be happy or troubled by this development. Maybe he could be husband number three, she thought. Katherine remembered a strong dislike for her back in high school.

"Two beers and a bourbon," said Whitcomb. "On the rocks." He stared at her chest, mesmerized by its bobbing as she wrote in her notepad.

She giggled and left to get the drinks, wiggling all the way back to the bar. Whitcomb's eyes stayed fixed on her bottom until she went around the corner.

Snapping out of it, he turned to look back at Katherine who sat with her hands clasped on the table. She smiled politely at him. She was definitely glad for this development. That floozy could keep him distracted, and all she had to do was eat and then drive them back home. Then, thank God, the evening would be finished.

"I know you," Loretta nodded to Katherine as she returned carrying a tray with their drinks, "but where are you from, sailor?"

"Well, gosh" chuckled Whitcomb, looking sheepish. "I'm not really a sailor, I'm a GI. And I'm from New Mexico."

"Oooh," she crooned, "a foreigner."

Katherine rolled her eyes. Whitcomb looked puzzled. Loretta giggled but didn't know why. "Here's menus," she announced, handing them each a vinyl bound folder, leaning across the table so Whitcomb could get a full look at her chest.

"I'll be back in a minute," she said, fluffing her hair and winking at Whitcomb.

There was silence for a couple of minutes as they scanned the menu.

"What're you gonna have?" he asked.

Something quick, thought Katherine.

"I'm think I'll order the pork chop special," she said instead.

"You said they've got good steaks?"

"Yes." It was Katherine's suggestion about the steaks that got her in this whole mess in the first place.

"Well, I'm getting the fried chicken," said Whitcomb, closing his menu.

The meal itself passed mercifully fast. The steady crowd of diners waiting in the front room to be seated wasn't entirely lost on Loretta, and she hustled out their plates, kept them moving, wanting to turn tables as fast as she could. They ate mostly in silence, the only interruption Loretta's bold flirting with Whitcomb each time she stopped by their table.

When the bill was presented, Katherine excused herself to use the ladies room while Whitcomb pored over the tab.

"Sheesh," he muttered as she walked off. "Who ordered all these drinks?!"

Inside the restroom, the wooden door held the noise of the dining room at bay. Katherine wanted a moment to herself. She had lost count of Whitcomb's drinks after a half-dozen, and she knew getting the keys from him would be a struggle.

She leaned over the sink, splashed water on her face and looked at herself in the mirror. She looked older, tired, and saw the dark circles that had formed underneath her eyes. The stress of the evening had taken its toll on her already but the worst was yet to come.

The din of the dining room washed over her again as she opened the door and picked her way back to the table. Whitcomb was standing now, talking to Loretta, who was writing something on her notepad. She tore off the sheet of paper as Katherine approached and pressed it into Whitcomb's hand.

"Um, hello, Katherine," smiled Whitcomb, trying to fold the paper with one hand and slide it in his pocket. Instead he dropped it on the floor. He tried to pick it up, and Loretta giggled again, smirking at Katherine.

Katherine smiled at Loretta. The waitress stood before her, still giggling and smirking, clutching Whitcomb's arm.

"Go to hell," Katherine said pleasantly, still smiling. Loretta's mouth fell open.

Katherine turned to Whitcomb and held out her hand. She wanted the keys to the truck. He turned white, then red, the look of a boy who'd been caught by his mother. He reached into his pocket, slowly extracted the paper from the waitress' notepad, and laid it on Katherine's palm. "Loretta" it said. "332 South Water Street." A heart surrounded the words.

"Not that, you dope," Katherine laughed out loud. "The keys."

Whitcomb turned a deeper shade now, a purple she hadn't seen before.

"Let's go," he said, snatching the paper back and jamming it into his pocket. "I'm fine."

He tried to march to the front door but Katherine put her hand on his chest. "You're not fine. You're drunk. That's why I'm driving."

Loretta tried to step between them. "You leave him be," she warned Katherine, her voice growing louder. "You should know better'n to act like that towards a man who took you out to a nice dinner."

Katherine looked around, heard the restaurant grow quiet. Conversations stopped in mid-sentence.

"He just had one beer. It's you who's drunk. You ought to be ashamed of yourself going on like this." Loretta's voice rang in the room. "No wonder you ain't got a man."

Katherine heard Stella Wade gasp clear from her station near the front door, saw the old woman's hands fly to her face. Silence hung in the air and she felt the entire room of diners staring at her. Katherine felt dizzy and her face grew hot. She turned and headed quickly for the front door, weaving through the crowd of diners and out into the cool night air.

(Bilfung)
Seben Inspektionsstelle in R.O.A.
vor der Geinreise 1946

Chapter 13

Stefan boarded a train in the pre-dawn drizzle, and stared out the window as the rails carried him toward Munich. He was glad at least that Maria had come with him to the station.

"Good God, Stefan," she had complained. "It's raining. Can't I just say goodbye to you here?"

He thought back to their embrace that morning, just before he stepped onto the train. He promised to return, his face pressed so tightly to hers that she could taste his tears.

Stefan shifted in the uncomfortable seat, tried to find a way to prop his leg up on the thin suitcase that carried his stuff. Though the train had been mostly empty early on, the cars picked up draftees at stops along the way. They were all headed to the same place, one of the army's training camps for new recruits. Most were younger than Stefan, barely out of high school. They sat silently on the train.

Mid-morning an older man got on, someone closer to his age. The man had a pleasant look about him, curly red hair, an easy smile and an ample gut. Stefan motioned to the empty seat next to him, glad for the company. At thirty he felt like a grandpa compared to these 18- and 19-year-olds.

"Stefan Biermann," he said to the man, and stuck out his hand. His new friend took it in his own and shook it.

"Otto Haertling," he replied. "Did the draft get you, too?" he asked as he settled into his seat.

"I was a teacher," Stefan offered. "Never thought this day would come."

"Nor I," said Otto. "I was a mechanic. Wife, two girls at home." He shook his head wistfully. "Guess we'll have to make the best of it."

The train rolled on, finally stopping around noon at an army training camp in the middle of nowhere. Stefan looked out at an empty depot next to drab buildings that crowded the tracks. A sergeant stood there frowning.

"Let's go," he shouted impatiently ordering the men to climb out of the train cars and the recruits were swallowed up by army life, wholly owned by instructors who controlled their every minute. The first days were devoted to rudimentary drills like marching and practicing salutes. Next marksmanship, map and compass work, filling the days from morning to night. Stefan hated it, but what choice did he have? He could never fake the enthusiasm for the shouting, the crawling through the woods that captivated the younger recruits, but at least he had a friend to commiserate with. And Stefan and Otto found that things went best when they stayed below the radar of the brutal sergeants who ran the training camp.

The recruits took their meals in an enormous dining hall with a high ceiling, criss-crossed by heavy wooden beams. Though the ancient hall was jammed with hundreds of new troops, it was silent other than the feverish scraping of forks and spoons on metal plates as the recruits hurried to finish eating. Sergeants prowled about, hatefully eyeing their charges, looking for any whisper of conversation, any excuse to seize a man and drag him from the hall.

However, one day during the fourth week that silent routine was broken, when suddenly the massive double doors at the back of the hall burst open, smashing into the wall with a thunderous crash. Six men with jet-black uniforms and high black boots came barreling in.

"Recruits, attention!" someone shouted, and all jumped to their feet, the wooden benches scraping back behind them. The room was completely silent except for a fork, clattering to the floor on the opposite side of the great hall.

Clump. Clump. Clump.

Stefan could hear the slow, deliberate steps of a single pair of boots in the long hallway outside. Otto standing next to him looked nervously at his friend but said nothing.

Clump. Clump. Clump.

There, framed in the doorway, stood an SS officer. He wore a jet black uniform with the lightning bolt SS and the death's head emblem on his lapels. His dark hair was combed straight back, and his coal black eyes slowly scanned the room.

"Sit down, recruits," said the officer. He slowly walked the length of the long room until he reached the front. He turned to face them, and a slow smile crept across his face as his eyes went around the room, sizing them up. It was not a friendly smile.

"I am Major Leider," he said. "I am an officer in the SS."

He paused for a moment.

"You are familiar with the SS, no?"

Of course they knew the SS. Everyone did. The SS ran the death camps. They were fanatical in their loyalty to Hitler.

"Good. Then I know that you want to be a part of the SS and our proud tradition of service and defense to the Führer and the Fatherland. And I am here to invite you today."

The room was completely silent. Leider looked around the room. The air was thick with anticipation.

"Would all those who do not wish to volunteer for the SS please stand up."

Stefan thought of Michael. How he suffered at the hands of these bastards. He felt his legs lifting him from his chair. He could not stay seated, could not "volunteer" for the SS though he knew that to defy them was insanity. Stefan stood.

"Are you crazy?" Otto hissed.

Stefan felt his head grow light and he started to sweat. He was probably 30 feet from Leider and he felt the man looking right at him. There was an uncomfortable shifting in the room. Somewhere somebody coughed and Stefan looked around. There were two others also standing! Stefan could not believe it. There was strength in numbers, even if it were just the three of them. At least he was not alone. And then Otto took a deep breath and stood next to his friend.

"You, in the back." Leider was looking past Stefan now, frowning at a slight young man with pale skin and blond hair. "Why don't you want to volunteer for the SS?"

"Sir. I have already volunteered for the *Panzerkorps*," he said in a high voice, looking down at his feet. "I want to be a tanker."

"We have tanks in the SS," said Leider, smiling again slightly. "Sit down. And you?" he asked the next one, a fellow closer in age to Stefan.

"I also volunteered for something else, sir. I signed up to be in the artillery."

"We have artillery, too, in our SS units," said Leider. "And they are a far sight better than those in the regular army. Sit down."

He turned to face Stefan and Otto, now standing alone near the front. Stefan felt every eye in the place on them.

"And you two?"

Stefan tried to think. His mouth was dry and his mind was blank.

"We want to be submariners," came Otto's strong, clear voice. He was looking Leider right in the eye. He knew the SS had no submarines. "It's been a life-long dream."

Leider stared back at them for a moment, the disgust evident.

"Hmmph. That's a fine way to go pissing away a chance to really serve your country," he growled at Otto. "Sit down, submarine boy."

The other recruits twittered quietly until he shut them down instantaneously with a fierce glare.

Stefan felt his legs fall from under him, and he collapsed into his seat. Otto sank down next to him and gave him a weak smile.

"And for the rest of you, we shall see if you are good enough for the SS to take you," said the Major. "Only the best of the best are accepted."

All was quiet. Leider stared around the room one last time, then nodded to the men standing behind him. Three quickly moved in front to escort him out of the room while the others fell in behind. The light gleamed off the black polish of their leather.

"Recruits, attention!" shouted one of the sergeants. They rose as one.

"Honor to the Fatherland!" shouted Leider.

"Honor to the Fatherland," shouted the recruits back to him.

"Honor to the Führer!" shouted Leider, and the call came back in return.

"Honor to the SS!" Hundreds of voices roared back their answer and the building shook with the volume. The heavy boots began to clump again across the floor of the dining hall as Leider and the six men in his company marched out of the room, the huge doors slamming shut behind them.

Still in his chair, Stefan's legs felt weak and his hands trembled. His palms and his armpits were soaked with sweat but his mouth was dry. He wanted to sit there for just a minute to regain his composure, but the sergeants were already shouting that it was time to go.

Chapter 14

On the square, Katherine felt panicky and out of breath. She ran first toward the truck, but then turned for the opposite direction where she found herself framed in the headlights of passing cars. She hurried along the sidewalk, glad to turn the corner onto the quieter street that headed toward home. Soon, a truck pulled up next to her.

"Hey cutie," Whitcomb hollered through the window, grinning as he idled alongside. His face showed no trace of the anger she had seen before. "Want a ride?"

She kept marching down the sidewalk, ignoring him.

"It's a long walk back to the farm." The truck idled alongside her, following her. "It'll take you all night."

Katherine stopped. She glared at him. She wanted to be home, but she knew she could never walk there. And she sure wasn't calling her mother. That truck seemed to be the lone option.

"The only way I'm getting in is if you hand over the keys."

"Here. Hop in. You watch me drive and if there are problems, you take over. Promise."

Katherine hesitated. He stopped on the gravel shoulder and set the brake.

"Promise." His face was serious, sincere.

Katherine opened the truck door and climbed in.

"Yeeehaaaaa!" shrieked Whitcomb. He stomped on the accelerator, and the truck's tires screeched as he peeled out. The rear end swung wide into somebody's yard, shredding a flowerbed as he spun through the grass. Whitcomb cranked the wheel the other way and the truck slung back into the street, fish-tailing in the opposite direction, leaving black ribbons of scorched rubber on the concrete. He spun up into the lawns on the other side of the street, thumping a mailbox before finally bringing the truck straight again.

"Stop it!" screamed Katherine, but Whitcomb grinned and laughed like a maniac as he clutched the wheel. "I mean it!"

"Aw, darling, just having fun," he said, winking at her and easing off the accelerator a bit. Though they still buzzed along the narrow road a bit faster than she liked, Whitcomb kept the truck in the lane. Now all she had to do was get home.

"So you know Loretta?" he asked as they left town. "She sure seems like a sweet gal."

Katherine turned to look at him in astonishment. She thought he was joking. But Whitcomb said nothing, kept his hands on the wheel, just driving. He was oblivious to pretty much everything that had taken place back at the restaurant.

"I knew her in high school," said Katherine, settling in her seat. "We weren't really friends or anything."

"Oh."

They were nearing home, just another ten minutes or so. Almost done with the night. Whitcomb hummed along as music played softly on the radio and Katherine took a deep breath and exhaled, looking out the window. Stars filled the clear night.

"Um . . . what are you doing?" Katherine asked, glancing over at him. Whitcomb, feeling smooth, had casually draped his arm across the seat behind her shoulders.

"Nothing, hon. Just trying to be comfortable."

"Would you please put your arm down?"

He looked at her, smiled and removed his arm. "Sure."

As Whitcomb turned into the drive, Katherine saw her mother's face silhouetted in the window upstairs. The light was quickly extinguished but Katherine knew she continued to watch. Whitcomb cut the motor in front of the house and they coasted to a stop, the wheels crunching on the gravel.

Katherine grabbed the door handle and pulled. She couldn't believe it was finally over.

"Wait," said Whitcomb. "I had a really nice time . . ." He blew out a boozy breath and looked at her meaningfully. "Katherine."

"Good night," said Katherine. She was in no mood for this. She stepped out of the truck and closed the door. As she turned toward the house, she heard Whitcomb's door open, and his heavy steps circling the truck.

"Hey doll," he said, following her quickly, "don't go so fast. Don't I even get a good-night kiss?"

He grabbed her arm and stopped her. His big rough hand gripped her too tight. She looked at him, feeling her anger mixing with cold fear in her stomach as she read the man's intent.

Oh God, no, she thought. Not another scene.

She didn't need any more drama, especially with her mother watching.

I'll scream if I have to, but please God, help me figure out something here.

From the darkness next to the porch came a deep growl, a threatening, throaty noise whose meaning could not be mistaken.

"Boomer, come," she said, calling out into the night, joy and relief washing through her.

The jingling of the dog's collar sounded through the darkness as the big animal trotted quickly toward them.

"Get your hands off of me," Katherine said. "I told you that once already."

The dog stood next to Katherine, his muzzle inches from the man's crotch, a deep growl still rumbling its warning to Whitcomb.

"Heh, heh," said Whitcomb. "Nice dog."

He released his grip on Katherine's arm and bent as if he were going to pat the dog's head. He only got halfway there with his hand when the growling doubled in pitch and volume and the dog bared his teeth.

"Okay," said Whitcomb, standing quickly. "No pet."

"We're done," said Katherine. "Time for you to go."

"But – "

"Now. Unless you want that dog to take a big chunk right out of your backside."

Whitcomb hesitated for just a second. "I just wanted one ---"

"Now," repeated Katherine, patting the dog's head. Boomer's growling continued, only reinforcing her command.

"Fine," Whitcomb huffed. He walked slowly backwards, still eyeing the dog. "You take a girl out," he grumbled as he returned to the truck, "just want to say goodnight, and she goes all cold fish on you."

He climbed in the cab, slammed the door, scowled at her, and fired up the motor. She could hear his angry mutterings continue out the open window as he left the driveway.

With Whitcomb finally gone, the strain of what she had been through finally caught up with her. Katherine felt weak in the knees and weak in the heart. She knelt and wrapped her arms around the warm dog, and buried her face into his soft fur.

Ж

Avoiding Whitcomb for the next few days was the only concern Katherine had. She planned to keep her distance, reckoning she could dodge him easy enough until the camp was closed and the men were all gone.

But sure enough, first thing Monday morning, there he was waiting for her outside the house when she opened the front door to cross to the office.

"Good morning, lovely Katherine," he said loudly, doing the same goofy sweeping bow. "I surely had a wonderful time with you Saturday night."

The small clutch of farm hands gathered on the other side of the courtyard stopped to watch and listen. They could only adore Katherine from a distance and the notion of a night out with her got their imaginations running hot.

The anger and embarrassment of that evening came flooding back over Katherine. She bit her lip, willed herself not to cry.

"Sergeant Whitcomb, please don't talk to me again."

"But Katherine," he looked shocked and hurt. "I felt a spark between us. Didn't you feel it, too?"

He dropped to one knee like he was going to propose, hands clasped, extended toward her.

"I'd like to see you again before we go," he said. "Tonight. Tomorrow night. Any night."

Katherine couldn't help it. She laughed out loud. As much as she detested this jackass, in a way she felt sorry for him, too.

"Listen. Saturday night was horrible in more ways than I can even remember." She shook her head in amazement, couldn't hold back the words. "No. Not for a million bucks. Not if you were the last man on earth."

His face froze, flashed that purple shade, but only for a moment.

"Fine," he said, standing stiffly. "If that's the way you feel. But you're making a mistake, sweet Katherine."

"Perhaps," said Katherine, walking past him. "Just leave me be."

Ж

After that, she only saw him from a distance. Things were busy with the POWs preparing to leave, and Whitcomb was fully occupied. Katherine did her part too, making herself as scarce as possible while still attending to required farm business.

On the morning of the POWs' departure, Katherine stood with John and Caroline on the front porch of the big white house. It was a clear and sunny day, and a half-dozen olive drab army trucks waited in a long line. The three GIs swarmed around the trucks, making last minute adjustments to their loads, shifting boxes of equipment, retying ropes that held the canvas tops on the back.

"Time to roll," shouted the soldier standing at the lead truck. One by one the truck engines roared to life, rumbling blue clouds of smoke across the courtyard. The Germans ambled from their loose group by the fence to the trucks where they swung themselves into the back.

Like a parade of elephants, the trucks pulled slowly out of the barnyard and into the lane. Some of the men—Germans and Americans like—gave a nod or a wave to the Lorbergs as they passed by the big house. Katherine saw Whitcomb riding shotgun in the third truck. He gave no reaction, just looked blankly at them as he rolled by. And then they were gone.

Chapter 15

Even before he opened his eyes, Stefan felt the bombs shaking the ground, heard distant booms over the grumbling engines of the Allied planes far above him.

He sighed, stretched, and rubbed his eyes. With only his blanket for a cushion, Stefan had spent the past few nights in an empty wooden potato bin in the cellar of an old farmhouse. It was barely long enough to hold Stefan's lanky frame and hadn't seen potatoes since the first year of the war, but still stubbornly held its smell of must and lime.

Climbing out, Stefan began the morning the same way he began every other since being drawn into the war. He took a stale cigarette from the box in his breast pocket and lit it, inhaling deeply as he sat on the broken kitchen chair he had saved from being used for firewood. The chair had no back, but Stefan didn't mind. It was one of the few places left to sit in the farmhouse.

He had begun smoking again after basic training. He knew it wasn't the best thing for his health, but then neither was being in a war. Stefan figured he could worry about quitting later. Right now, it was one of the few pleasant things left.

As he exhaled blue smoke, he pulled out his worn leather wallet and extracted the picture of Maria he had received just a month before. Although the photo was creased and crinkled, the words on the back were as clear as when she had written them: *Stefan, I think of you often. Maria.* Not exactly the most romantic words ever written, but he wasn't complaining. At least she had sent something.

Stefan folded the photograph carefully and tucked it back into his wallet. He breathed in the last bit of nicotine from the cigarette and stood, readying himself for another day of this wretched war.

Two steps from the chair was an old box of rusty canning lids. Stefan kicked at the box hard enough to rattle the rings. This elicited a sleepy mumble from the lumpy mass curled up in a drab wool blanket on the floor on the other side of the narrow cellar. A stray lid lay apart from the others, and Stefan kicked at it, sending it clattering into the stone wall an inch or two above the tousled mass of red hair. A resigned chuckle escaped from the mass.

"Damn, Stefan. I don't know what's worse - those bombers or you."

With that, Otto turned over and gave Stefan a grin. He picked up the ring and flung it back at Stefan, missing by a good bit. Raising himself first to hands and knees, with a hearty grunt Otto huffed himself the rest of the way to his feet.

"Hell of a way to wake up," he continued, still smiling. He was dirty from lying on the floor. Beginning with his expansive belly, Otto tried to brush the cobwebs and dust off of his uniform, as if he could somehow improve on its present soiled state. "If those bastards are going to insist on hitting us every morning, at least they could be consistent on the timing. Maybe then I could get used to it. This is like having an alarm clock…that explodes."

Stefan and Otto were now in their third month in the war. After their initial training, they and a dozen other recruits had piled into a truck that meandered through the French countryside, dropping men here and there along the front as replacements for those who had been killed.

It was late September 1944, and things were going poorly. Defeats in North Africa and Russia had sapped the German army. After the Allied landing in Normandy four months earlier, they had been pushed back through France, and now were fighting just to hold their ground.

They rolled along in the back of the truck, packs and rifles at their sides, no one speaking as they bumped and jostled over the rough roads. Finally the vehicle stopped long enough to let out Stefan and Otto. Without so much as a wave, the driver took off to the next site, leaving them at their new home.

The pair found themselves as part of an infantry company assigned to hold the line against the advancing Americans. Their platoon of thirty-odd men was huddled in and around the village of Fontaine-le-Bourg, and the other platoons of the company were thinly spread around them across nearly five miles of rolling terrain. Communication was difficult, isolated as they were in the countryside. The men knew that they'd be squished like ants if an attack of any size came their way.

"Biermann! Haertling! Get up here! You've got stuff to do," came a voice shouting from the first floor.

The yelling meant they'd have about thirty seconds to choke down some breakfast, then head for their rotation on the line. Twenty-four hours in an observation post, peering into the valley, squinting for signs of the advancing Americans. It was a monotonous yet terrifying chore. In the depths of the night, every rustle in the distance was a squad of advancing Yankees, and every shadow in the valley was an American GI coming to take their lives.

The pair trudged up the creaky stairs from the basement, careful from painful experience to avoid steps that had been pried away long ago to become firewood. Stefan, blinded for a moment by the morning sun, could see only the silhouette of Buchholz, the sergeant who had called to them.

"You guys are too damn slow," grouched old Buchholz, shoving a crate with a few bits of stale dark bread toward them. "It's your turn to head out again, and it's already past seven."

The two went into the damp morning to join the other soldiers standing together in the front yard of the farmhouse, eating over the hood of a truck. Otto chomped lustily on the bread, washing down great bites with equally big gulps of cold and watery coffee from a tin cup. Stefan picked at a few bits of crust and looked around at the grimy men. Sometimes he just couldn't believe where he was now, what he was doing. It seemed a million miles, a million years from his life as a professor.

"Hey, don't forget lunch," said Otto. He pushed a knapsack toward Stefan, and then handed him a canteen, a bit more bread and a chunk of dried cheese. Stefan flicked at the mold growing on the cheese with his fingernail, trying to scrape it off as best he could while Otto scavenged a single tin of canned wurst that would be their main course while on watch.

Heads down, they shuffled and ducked from tree to house to fencerow to barn. Though the trip from company headquarters to the observation post was normally uneventful, Stefan and Otto both knew that it was a good idea to be careful. The Yankees on the other side of the valley were watching for activity, and didn't mind sending an occasional bullet zinging their way just to remind them of their presence.

"Wendlandt! Auth!" Stefan called softly as they approached the observation post. It was wise not to startle men with weapons.

"Yoo-hoo! Your replacements are here!" trilled Otto as they came around the side of the building to the doorway partly hidden by a tree.

"Haertling? Damn. About time you got here," said Auth, a skinny kid of about twenty. "Biermann with you?"

"Yeah, it's us. Sorry we're late," said Otto, poking his head inside. "We hurried as much as we could."

"Anything happen last night?" asked Stefan, following Otto inside as

Wendlandt and Auth began to collect their stuff.

"Nah, not much," said Wendlandt. "We heard the Yanks coming and going about eight o'clock last night. Don't know if they're bringing in new guys, resupplying or something else."

"Probably just messing around," agreed Stefan, noticing Wendlandt and Auth eyeing his pack with the bread and the cheese. "Hey, no sense hanging around here if you're hungry. Head on back."

"Right." Auth turned to go, then paused to look at Stefan and Otto one last time. "Good luck. I'm sure it'll be quiet."

The building was a relic; an old pump house nestled into the hillside at the edge of some woods. Built over a well, the small building was damp and cool, and moss grew on its perpetually shaded stone walls. Other than the slight gap for the doorway on the left, it was covered with overgrown bushes and trees. The front, facing away from the farm and down the hill, was more open. Two rectangular windows, glass and wooden frames long gone, allowed a broad view of the valley below.

"I'll watch," said Stefan. "You get your stuff settled."

While Otto fiddled with his gear, Stefan took out his field glasses and slowly scanned the valley. The area had once been a peaceful patchwork of meadows and fields, but with the war came the end of its cultivation. Now weeds and scrubby brush grew where cattle once grazed.

"Doesn't look like anything new," he said.

Peering up the hill on the opposite side of the long low valley, Stefan could faintly make out the enemy positions roughly a mile away. From time to time, men would appear briefly in the far distance before disappearing again, vanishing like a mirage on a hot summer day.

After a while, Otto took a turn scanning the valley and morning slowly drifted into afternoon. Stefan hunted deep in his pack for a blank sheet of paper. Though it was rumpled and already dirty, he spread the sheet on his leg and did his best to smooth the wrinkles from it.

"*My dearest Maria*," he wrote, beginning yet another letter to her. "*How often I think of you, and wonder when we'll be together. I long for the day of my return. . .*" Stefan stuck the stubby pencil between his teeth and stared at the ceiling. There hadn't been much remarkable to tell about his time in France but he managed to write at least once every day. The letters all said the same thing - he missed her dreadfully and longed to be home, on and on.

"Hey, know what occurs to me?" asked Otto.

"What's that?"

"These letters you're writing all say just about the same thing, right?"

"Well, yes. Pretty much."

"You should consider just making a bunch of copies, perhaps 30 or 40 sheets," offered Otto. "Then when you're ready to write, just date one, sign it and you're done. Save you a lot of time."

Otto's good-natured harassment made no difference to Stefan, and the two drifted into a comfortable silence. A half-hour passed before Otto spoke again.

"Stefan, what do you think is going to happen with all this?" It was the question that always seemed to come up.

"I don't know," Stefan replied, fishing in his pocket for a smoke. Otto's question had nothing to do with the scene in the valley or the possibility of any coming fight. It was about home, and the wife and two small daughters he had left behind. "Just depends on what the Führer decides to do."

"Did you know that Margarite turned four last week?" Otto asked. She was the littlest one, with red hair like her daddy. Margarite had been just a baby when he left. Her sister, Helene, was fair and beautiful, favoring Otto's wife, Elise. She would now be nearly six.

Stefan took a deep drag from the cigarette, held it in, then exhaled and continued talking as he stared out the window.

"The way I see it, if we just settled in, everybody'd sign some pact and it'd all be done. The British aren't in any condition to push the issue and hell, if you took the Americans out of the picture, we'd be on the island right now, eating crumpets and dancing with the queen at the royal ball."

They were both silent again, thinking. Stefan looked at his friend.

"I love them more than anything in the world," Otto said. "I just want this to be done."

In those rare moments when Otto let on how low he felt, it was always because of the awful emptiness and longing to be with his girls that filled his heart.

"I don't know what's going to happen," said Stefan, looking at his hands, slowly rolling the cigarette between his fingers. "I mean, it can't go on like this forever. Things are starting to crumble for Hitler. Somebody even tried to assassinate him. Maybe he's not got the grip on things he used to."

Out here in the woods was the only place where Otto and Stefan dared talk like this. You just didn't second-guess the Nazi leadership. What happened to Michael and the others was proof of that.

"What about you and Maria, Stefan?" Otto asked. "Marriage in your future?"

Even though they'd had the same conversation at least a dozen times, Stefan didn't mind. It was his turn to talk, to think out loud, and he hoped that, if nothing else, maybe it would help him figure out that confounded woman. He looked into the lengthening shadows outside, heard the evening breeze and thought of Maria.

"I love her a lot. Enough to marry her? Absolutely. But, that's where she's different. She didn't want to get married before. Wasn't ready, she said. "

Stefan snuffed out the smoke on the stone windowsill and turned toward his friend.

"I'm ready to settle down. I had a secure teaching position at the university. Not tenure yet, I know, but a well-paying combination of both teaching and writing. And Maria was a perfect part of that picture..."

His words trailed off and he looked back out the window, past the thin trail of smoke that still curled up from the crushed cigarette. They both thought about the people they loved back home, a world away from the French woods.

No matter what happened, Stefan thought, he'd return to Maria and he'd marry her. He may not get his teaching position back, but at least he'd have her. He could make her love him, and they'd be happy together, he was sure. She told him once that he didn't exactly set her heart aflutter when she looked at him. That stung him a bit, but hey, they didn't live in a fairy tale world. You couldn't expect everything to be perfect.

"Sorry," sighed Otto, "didn't mean to bring you down. Listen, you've got the midnight shift, so why don't you try to sleep some now. It'll take your mind off that same old crap we kick around every time we come out here. Christ, you'd think we could find something else to talk about. Football, or the opera or trees or something."

"Sounds fine. Wake me when it's time." Stefan positioned his pack for a pillow, pulled his cap over his eyes and he slept.

X

A couple of weeks before shipping out, he and Maria had gone to the countryside to his grandparent's farm, a place on the hills high above the Rhein where Stefan had spent his summers as a youth.

"Why do you love it so much?" Maria asked him on the drive out. Even after he began teaching, Stefan still went out to the farm as often as he could.

"Hard to say." He smiled. "It's just different from the university."

He savored the labor in the vineyards, the way the dirt felt in his hands and the soreness that stayed in his muscles after working there. The most strenuous thing he ever did in academia was stand behind a lectern, trying to keep drowsy coeds from nodding off.

They ate lunch with his grandparents on the balcony, watching the river far below. The sun shone on them and the ominousness of the war seemed far, far away. It was peaceful and lazy and after coffee and dessert, Grandma started washing the dishes and Grandpa announced that he was going to take a nap.

"Go for a walk?" Stefan asked.

She nodded, and they went into the fields, following the paths that led through the terraces lining the hillsides, where the rows of grapevines grew. He was glad to be with her, as always, but especially eager to show her around this place he had loved so long.

"Oooh, it's hot," she said, fanning herself as she tottered on the rocky path soon after they left the house.

"It'll be cooler when we get higher up."

"And your grandparents' house," she said, "what a place."

"Yeah," said Stefan, smiling, "Isn't it, though?" He loved the knickknacks that crowded the shelves and the quaint pictures on the walls of their little home. Nothing had changed since he was a small boy and visiting always carried him back to his childhood making him feel warm and secure inside.

"What a bunch of junk they've got," said Maria. "And God, the decor. I don't think it's been updated in the last forty years."

Stefan said nothing, just frowned.

"And what in the world was that stuff she served for dessert?" asked Maria, wrinkling her nose, "Ugh." she concluded. "Must be some country thing."

"That," said Stefan, "was rhubarb with sugar and cream, one of her specialties."

"Rhubarb?" asked Maria. "I didn't think anyone actually ate that stuff."

"Maria, it's my favorite dessert. She made it especially for me."

"Well, goody. How much longer do we have to walk? My feet hurt."

Stefan didn't reply.

"I'm sweating," she said. "I want to go back."

Stefan gritted his teeth.

"Do you even know where you're going?" she asked. "Stefan, this path is too steep."

They continued on in silence until she stopped completely, arms crossed on her chest. He turned and looked at her.

"I know you think this is great, Stefan, but I just can't get thrilled about walking around on a hillside looking at grapes." She gave a big huffy breath. "Are you ready to go back now?"

Stefan glared at her. He could wander for hours among the grapevines and the terraces, and it never got old. He loved this place more than anywhere on earth.

"Maria, just look at that," he said, pointing out into the valley, with the river a ribbon below them. Farther upstream the turrets of a 16th-century castle were visible over a bend in the river. "How can you complain when it is so beautiful?! Christ." He turned uphill again. "Let's keep going, just a little bit more."

In a few minutes, they'd reach a spot close to the top of the massive bluff where the view was absolutely spectacular. The hillside dropped sharply there, spilling down almost a hundred feet where a cool spring had etched itself into the rock, drip by drip, through the centuries. They could sit together there and look over the valley. He knew that there she would finally see what made this such a magical place.

"We're almost there. You're going to love it."

The path flattened as they drew near and Stefan took Maria's hand. The place was just around the curve of the hill, not a hundred yards away. Stefan felt his excitement growing as they made the last few steps. It had been a long while since he had been up here, and he prepared himself to be overcome once more by the beauty and peacefulness of the idyllic spot.

As they finally walked together onto the overlook, the spring dripped from a mossy opening in the hillside, forming a clear dark pool. A light breeze came from higher in the hills, tickling the leaves around them. Leading her by the hand, he took her to the edge, where the ground dropped away sharply to reveal the majesty of the entire landscape spreading out in front of them.

"Here we are," he said softly.

Tiny farms dotted the mountains with brown cattle and red barns interspersed between the rows and rows of grapes covering the hillsides with green. Far below, they could see boats puffing slowly along the dark green ribbon of water toward the faint confluence off in the distance where the Rhein and the Mosel came together at Koblenz. To Stefan, it was the most glorious place on Earth.

She squeezed his hand and looked up at him. He turned to her, gazing deeply in her eyes.

"Wow, Stefan," she said. She scrunched up her face and frowned. "This is really dumb. You mean to tell me we climbed all the way for this?" She turned and started to walk back down the hill.

Stefan took three steps toward her, quickly closing the distance between them.

It had been too much. Rage formed a boiling pressure between his eyes, and he went toward her with every intention of shoving her off the ledge and down onto the lovely green fields spread out below.

But then she stopped, and he did too. Maria turned slowly in the path to face him. She smiled and suddenly he felt hopeful, his heart lifting again.

"Well, are you coming?" she asked. She stood, hands on hips, square and unmoving in the middle of the path. "Or am I going to have to walk back from this thrilling little adventure all by myself?"

Stefan suddenly felt very tired.

"Sure," he said finally. "We can go."

X

Stefan lay in the darkness and listened to Otto cough a couple of times and fiddle with his equipment as he peered out the front. He had been awake for a while but in no hurry to sit up. The coming watch would give him plenty of time to chew on all these things rolling through his mind.

"Psssst, Stefan," whispered Otto after a little while. "Wake up. It's your turn."

Stefan remained silent.

"Stefan," Otto whispered again, this time with a nudge.

Stefan sat up, pulled out the white handkerchief he always carried and loudly blew his nose in it. Right before he left, Maria had given him a half dozen, all embroidered with his initials. It was the only thing remotely sentimental she had ever given him.

"Maria give you those fancy hankies?"

Stefan nodded.

"They linen?"

Stefan nodded again.

"Rather precious for out here, don't you think?" asked Otto.

Stefan shrugged.

"I guess it's always good to keep one handy," said Otto. "You flap that thing for surrender at anyone who'll take it and we can be out of this mess."

"I'll keep that in mind," said Stefan. He smiled, and they traded places so that Stefan was by the window. Otto stretched himself on the floor, shifting and scratching. He put his head on his backpack, using it for a pillow, trying in vain to get comfortable. There was no moon, but they'd had dark nights before. What they could hear was more important than what they could see. Even in broad daylight, the noise of engines and men moving in the distance carried well beyond what they could see from their perch.

An hour passed perhaps, and Stefan sat chin on hands, thinking and watching, when a sudden snap, a stick breaking maybe, jerked Stefan back to the present. He tensed involuntarily, feeling the instant race of cold panic and adrenaline in his veins. He took a deep breath, let it out slowly and tried to relax. Noises happened a thousand times a night when you really listened, but they usually meant nothing. "It's good to be alert," Buchholz, the old sergeant always said, "but you don't want to fill your drawers every six minutes either." Stefan lit a smoke and sat back, ears straining against the silence.

Just as he heard movement again, this time much closer, gunfire broke out on the hillside farther down the valley. Suddenly shooting was everywhere. Once the volleys began, they erupted in a deafening crescendo until the roar was everywhere around them. At the first sound of firing, Otto sprang from where he lay and tried to jam a magazine in his weapon through the daze of deep sleep from which he had been yanked.

The Yankees were clearly moving toward them across the valley but whether it was an out-and-out attack or merely a feint to divert attention from elsewhere, he wasn't sure and really didn't care. Dead was dead, whether the pushpins on the planners' boards showed the main American force here or ten miles south.

Stefan stuck his rifle through the window and sprayed with rapid left to right bursts down the hill. He didn't know exactly where the bastards were, but figured he might hold them back a bit. That was a mistake as immediately return fire zinged in on them from no less than four different places, shown by the little orange tongues of fire flickering from gun barrels scattered through the trees.

"Oh boy," said Otto. "We're in trouble."

The radio crackled with sounds of the attack mixed with shouting and shooting from the posts scattered up and down the valley. Otto and Stefan continued the furious exchange of gunfire, aiming quick bursts where they thought the attackers might be, and then ducking again just as fast.

Despite their efforts, he could tell the Americans were getting closer. He didn't realize just how near they were, however, until he heard the clunk of a grenade hitting the floor of the pump house, tossed through the window in front of him.

"Look out," screamed Otto.

Stefan watched in slow motion as the grenade rolled between his legs and dropped into the slight trough that drained the hand-pump. He only had time to dive to the far corner before the explosion rocked the pump house and knocked him unconscious.

Chapter 16

When Stefan came to, it took him a moment to figure out what had happened. He was still in the pump house, though now lying on his stomach on the floor. A soldier holding a rifle stood in the doorway, framed by the sun pouring in behind him. Their own weapons were missing and the sounds of the fighting were long gone. Though Stefan couldn't see the man's face, he recognized the American uniform.

Stefan's head throbbed and one of his eyes was swollen shut. He coughed, trying to spit out the grit of dirt and blood that filled his mouth. Hearing the noise, a soldier came and stood over him, keeping the gun trained on him.

"Speak English?" asked the man. Stefan nodded. He could see the GI more clearly now. He was short and broad-chested, a sergeant who looked to be about 25.

"Get up," the soldier told them. Otto lay nearby and he nudged him with his foot to ensure a response. Though he was groggy and had powder burns on the side of his face, he seemed otherwise unhurt.

The soldier marched them at gunpoint, hands on their heads, up the ridge towards the farmhouse, where three others captured from their company waited below an elm tree next to the house. The GI motioned for them to stand and fall in next to Otto and Stefan.

"This way," said the American sergeant, and he swung his rifle toward the little village. Shuffling along single file, they spent the rest of the morning on foot, following the dusty country roads to Fontaine-le-Bourg, adding others who had been captured as they went.

At the village, the GI marching them stopped the group outside a barn, where two more American soldiers sat at a pair of field desks just inside the door.

"Okay," he said. "We need to get you registered." The first two POWs entered the barn and approached the desks.

Stefan waited, shifting his weight from one foot to another as the Americans worked their way through a stack of forms, asking the newly arrived Germans one question after another. When the prisoners finished, they moved farther back into the barn, and finally Stefan was called. He stood at the desk, waiting for direction. The prisoner already seated to his right looked up at Stefan and scowled. He was a man with jet black hair and burning dark eyes who looked vaguely familiar.

"Setzen Sie sich," said the man sitting behind the desk. "Sit down." Though he appeared to be almost forty, the American was just a lowly private. He wore wire-rimmed glasses and carried the manner of a schoolteacher. Stefan thought he saw a bemused sympathy in the man's eyes.

As Stefan sat in the wooden folding chair, the man reached into the top drawer of the desk and pulled out a blank form. He licked the tip of the pencil and got started, looking at Stefan over the tops of his glasses.

"Your name?"

"Biermann. Stefan Michael Biermann."

"Date of birth?"

"November 17, 1912," said Stefan. He would be thirty-two next month.

"Where? What city?"

"Heidelberg."

The American scratched the information on the form.

"Do you live there now?"

Stefan nodded.

"Married?"

Stefan didn't say anything. He was thinking of Maria. He remembered the day he received his induction letter from the military. He figured they would get married at once. They had three days before he was to leave but Maria would have nothing to do with it.

"Married?" the man asked again, and it pulled Stefan back to the present.

"Um, no." he said.

"Civilian occupation?"

"I was a teacher at the university," said Stefan. The man looked at him.

"I taught, too," he said. Stefan had been right. "High school." He continued. "What unit were you with?"

Name, rank, and serial number. That's all they had to give, said their instructors at basic training. Back then, being taken by the enemy had a terrible mysteriousness about it. Stefan always imagined that he'd face heinous torture in an attempt to force him to reveal such information. This was like filling out a form at the doctor's office.

"Part of the 716th Infantry Division," said Stefan.

"Next!" came the command at the door. Stefan looked up. The German prisoner next to him with the jet black hair was finished. He scowled at Stefan again as he stood. His eyes narrowed as he remembered this "submariner" who with his fat friend stood quaking before him that day in the dining hall.

"Bastard," the man muttered. "You never wanted to be here."

The man spun on his heel with disgust and departed. Though the paperwork he carried still called him Leider, he was no longer an SS major. He had torn away his officer's rank and replaced it with a private's grade. The Allies had a special interest in catching the SS men, but a set of doctored documents had allowed him to slip past. To the American GI's who had captured him, he was an ordinary enlisted man in an infantry unit.

"Wonder what's with him?" Stefan thought, trying to place where he had seen the man before.

"Last thing here," said the man asking the questions. He slid him a postcard along with a stubby pencil that looked like it had been gnawed on.

"Fill this out and address it to someone back home. Someone responsible for your affairs," said the American. "It tells them you're now a POW. Write that you've been captured but are okay. If you put down anything else the censors are gonna trash it."

Stefan took the postcard and pencil. The card offered about four lines in which to compose his message. He closed his eyes for a moment to think, then started to write in the limited space. *"Dear Mother and Father; I am a prisoner of the Americans, but am in good health. I will write again. With love from your Stefan."*

He looked at what he had written, flipped the pencil over and tried to erase his grandparents' names. How could he have been so stupid? Maria's name belonged in that spot. But the blasted pencil simply smeared the words. No matter how he tried, Stefan couldn't erase the dark smudge that filled the spot, couldn't add anything more.

"Sir, I've made a mistake," Stefan smiled at the man, pleading. "May I have another please?"

The GI frowned at the line of men stretching outside and shook his head sadly. "Sorry," he said. "That'll have to do."

Next to him, Otto leaned over. "I'm sure it'll be fine," he said. He showed Stefan his own postcard.

"Dear Darling," Otto had written. *"It looks like I'm going to be the guest of the Americans for a while. Hope they're as good to me as you are. Except in that way. More later. Yours, Otto."*

They sat and waited in the barn, and after an hour, one of the Americans called them to their feet. He spoke in German. "Who is the highest-ranking one here?"

A sergeant named Müller raised his hand.

"Okay, march these men to the other side of the town. A guard will show you the way. There's a mess kitchen set up, and there you'll eat."

"That's the most positive development I've heard in a while," said Otto. Stefan said nothing. His brain felt fuzzy and faint from hunger. He fell into the column behind Otto and stumbled through the dusk, following the ragged line marching toward the kitchen.

After a few minutes they reached the mess tent. Inside were the cooks, hired French workers who stood, ladles ready, behind great pots of steaming soup. Stefan didn't know what kind it was and didn't care. All he could tell was that it was hot and smelled great. Large chunks of tender meat floated throughout and the men could have as much of the soup as they wanted. As the cooks filled and refilled his bowl, Stefan finally began to fully feel the weariness that had settled so heavily into his bones.

Finally sated after about his sixth helping, he and Otto and the other men staggered to an empty warehouse next door. Stefan curled up as best he could in an unclaimed corner, and plummeted directly into a deep and mercifully dreamless sleep, sedated by the past days of stress and a bellyful of hot soup.

※

The next few weeks were a blur. The prisoners moved through a string of holding camps, each one taking them closer to the coast.

The biggest annoyance was that with each move to a new camp, another group of Americans set upon them scavenging for souvenirs, eager to peel every button and patch they could find off the Germans.

"Cripes," muttered Otto, rubbing his neck after a private nearly tore the collar off his shirt trying to get at one little patch. "I'll be standing here naked

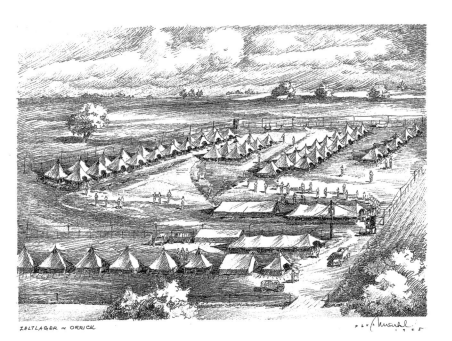

ZELTLAGER IN ORRICK

before long. Hope they're still not grabbing for souvenirs then."

Another troubling thing was that as the days went on, Stefan noticed the man with the jet-black hair time and time again.

"I still can't place him," Stefan said. He and Otto stood in the twilight one chilly evening in a large camp near the coast, a collection point to send the prisoners overseas. "But it's odd. He's always staring at me."

"Can't say that I know who you're talking about, Stefan. There's what, a thousand men here?"

"Wait," said Stefan, looking up. "Here he comes now."

By chance the man had appeared down the way and the pair watched him walk across the broad gravel of the compound. He wore a cap and was too far away for Otto to see clearly.

"Let's follow him," smiled Otto, and before Stefan could respond, Otto had taken off after him.

From a distance, they trailed Leider to a remote corner of the compound. A campfire burned between some tents and several shadowy forms huddled around the flames. He approached the blaze and joined the men gathered there, taking his place at the center of the circle.

Stefan and Otto continued their approach, more stealthily now, wending their way around the back, creeping between the rows of tents to avoid being seen.

Moving in closer, Otto was finally able to get his first good look at the men around the fire.

"Those are the Nazis," he whispered.

Stefan shrugged. Seemed like there were always a few around. Though the bulk of the soldiers in the army were mere draftees, ordinary citizens who loved their country, about 20% were true National Socialists, card-carrying members whose loyalty to the party and the Führer was fanatical and unfailing.

"That guy in the center, I can't believe you didn't recognize him," hissed Otto. "That's the SS major who came into the dining hall back at recruit training."

Stefan froze. This was something different. He remembered the fear that had gripped him that day as Leider stared him down while the shouts of praise to the SS had thundered through the great hall.

"*Kameraden*," Leider said, quieting the men around the fire. They leaned in closer as he began to speak in hushed tones. Snippets of the conversation floated over as Stefan and Otto listened.

"How do we influence these others...?" asked Leider and the others murmured in response.

The fire crackled and the wind picked up. Stefan shivered and tucked himself closer to the tent as he continued to listen.

"...too ambivalent about things...," said another, as the conversation continued.

"...make the traitors pay," said Leider fiercely, angrily smacking his fist as the others nodded their agreement.

"Let's go," whispered Stefan and the two crept back to their tent.

"How the hell did he make it through" asked Otto.

"Beats me," said Stefan. "But we gotta keep an eye on them. It's dangerous when they get together."

Ж

The men passed the days in the camps as best they could, waiting for an available ship to take them onward.

Meals were the only scheduled activity, and invariably they were a disappointment - usually got a single bowl and a crust of bread. It was enough to keep them going, but just barely. Certainly none came close to that grand introduction on the first night.

"What's with this?" Otto frowned one day at lunch, peering into his metal bowl. The cook had filled it with watery cabbage soup, one lonely bit of ham sunk forlornly on the bottom. He continually hoped for another go with the great pots of soup they had the earlier.

"What do you mean?" cackled a toothless French woman who was working the line. She looked to be about eighty, and so tiny only the kerchief covering her head rose above the pot. She had to stand on tip-toes to dip her ladle into the soup.

"It's not like we had the first night. That had meat. This is barely more than broth."

"You won't get fed much like that," said the woman, waving the ladle at him. "That was left-overs from the guards. One of them had hit an old donkey with the truck on the road the day before. That was what you were eating."

Stefan felt like he was going to vomit. Otto stuck up his index fingers and put them behind his ears.

"Hee-haw. Hee-haw," he brayed at Stefan and the French woman. Stefan didn't know whether to laugh or cry.

And so on it went, aimlessly for days. Stefan wondered how much longer this could last. Then suddenly one morning word came that a vessel had arrived in the harbor to take them on, and preparations to move the prisoners aboard a freighter for a long ocean voyage shifted into high gear.

"Word is we're headed for America," said Otto, nervously rubbing his hands together as they waited to walk up the gangplank.

"America! That's crazy," Stefan replied. "No way they'd send us all the way there."

And he doubted up until the moment it became clear the ship was steaming right on past England and into the open sea. Turns out the rumors were true. With the camps in Great Britain already stuffed full of POWs taken earlier in the war, the Americans had agreed to take on the thousands more prisoners being captured each month simply because they had the space to keep them and a desperate need for their labor. And before they knew it, the pair had crossed the Atlantic, and were waiting in a New York rail yard to climb on board an old train car, beginning the next phase of a trip that never seemed to end.

Chapter 17

The shifting of the train bumped Stefan gently awake. He had lost track of the days but could tell from the light it was early morning, perhaps approaching 7 a.m.

"How much longer do you think it will be?" asked Otto, sitting next to him, eyes still closed. "I'm afraid my rear is permanently stuck to this seat."

"Coming through St. Louis, we turned this way, I think," Stefan said, his finger drawing the train's route on the seat in front of him. "I could tell where we were when we crossed the river. We're headed southwest now."

"Wonder where all the damage is?" asked a POW sitting behind a couple rows them. Stefan glanced over his shoulder, then looked at Otto, shaking his head. It was Leider. Would he never get away from the guy?

Leider stared eagerly out the window, continued his muttering. "Bombing must have been in other places."

Otto rolled his eyes. The German propaganda machine had cranked out news about the destruction in the United States. "American countryside pummeled by German Air Force," read the dispatches. "Neither cities nor farms can escape the hail of devastation." They both knew it had been a giant load of baloney, but apparently Leider hadn't figured it out.

After a time, a guard circulated through the train car, doing a head count and carrying a wooden crate. From it he passed a piece of bread and a thin slice of salami with an apple for each POW. It was never enough but would keep the hunger away for a while.

"Make sure you eat this," he said in English to Stefan and Otto. "We'll be there soon but this will have to last until dinner."

Otto didn't catch what the man said and looked at Stefan for a translation. From the other side of the car, Leider sat up.

"Where are we going?" he asked the guard. He could understand and speak a little English.

"Fort Leonard Wood," said the GI, pausing from handing out food. "We'll be there in another two or three hours." The guard continued toward the back of the train.

"What did he say?" asked Otto.

"We're in Missouri now," Stefan told him. "Going to Fort Leonard Wood. It's a new place, only a couple years old. I was by there during my last visit."

"What's it like?" Otto asked, gazing out the window.

"It's pretty far out in the country, and there wasn't much there," said Stefan, remembering his trip, and the day he stopped in the dusty café parking lot. He remembered the waitress, the farmer. And he remembered Katherine Lorberg.

The two friends resumed their silence. Stefan thought about Maria. Had she been getting his letters? Probably not, he figured, given what the war had done to the post in Germany.

Of course there was no way for Stefan to know, but as it turned out, mail service still functioned in Heidelberg. And just about every day, the postman delivered a letter from Stefan to Maria's apartment, sometimes two or three. She wasn't reading them though. They were going straight in the trash unopened. Her mind was occupied with other things.

※

At last, the train turned off the main tracks, passed through a big fence and approached a concrete platform. A sign stood nearby: WELCOME TO FORT LEONARD WOOD, MISSOURI. About a dozen soldiers stood around outside. Stefan guessed they were guards, but none seemed particularly excited about the train's arrival.

"Just stay seated," shouted the guard at the front of the car. "It's going to take us a while to get unloaded."

Stefan looked at the guards slouched against the walls of the depot. One soldier's gut lopped over his belt in impressive fashion. Another seemed to have polished his boots with cow manure. A third looked like his uniform had been wadded up under his bed. Stefan knew that they weren't on parade, but this was ridiculous.

The guard who appeared to be the leader of the welcoming committee stood on the platform watching them.

"Does that guy have a glass eye?" asked Otto, nudging Stefan. Its poor fit made it bulge from the socket and the man fiddled with it repeatedly, dialing at it with his finger to make sure it was still in place.

The first cars began to unload and a guard counted the men as they exited the train and marched off the platform. Four cars were emptied, and then it was their turn.

"Okay," shouted the guard from the front of the car. "We're next. Everybody up!"

The men rose from their seats and filed to the end of the car and out onto the concrete platform, standing silently in the late afternoon sun. Their legs were stiff after sitting for so long. There were no sounds other than the occasional cough or the distant call of a train whistle.

The guard with the glass eye pulled out one of the German sergeants, a man named Bunzek. On the surface he seemed to be a decent fellow, a quiet guy with thin brown hair, but Stefan knew he was tight with Karl Leider.

"March these men to their barracks," he told Bunzek, pointing to one of the guards waiting nearby. "He'll show you where to go."

The POW compound was set away from the main part of the post, standing alone and isolated in the middle of a broad and barren expanse, a brightly illuminated island of razor wire. A half-dozen guard towers, huge thick wooden structures, stood sullen and foreboding at the corners and midpoints of the fence line, each with the dull black barrel of a .50 caliber machine gun, big as a man's fist, poking from the top.

"Stop the men here," said one of the guards to Bunzek, as they approached the gate. The rhythmic clump-clump-clump of their boots fell silent. Stefan could see men inside the wire, fellow Germans, looking through the fence at the new arrivals.

"Bringing in a fresh batch here!" shouted the lead guard, the one with the glass eye. The name on his uniform read *Whitcomb*.

He waited outside the gate until another GI guard emerged from within. The man held a clipboard and wore thick glasses, and hurried over to Whitcomb.

"How many are there?" he asked, squinting at the Germans, then squinting at his clipboard.

"We brought 198 in on the train," said Whitcomb. "Don't know what happened to the other two. Har har." He laughed at his own joke and slapped the gatekeeper hard on the back.

"You lost some prisoners?"

"Never mind," said Whitcomb.

The men shuffled in and stood waiting on a small patch of grass, where buildings on three sides formed a courtyard of sorts. A couple of American guards stood behind them, weapons dangling loosely at their sides. Whitcomb turned and went into one of the offices, emerged with an officer, a big guy, over six-foot with a square jaw and close-cropped blond hair. If you put him in a German army uniform, he might well have passed for one of Hitler's Aryan heroes. A translator stood at his side.

"Welcome to Missouri, and the internment camp for prisoners of war at Fort Leonard Wood. I am Captain John Lorberg." He stopped and smiled as the German standing next to him translated his words. Stefan wondered about the name, figured it was a coincidence or a distant relative. An influential family like Senator Lorberg's probably had branches throughout the state.

Lorberg looked at Bunzek. "Have your men stand at ease." Bunzek repeated the command and the Germans relaxed in formation, now standing more comfortably before Lorberg. Stefan looked at Otto, who nodded once. The courtesy of this American officer was not lost on them.

"Things are simple around here," Lorberg continued. "Follow the rules and you will have no problems. If you don't, you will end up there." He gestured to the guardhouse, a solitary building with barred windows. Through one of them, Stefan could see a silhouette pacing slowly back and forth.

"It usually works best when we leave you to manage your own affairs," said Lorberg, eyeing the prisoners standing before him in the growing darkness. "Problems are handled first through your chain of command. It's only if you screw up really bad that you'll hear from me directly. Hopefully we won't see too much of each other."

He paused.

"Ha ha," said the captain.

"Ha ha," repeated the interpreter with unconvincing enthusiasm.

"The United States follows the Geneva Conference regarding treatment of prisoners of war," continued the captain. "This is very important for you to understand as it outlines your rights and obligations as prisoners."

"Cigarettes and beer," said Otto, standing next to Stefan in formation."

"What?" Stefan did not look at his friend. They stood in the second row but as Lorberg went on with his talk, he didn't seem to notice their exchange.

"That means we get cigarettes and beer and all the other stuff the GIs get," said Otto. He was talking quietly, trying not to move his lips. "Geneva Conference says they've got to treat us the same. If they can get it, we do, too."

"It's true," shouted Lorberg, startling everyone as he crossed the short stretch of grass to confront the two. Leaning into the second row, his face close to theirs, he grabbed the front of their uniform shirts.

"You can get cigarettes and a can of beer each in your camp stores at the end of the day. But not for you two if this is how you're gonna act."

Bunzek turned and glared furiously at his charges. The last thing he wanted was for his men to be screwing things up so soon. The guards behind the Germans suddenly stepped closer, pulling their weapons up, hoping to finally get some action.

"Geneva Conference says we gotta feed you guys the same, house you the same, and sell you the same stuff in the canteens," said Lorberg. He was shouting now, and flecks of spittle gathered at the corner of his mouth. "I don't like it a bit, but that's the damn rules. Plus, there are always these Swiss inspectors and a bunch of other nags snooping around to make sure."

The men stood silent.

Captain Lorberg waited for a moment, let his words hang in the air, then released his grip. He smiled blandly, and the anger vanished from his face. He walked back to his position at the front of the formation, then began again.

"The good news, however, is that the Geneva Conference says we can work you while you're here," continued Lorberg. "No sitting on your ass. If you don't work, you don't eat. It's that simple. We'll put you in the guardhouse if you don't want to cooperate."

Stefan waited for the "ha ha" again, but the captain was not joking.

"First thing Monday morning you'll all get jobs. Maybe in the laundry or the mess hall. Maybe on a road crew. There's all kinds of work to be done."

Lorberg stood silent for a moment. It was increasingly difficult to see him in the deepening darkness. The sun had long since gone down in the west and all that remained was a mixture of deep pink and light purple on the horizon.

"Just play along and everything will go fine," he said, his words hanging in the darkness. "And don't think you can get away with pulling any shit. I always find out what happens here."

Bunzek called the Germans to attention, and then with the translator trailing behind, the captain went back into his office.

Chapter 18

The barracks were single story, long and narrow, with a dozen beds on either side of a center aisle. Each bed featured a brown woolen blanket, a sheet and a pillow, all folded and stacked at the foot of a thin army mattress.

"Here's my bed," shouted Otto and he dove headlong over the end of the metal frame onto the bed. His heft overwhelmed the spindly frame and the springs gave way with a crash, dumping him to the floor in a heap.

Stefan tried to dislodge his friend from the tangle of springs and blankets while the other men roared with laughter. Leider glared and stomped to the far end of the bay.

With the bed fixed, they joined the loose formation of men who had drifted outside. Stefan's stomach was aching with hunger; the last time they had eaten was on the train, more than eight hours ago. Standing there in the darkness, Stefan heard another stomach growling and looked sideways at Otto, who smiled sheepishly back at him.

As if on cue, Whitcomb's voice called from the darkness behind them. "Bunzek, march these men to the mess hall for dinner."

Faint traces of the evening's menu lingered in the air as the men approached the mess hall. As the soldiers filed in, the spread laid out far exceeded their expectations. Pork chops, boiled potatoes, green beans. Great jugs of cold milk, real butter and fresh baked bread. Canned peaches and chocolate cake. Most of the men had not had a meal like this since they sat at their mother's tables back home. The last meal even remotely close was the soup at the French camp.

"That's not donkey, is it?" Otto asked the man behind the counter. He shook his head as he speared a choice cut from a tray loaded with great slabs of meat and plopped it onto Otto's tray.

"This is a trick," muttered Leider, who stood behind Stefan and Otto in line. "Some kind of propaganda. They can't feed us like this all the time."

"Well, maybe so. Guess the joke's on me and I don't mind a bit," said Otto. "More potatoes, please."

The server gave him a second heaping scoop of mashed potatoes and Otto smiled in satisfaction.

The Germans ate quickly, greedily, though their stomachs weren't accustomed to such a rich load of food. Only ten minutes after eating, Stefan felt full and bloated.

The two friends finished, then staggered like drunkards back to the barracks, hands caressing their too-full bellies. They fell into bed fully clothed, passing out as their weary bodies finally succumbed to the stress they had carried since being captured. They were now "home," whatever that meant. They did not know how long they would be in Missouri, but any worries they had vanished quickly as they fell into a dreamless sleep that held them through the night.

X

The next morning came quickly for Stefan. It was dark when he first awoke, so he lay silently until light played through the window and gradually brightened the room. Stefan swung his legs over the edge of the bed and looked around the long narrow room. Though Otto still snored next to him, Leider was up and busy, moving about his bed on the other side of the aisle. Their eyes met, but Leider frowned and looked away.

"Asshole," thought Stefan.

Stefan watched Leider finish folding his last couple pairs of socks, laying them smartly in the footlocker next to his bed like little soldiers in formation. He had arranged all of his newly issued clothes with the same precision, as if preparing for an inspection. Of course, Leider would be concerned about that sort of thing, thought Stefan, especially when it didn't make a damn bit of difference now.

From instinct or habit, Stefan reached for the packet of cigarettes in his breast pocket, patting at the empty space. He wondered if what Otto had said was true. Cigarettes and beer. Though even Lorberg confirmed it, Stefan still doubted they'd be sitting around chugging beer and having smokes in some sort of POW social hour.

"What do you think of things so far, Biermann?" It was Leider asking from across the room. He was casual about it, but there was danger in the question.

Stefan wasn't sure what to say. The man had closed the lid to his footlocker and was standing now, looking at him, expecting a response.

"You know, it's not the worst place we could be," he offered neutrally. "We'll just have to see how it goes."

Leider frowned. "Seems like it's going bad already, don't you think?"

"Pardon?" stammered Stefan.

"We're off to a damn poor start, and you and this asshole get most of the blame." Leider gestured at Otto, who had pulled the wool blanket over himself at some point during the night, only the top of his poking from underneath.

Bunzek glanced up with surprise. He was kneeling on the floor, starting to pull his clothing from the duffle bag. Following Leider's lead, he was folding the items and placing them in his footlocker.

"What are you talking about?" Stefan knew he shouldn't respond, but was surprised by how quickly the man's anger came.

"I'm talking about you two last night in formation. You want more? How about the way that fat ass flounces up and down the street. Makes us all look pathetic."

Stefan caught the barely perceptible shift in breathing from the bed next to him, and he knew that Otto was no longer asleep.

"Hey, Karl," Bunzek interjected. He spoke hesitantly as he looked at Leider. "Why don't you lay off them a bit. . .?"

"You shut up, Bunzek," snapped Leider, cutting him off. "You're part of the problem if you can't get this fixed. Just because they put you over this sorry-ass group doesn't mean you'll stay there."

Three of Leider's Nazi thugs moved quickly from their bunks at the far end of the barracks. They slid silently behind Leider, making it obvious who was really in charge.

"Listen to me, damn it." Leider turned from Bunzek, addressing everyone now. "We're not a bunch of boot-lickers, doing every last thing they say. We're still Germans, and still soldiers. And we will start acting like it again. We are still in the fight with these people."

Leider moved to the middle of the aisle so that he could face the length of the room and see every man. Breathing hard, he paced back and forth between his bunk and where Otto still lay.

"We're Germans, damn it!" he shouted again, punctuating the air with his fist. "We're soldiers!

Leider stopped at the corner of Otto's bed. His fists clenched as his voice dropped to a disdainful whisper.

"We're not a bunch of screw-ups. We're certainly not going to mess things up for ourselves like this worthless piece of shit did for us last night."

As he finished, Leider sneered, cocked his arm quickly and swung at the side of Otto's head. At that moment, Otto jerked the blanket off his face, and Leider's blow glanced off his raised arm instead.

"What the hell, Leider?" said Otto, sitting up and rubbing his forearm.

At the same time, Stefan leapt off his own bed and threw himself at Leider. Knocking him off balance, Stefan drove him backwards across the barracks. Leider cursed and pounded Stefan's back with his fist as he careened into the thin side wall with Stefan's shoulder driving hard into his stomach.

The two hit the floor, throwing punches, scraping and gouging at each other, trying to inflict whatever pain they could. Instantly the other men were on them, shouting and trying to separate the two. Finally pulled apart, Stefan and Leider glowered at each other, breathing hard as the other men held them.

"You and you," whispered Leider to Otto and Stefan, pulling himself free from the men who held him. "Better watch out."

Leider spun on his heel and headed for the door, with Bunzek and his three lackeys following. He slammed the door behind him. It was silent for a moment until the men in the barracks went back to what they were doing, as if nothing had just happened.

Stefan sat back on his bunk, and Otto turned to face him.

"Wow," said Otto, uncharacteristically at a loss for words. "Wow."

"Yeah, well, we knew it was coming with him, didn't we?"

"I guess so, but sooner than we thought," said Otto.

Stefan noticed his hands were trembling. Otto saw it, too, and smiled.

"Hey, you were pretty impressive there. I mean, I've been in a scrap or two in my day, but I was never sure what you'd be like in a fight."

Otto held up his fists and jabbed them in the air like a boxer, bobbing and weaving.

"Yeah, I thought a delicate academic wouldn't be able to mix it up like that. But you got in a good lick or two. Definitely held your own."

Stefan shook his head grimly. He knew that they had just tangled with the worst person in camp to have as an enemy.

Chapter 19

That afternoon was quiet. Some of the prisoners engaged in a half-hearted game of soccer in the space behind their compound. A few played, a few watched. Others simply sat outside the barracks, doing little of anything.

Stefan figured he'd use the time to compose another letter to Maria. He parked himself on the wooden front steps of the barracks, sitting in the sun with paper in hand, ready to write when a guard approached. It was Whitcomb. He stopped in front of Stefan and pulled a piece of paper from his pocket and frowned down at it.

"You Stefan Biermann?"

Stefan squinted into the bright afternoon sunlight, nodded.

"Where's your buddy? Haertling?" asked Whitcomb, fiddling with his glass eye.

"Over there," said Stefan, gesturing with his head to the soccer field. Otto stood on the sideline, a one-man pep squad, yelling and dancing.

"Go get him."

Stefan felt a press of worry as he went to fetch Otto. Surely they couldn't know this quickly about the fight. It was in the barracks, there were no guards around. The two returned to where Whitcomb stood waiting for them by the steps.

"We're going to see Captain Lorberg," said Whitcomb. "C'mon."

"What does he want?" asked Otto. "I don't remember him requesting an appointment with me."

Whitcomb glanced at Otto. He wasn't sure what to make of the man.

"That's not backtalk, I hope."

Stefan and Otto walked side by side with Whitcomb following a few steps behind. Soon they were at the front of the camp. Whitcomb walked to the door of Lorberg's office and rapped sharply. Captain Lorberg opened the door, swinging it wide to assess the two men standing before them. The butt of a .45 pistol poked from the shiny black leather holster on his belt.

"Come in," he said. Lorberg stepped back in and Stefan and Otto followed. Whitcomb lingered just outside the door.

"Hey Whitcomb," said Lorberg, and the man poked his head into the small room. "See if you can find the translator."

Inside the plain office, Stefan and Otto stood at attention, waiting by two straight-back wooden chairs.

"Please sit," said Lorberg. He went behind his desk and took a seat. Otto and Stefan sat stiffly, waiting for the translator. A minute passed. Then two. Lorberg leaned back in the chair, looked up at the ceiling, shuffled his feet and drummed his fingers on the wooden surface.

"Well shit," Lorberg finally spoke. "Who knows where that guy is. Either of you speak English?"

"I do, sir," said Stefan. "A bit."

"Okay. There was a fight in your barracks this morning. True?" Lorberg looked at Stefan first, then Otto. The two glanced at each other, Otto searching Stefan's eyes for meaning.

"The fight," Stefan said in German.

Both turned back to Lorberg. Both nodded.

"What caused it?"

"A simple disagreement, sir," said Stefan. "Nothing serious."

"I've already talked with Leider. He said the same thing. You comedians have a script?"

The officer picked up a pen lying on his desk and twirled it between his fingers, considering what he should do.

"I'm going to separate you and Leider. Different barracks, separate work details." He looked at Stefan. "It's either that or the guardhouse. Can't have fighting in the camp. Sound good to you?"

Stefan nodded.

"But boys," Lorberg said, "I'm still concerned. The problems last night in formation. And now this."

He leaned forward, hands on the desk, looking from Stefan to Otto, and

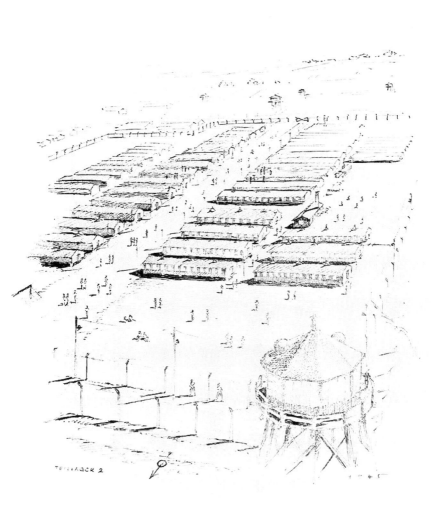

back to Stefan again.

"You're new here. Haven't quite figured out how things work. I hope that was just a release of stress after your trip. Christ, was it five days on the train from New York?"

"Yes sir." Stefan nodded.

"Well, I'd be full of roar, too, after that misery," said Lorberg, his face growing serious again. "But no more. Else you'll be seeing the guardhouse."

He straightened himself, crossing his arms on his broad chest.

"Okay?"

"Yes sir," Otto and Stefan said in unison.

"Good."

They stood, and Whitcomb led Stefan and Otto back to the barracks, where they collected their stuff in anticipation of the move.

Chapter 20

After the initial excitement of those first days at Fort Leonard Wood, things settled down and the next few months passed without incident. Stefan and Otto got settled in their new barracks and though they didn't see Leider again, they knew he wouldn't forget what had happened between them that morning.

Soon enough the days began to run together, an uneventful cycle of work and rest. Stefan was assigned to the laundry running a steam press and Otto washed dishes in the mess hall. Neither minded the work. It made the days go more quickly, and while the 10 cents an hour the POWs earned for their work didn't make millionaires out of anyone, the whole *zigaretten und biere* legend turned out to be true. The POWs could buy a single can of beer in the canteen each night along with tobacco when it was available. Plus they could save the rest of their earnings in an account they'd eventually cash out back in Europe.

One Tuesday evening after dinner, Stefan and Otto wandered through the barracks toward the canteen. Otto wanted to get a beer and see what else was there. The POW store carried the same merchandise available to GI's, everything from stationery to socks, cologne to candy, an assortment of goods that never failed to surprise Stefan.

"You buying anything?" he asked Stefan as they approached the canteen.

"Maybe." He planned to pick up another note pad. Just a couple of pages remained in the one he had now. He had used it writing letters to Maria, and he had just bought it a week ago. "Some smokes for sure if there's any there."

Otto pulled open the door and the pair stepped in. A couple of POWs lounged behind the counter. One looked to be about 20; the other a bit older. The older man yawned as he leaned over the counter, resting on his elbows and flipping through a magazine.

"Evening, gentlemen," said Otto, tipping an imaginary hat to them as he headed to the cooler for a can of beer.

"Got any smokes?" asked Stefan.

"Nah," said Knehans, the younger man.

"Like always," replied Stefan with more than a trace of irritation. "Thought you said they'd be bringing some in."

"They were supposed to," said Weeke, the older man, looking up from his magazine. "Earlier this week. Not sure what happened."

The situation with cigarettes was a bit of a frustration and a mystery. Though the GIs always had plenty, tobacco was invariably in short supply in the POW store. If there were smokes, it'd maybe be a couple of cartons at most, and they'd be gone within an hour.

"Another shipment's supposed to be here in a couple days," offered Knehans.

"Bullshit," said Stefan "Those 'couple days' never seem to materialize."

"What can you do?" Knehans shrugged sympathetically.

Leaving the canteen, they went back to the barracks. Otto went inside to see if he could get in on a card game while Stefan sat on the front steps, enjoying the last of the cool evening light. He pulled out the new notebook and started another letter.

"My dearest Maria...," he wrote, and he was soon lost in thought. "Working in the laundry today, I passed the hours like I always do, just thinking of you and longing to be with you. All day long the pants and shirts pass by as I make the steam press go, but I only see your face. I thought of that day early on when we took the row boat on the lake. That memory was enough to carry me through the day."

Stefan's mind took him again to that summer Sunday afternoon. They had gone out together to a lake at the edge of town carrying a picnic basket and a bottle of wine. With their blanket spread on the neatly-mown grass, they had laid together in the warm sunshine, enjoying an ease and peacefulness rarely found in the busyness of everyday life. Families with small children splashed in the water, their laughter carrying over to Stefan and Maria. Rowboats carried young lovers out over the calm waters closer to the beach while farther out, sailboats made the most of a gentle breeze to cut crisply back and forth on the sparkling water.

For two hours they talked and laughed and ate. When the wine was gone, Maria stood up, and took his hand, pulling him upright next to her.

„ DIE SKATBRÜDER "

CAMP CLARK, MISSOURI, U.S.A.

"Come on," she said, her dark eyes sparkling at him. "Let's see if we can take out a boat."

She danced off ahead, laughing mischievously as she dashed away, skirt lifted, feet flying across the grass. Stefan followed, running behind her, enjoying the simple joy and freedom of a chase across the lawn.

Maria looked back and he caught her hand, and pulled her gently to a stop. They stood, facing each other still and alone in the middle of the broad green expanse, hearts pounding. She looked at Stefan, laughed. They were both breathless from the dash. The calls of the children still carried over to them from the water. She covered her mouth with her hand, laughed again and looked down.

Stefan reached to her, lifted her chin with two fingers so that she was looking at him again. He leaned forward slowly to kiss her, feeling the gentle pounding of her heartbeat through his thumb on her slender wrist.

"Biermann!"

Stefan, jerked from his thoughts was still perched on the steps of the barracks. He glanced up from his notebook.

"Biermann!" called the sergeant again. Time for the mail. A dozen men crowded around the sergeant, waiting anxiously to claim some hoped-for letter or package from home. Stefan never got mail and hardly bothered to listen.

"Biermann!" hollered the sergeant a third time, starting to get irritated. He thrust an envelope toward him. "Something for you."

Stefan stood quickly and wiped his hands on his pants, eager to see what it was. He dared not think it was a letter from Maria; maybe something from his parents. He had received a single letter from them since arriving in the States. It was months old, sent even before his capture.

The crowd parted so Stefan could lean in for the letter. He took it in both hands like a fragile treasure and held it up. Maria's delicate handwriting was on the envelope and the postmark showed it had only been written six weeks before.

Stefan trembled with excitement as he returned to the steps and sat. He slid his shaking finger gently through the flap of the envelope, applying every bit of self-control he could muster to avoid damaging this precious envelope. He held his breath as he eased the crisply folded letter from inside. It was a single page, but she had written a lot. The thin lines of her script marched row after row across the page.

"Dear Stefan." His eyes darted across the sheet following the sentences.

"I hope this letter finds you well. Thanks for the many nice letters you've

written me. And sorry for the delay in responding. I have been just so busy with school and other things."

Maria had written from her room. It was in the early morning and she sat at her desk, naked but for her white cotton bathrobe, hanging loose and open, her slender legs folded underneath her as she leaned over the desk to write. She was not alone.

"I've been doing okay, but of course, I miss you. Do you happen to remember one of your students, a fellow named Heinrich? He's been keeping me company and so that helps."

Heinrich stirred in her bed. He still slept, but rolled over to his side, tossing a withered hand on Maria's pillow.

"The big news around here is what happened at the university. There'll be some changes when you get back for sure. And that's why I'm writing. Dr. Goetz and five other faculty members were arrested not long after you left. Rounded up in the middle of the night, and no one has seen them since. Shocking, isn't it? And I always liked Dr. Goetz. Nobody knew why exactly, but apparently they were under suspicion."

Stefan's hands began to tremble so badly the paper shook. The words continued.

"And you won't believe what broke the whole thing. A ripped up flyer for the Nazi student rally in the trash outside of Goetz's office. It got torn down, and that's what made them suspicious. Heinrich is the real hero here. He found the flyer and turned it in. They started watching Goetz and the whole thing broke not long after that."

Stefan felt himself becoming dizzy, his breath coming in shallow gasps.

"Like I said, it's shocking about Goetz, but I say if you make your bed then you've got to sleep in it. And this could be a good opportunity for you. A promotion maybe when you get back. Keep writing those letters. I'll try to be better about replying. Love – Maria."

Stefan leaped off the steps, ran to the side of the barracks, scattering the men still lingering there. He leaned against the barracks, crying bitterly, head and arm pressed against the rough wood, retching and crying, unable to contain the bile in his stomach, unable to contain the guilt and shame. He had caused it all, he knew. And now Dr. Goetz was paying for his carelessness in writing that note.

Chapter 21

"You've got to stop thinking about it, Stefan," said Otto. The two stood at the edge of the soccer field watching a group of POWs kicking the ball back and forth. The grass was brown and a chilly wind blew from the north. "It's not your fault."

"How can you say that?" asked Stefan. He had his hands jammed in his pockets and he scuffed his feet as they talked. "I'm the one that tore that flyer down. That's what did it."

"But even if that's what gave him away, you know they must have had him under surveillance before that. It was just a matter of time. You can't blame yourself."

"Okay, maybe so, but what about me? They've got to know about me then, too."

"Nah," said Otto. "You had never been affiliated with the group. And Goetz would have been careful about how he got rid of the note you wrote. He's not a dope, you know, just pitching it in the trash."

Stefan snapped a glare at Otto.

"Oops. Didn't mean it," said Otto, a smile creeping across his face. "But seriously, if they wanted to get you, they already had plenty from that outburst in the classroom. And even a hint at a tie to Goetz and his circle would have been enough."

"I guess if nothing else, the letter shows that Maria still cares for me," said Stefan, looking into the distance. He was thinking about her skin, her lips, her hair. The faint scent of her perfume still lingered on the paper and he savored it each time he read the letter, the only positive piece of getting it. "She was never good about expressing that directly but you can read between the lines."

Otto frowned, bit his lip. The only thing obvious to him in the letter was that Maria seemed to have taken up with another man.

"But Stefan, I don't get it. Who is this Heinrich? And doesn't it make you a bit uneasy that he and Maria have been hanging around together?"

"Nah. He's a younger guy from her neighborhood. Their families are friends. He's more like a nephew than anything."

Yeah right, thought Otto. A nephew who's gone romping in Cupid's garden with your girlfriend.

"I mean, was it anything personal that he found the flyer? Course not. He's just eager to help out the cause."

"Okay, maybe so," said Otto. "But why hasn't she written until now?"

"She may not have had an address for me. She may not have gotten any of my letters. Who knows what mail's getting through?"

A stray ball came rolling out-of-bounds toward the pair, and Stefan kicked it back to the players.

"Stefan, let me tell you something. I just know that if Elise wrote me just a single letter in a whole year and it said that she's got another guy keeping her company, I'd be concerned."

Stefan turned from watching the action on the field to look at his friend.

"There's nothing I can do about what might be going on back home, so I'm not going to let myself worry about it. But I'm always glad for your opinion, Otto. I know I certainly appreciate what you said about Dr. Goetz."

He attempted a smile, but his mind still churned. Stefan couldn't get over the shock and sorrow of Dr. Goetz's arrest. He knew that Goetz – if he wasn't already dead – was condemned to the same kind of hell and horror that Michael had suffered. But what could he do from here?

"Ah, shit. Look who's coming," said Otto. He stared past Stefan toward the gate that led back into the barracks area. "Hello, Leider," said Otto in a polite tone. "Enjoying a nice walk this afternoon?"

"Hello *fettsack*," said Leider. Stefan turned to see him with two of his Nazi thugs in tow. "It's been a long time." He approached Stefan with an oily smile, his hand outstretched, offering to shake.

"What do you want?" Stefan ignored the handshake. "Need anything? Or just coming to remind us of what an asshole you are?"

"We were so very sad to see you leave the barracks," said Leider. He dropped his hand, but stood very close, almost nose-to-nose with Stefan. "The place hasn't been the same without you."

The smile vanished.

"We've lost the stench of you insufferable losers fouling the air," he said through gritted teeth.

Stefan's hands curled into fists. Tense silence hung between them.

"I haven't forgotten," said Leider. "Better watch your back."

"Eat shit, Leider," said Stefan.

His two goons stepped closer, each a head taller than Stefan.

"Better be careful," whispered Leider. "You're a coward and a traitor and you'll get your due."

He stepped away sharply, the two trailing behind him. Stefan exhaled, too soon.

"Oh, Stefan?" Leider paused, looking back after a few steps. "So sorry to hear about your dear Dr. Goetz."

The trio turned and left the yard. The soccer players still kicked the ball up and down the field, same as before. Someone scored and players cheered. Otto and Stefan stared at each other, dumbfounded.

Chapter 22

Stefan should have felt refreshed, but in truth he was exhausted. Since the encounter with Leider, nights had meant long stretches of lying awake, wondering and worrying. How could the man have known about Dr. Goetz? Stefan again feared Leider and his henchmen, even carrying a cot leg when he went to the bathroom at night in case he was set upon in the dark.

It was morning, after breakfast, and the sun shone brightly into the barracks. Everyone else was outside in the chilly sunshine before work started. Stefan sat with writing paper in front of him, while Otto watched nearby.

My dearest Maria,

Thank you for your letter. I was so thrilled to receive it. I have read and re-read those precious paragraphs, and it brings me great joy and comfort to hear from you. I saw that you have my current address, which means at least one of the letters I sent must have finally got through to you. I am sure that you wrote as soon as you heard from me.

Maria, my love for you grows stronger every day, and I eagerly await more letters from you. I know that you are busy and hope that you can find time to write me as often as you can. My heart longs to be with you again, and I know that you wait for me faithfully to until my return.

I was as shocked as you to hear about Dr. Goetz. I believed him to be a good man too, and loyal to the Party. What rot must have crept into his brain to lead to such perversion of his position of influence and authority. I hope he is now getting whatever punishment he so richly deserves.

"That's good, Stefan," said Otto, knowing how difficult this was for his friend. As he wrote, Stefan bit his lip so hard that he could taste blood. "You've got to put that sort of thing in there," he continued. "Obviously someone here is reading your mail."

Please give my regards to your family. I remain here, true to you and true to Germany and the Fuhrer. I close with the deepest expression of my unending love for you.

Yours,
Stefan

He folded the paper into thirds and tucked it into the envelope. A heavy sigh escaped him as he closed the flap and turned it over, writing her name and address on the front.

"All set," Stefan said. He gestured at Otto with the envelope. "I can drop this in the mail on the way."

Boots thumped on the steps outside and the door creaked as it swung open. It was the sergeant from their new barracks, an older man named Schultz. He poked his head in the door. "Fellas, time to go. Something different today."

He led the pair onto the parade grounds, where the other men were already assembled.

"Looks like half the camp is here," muttered Otto, looking around. Stefan heard the guards talking behind him.

"So, we're getting ready to send another bunch out?" asked one GI.

"Yeah," said another. Stefan looked back. It was Whitcomb. "So many new prisoners we've got plenty to spare. And with spring here, all the farmers need help again."

A murmur started among the waiting prisoners. The guards perked up, wondering about its source. Suddenly they saw what caused the disturbance.

"Would you look at that," whistled Otto. It was a woman standing next to the fence, just outside the gate. Heads snapped immediately in that direction. This woman was an absolute knockout, and the men stood transfixed.

To see such a beautiful woman around the camp was unusual, a rare treat. Though there were a few clerks in the main office, they stayed cloistered at the front of the camp. Another small clutch of women worked in the laundry, but intentionally separated from the POWs. The men saw them infrequently, but did not lament it. As Otto tactfully observed, if Attila the Hun had a sister, she probably worked in the laundry.

Stefan, too, found himself staring. The woman looked to be in her late twenties, trim, five-six with dark hair and dark eyes. She wore a felt coat, with a blouse open just a bit at the top, enough to certify that yes, this was a woman. She waited expectantly to be escorted in.

Whitcomb stood at the edge of the prisoners' formation with a handful of guards. Led by Whitcomb, a couple of them started to snicker and gape as she approached.

The woman didn't ignore them, didn't try to pretend that she was oblivious to their leering. She turned and glared at them, especially Whitcomb, taking two steps closer toward the fence, as if daring Whitcomb and the others to continue.

"Still the same," she muttered, shaking her head.

The comment didn't make sense but seemed to be directed at Whitcomb. He looked back at her, touched his finger to the brim of his cap in a mock salute and nodded, smiling broadly all the while.

Captain John Lorberg stood at the front of the formation, going over some personnel rosters. He also noticed the buzz, then followed the focus to the fence where he saw the woman waiting.

Lorberg nodded to the guard standing next to him, and the man sprinted to let her in. Lorberg followed with long strides to meet her at the gate.

All eyes followed as Lorberg and the woman approached one another across the brown grass and bare dirt of the parade ground, the woman in her dark coat, Lorberg in his fatigues. When just two steps separated them, the officer held his hand out as if to shake and she took it in both of hers. Suddenly, so quick he almost missed it, Captain Lorberg pulled the woman close and leaned over to kiss her. A brief peck on the corner of the mouth, done in a flash, but a kiss nonetheless. Stefan's eyes just about popped out of his head.

"Whoa!" Otto's eyebrows shot straight up. "Did you see that?"

The entire group was silent, stunned by this display of tenderness, so out of character for this place. The only noise came from the gusting wind whistling through the wire. A kiss from such a woman. Hearts ached at the thought. All through the ranks, virtually every man recalled a love left back home, a long-ago sweetheart, days when such kisses were routine.

Lorberg offered the woman his arm, and the two walked to the front of the formation.

"Attention!" shouted Bunzek as they approached.

Three hundred men snapped stiffly into place, standing ramrod straight as the chilly January wind kicked up around them, flapping collars, rustling hair. Stefan shivered, goose bumps rising on his arms as he watched John Lorberg and this woman crossing in front of him.

The POWs were sorted by barracks in front of Lorberg and the woman, a group stretching for a hundred yards. Escorting her on his arm, Lorberg walked her the length of the line.

"Wow," said Otto dreamily, "if I'd have known we'd be getting inspected by her, I'd have cleaned up better."

Otto's hands shot to his neck as he tried to quickly smooth the rumpled collars of his work suit. Bunzek, standing at the end of the row, leaned forward, eyes drawn by the motion. He scowled at Otto, whose hands snapped quickly back to his sides. Otto stood still once again, eyes straight ahead, collar now smooth, mission accomplished.

After circulating through the ranks of POWs, Lorberg and the woman returned to the corner nearest Stefan's group, where they stopped to talk. Though they spoke softly and in English, Stefan could hear what they said.

"If you want the same number as last year, this bunch would be good," said Captain Lorberg, nodding toward Stefan's group.

"Any problems with them?" she asked.

"Nope. They're still pretty new. Haven't been here long enough to be ruined by the Nazis, least as far as we can tell. If you take them now, Katherine, you'll be fine."

They moved to the end of the first row of Stefan's group. Lorberg waited as the woman walked slowly down the first row of prisoners.

"Oh boy," whispered Otto as the woman approached. "Here she comes!" His eyes were straight ahead, but a happy grin crossed his face as he threw out his chest and lifted his chin.

Stefan could smell her sweet, subtle perfume on the breeze as she drew near, now just a single man away. She stopped between Stefan and Otto, looking first at Otto. His collar had somehow become unruly again, its tips pointing up in the air like bat wings. She frowned at his rumpled appearance, but when he smiled his impish smile, her face softened and she leaned toward him.

"I think your uniform needs some help," she whispered.

Though she didn't return his grin as she said this, the seriousness disappeared from her face for just a moment. She took a step to the side to look at Stefan. They were eye to eye. The wind lifted a strand of her hair and pulled it down over her dark eyes. She raised a delicate hand to brush it from her face. Their eyes met, and he returned the gaze. She paused a second more but said nothing, turned, and went on.

When she got through the group, she returned to stand next to Captain Lorberg.

"All you've got are Germans?"

John nodded.

"No Italians?"

John shook his head, smiled. Walt had told Katherine that farmers in other parts of the state were sometimes getting Italian POWs. They might not work as hard, but they were a lot more peaceable and easy-going.

"Nope. None to be found around here. They're all working cotton in the Bootheel."

Katherine sighed. She wished that it wasn't Germans again. It wasn't that she hated them, they just made her uneasy. They were polite enough, to be sure, but there always seemed to be a layer just underneath, something calculating and heartless.

Glancing again at the troop gathered before her, Katherine realized again that only days before, these men had been fighting Americans, trying to kill as many possible. They were the very real threat her brother faced every day in the war.

She looked again at John. The farm needed workers if it was to survive.

"Well, I am glad we can get them. "There's just no other way we could get by."

He nodded, knowing that they all would have preferred to have the local hands still on the farm.

"You're busy, John," she said. "If you'll just show me out I'll work with Colonel Whiteside on the rest of the details."

They turned and walked to the gate, where they embraced again. Whitcomb and the other guards stared after her, and the POWs did, too. It had been a while since any of them had seen something so lovely.

Snatches of conversation wafted from the guards as the Germans stood waiting, and Stefan picked up bits and pieces.

"Who was that?" asked one standing with Whitcomb. "She was a knockout."

"That," said Robert Whitcomb, "was Katherine Lorberg. And YES, Captain John Lorberg is her brother. And YES, Walter Lorberg, the big-wig politician, is her daddy."

Stefan couldn't believe his ears. It couldn't be the same woman he had met in 1940 in that little diner slouched alongside the road. He remembered her perched on the stool next to him. The beauty of her eyes, her hair.

"What's she doing here?" crowed one of the guards, a little guy with a red face. His name was Morrison, and he looked like a bantam rooster.

"Well, with her dad spending all his time in hobnobbing at the capitol and her brothers off at war," said Whitcomb, "she's the one running the family business. Maybe you've heard of it?"

He arched his eyebrows and looked at the others, most of who were from the east coast or the deep south. Several shook their heads blankly. Whitcomb was proud of his expertise.

"Let me tell you then, friends, about Lorberg Farms and Orchards, the largest farming operation in the state of Missouri. Supposedly they do ten thousand dollars worth of watermelon alone. And that's probably the smallest of the crops they put out."

One of the men whistled.

"He's right," piped up a guard from Iowa. "Every grocery store in the Midwest worth a lick carries Lorberg produce."

"They're out in Augusta, on the river, and we had a camp out there last year," continued Whitcomb. "She's here to get a bunch of these Krauts to work out there again. Her daddy uses his pull to make it happen."

The guards started to all chatter at once, thrilled by the possibility of leaving Fort Leonard Wood and going someplace new. These small work camps dotted the state, including some in St. Louis and Kansas City.

"I'd love to be in St. Louis—"

"What about Kansas City?"

"Anywhere but here."

"How 'bout the country?"

"—long as there are women!"

"—and a dance hall or two."

"With beer."

"Cold beer."

Whitcomb began recounting his experience at Augusta the previous summer. Suddenly they were all silent again, listening intently to his every word. Stefan struggled to catch bits and pieces as well.

". . . when we were out there last year, she couldn't get enough of me . . .," said Whitcomb in a low voice.

The guards all roared and laughed, drowning out Whitcomb's next few words.

". . . mmm those titties," were the next words that Stefan could make out, and the guards laughed again. Stefan frowned.

"We'd be out sometimes in the evening, and start going at it, and that whore'd be begging me. 'Don't stop,' she'd say, 'Give it to me harder," said Whitcomb, leering at the others with his memory. "Said I was the only one man enough to satisfy her . . ."

The vulgar laughter of the other guards drowned out the rest, but Stefan knew what Whitcomb was talking about. He stood with jaw clenched and fists opening and closing.

Whitcomb's crude discourse and the accompanying coarse laughter from the other guards continued until Morrison piped up.

"Yeah, right, Whitcomb. I'm not buying it. A woman that classy wouldn't have anything to do with you."

The guards who knew Whitcomb's temper were shocked at the man's boldness. They fell silent, all eyes on him.

"Full of shit," he continued, his words hanging heavy in the air. "That's all you are, Whitcomb. I bet you told her you got that glass eye over fighting the Krauts, too."

Stefan watched as Whitcomb's face instantly flashed purple and hot, black anger rolling across it like thunder from a storm front. The glass eye bulged in its socket, as if his fury might pop it from his head.

"Listen, asshole. You don't talk about my eye," said Whitcomb, staring at him with hatred. "Ever. You got that?"

"Heh, poked in the eye by a stick," crowed Morrison, still laughing, looking around the circle, talking to the others. "That's right, a real fierce war wound. Walking through the woods at night at basic training, drunker than hell off homemade hooch. What kind of ass does something like that?"

In a flash, Whitcomb was on the man. He knocked Morrison flat on the bare ground before he knew what had happened, pummeling his face and chest wildly, brutally, with his fists.

"Hey! Knock it off!" shouted Captain Lorberg as he sprinted over from the fence. He waded into the tangle of guards trying to pull them apart. Whitcomb fought and screamed, tried to break free of the arms holding him, insane with rage.

"What's the matter with you?" Lorberg demanded once the two men were separated. He was frustrated and embarrassed by this conduct by his men on the parade ground in front of the prisoners. He especially hoped Katherine hadn't seen it.

Whitcomb was breathing heavy, shirt torn. Two men held his arms. He offered no response, just glared at the Morrison, still struggling against the arms that held him.

"Take him out of here," said Lorberg, shaking his head in disgust. "We'll talk once he cools off."

The two guards dragged Whitcomb from the parade ground.

"That little shit! I'll kill him! Swear I will!" Whitcomb started to shout as they frog-marched him out, his imprecations growing fainter but no less insistent as they went.

Morrison stood up, disheveled, scratch marks on his arms and face. He was bleeding from the nose.

"Wow," he said, wiping at his uniform, trying to smooth it out. "What a lunatic."

He looked at the other guards still gathered around him and tried to laugh off Whitcomb's irrational fury. The other men shook their heads.

"What the hell was that about?" asked Lorberg, looking at his clipboard. He didn't really expect an answer. "Let's get back to business."

He walked to the front of the formation, flipping through his stack of rosters.

"We're changing up the work assignments," he announced. "Some will continue in your present jobs, others will get different ones."

He and Bunzek began working through the formation, divvying up the prisoner groups. This group would now be working in the warehouse, this group would remain in the post quarry, that group would go dig ditches in a new housing area going up.

"You men here," said Lorberg, gesturing to the men in Stefan's group as Bunzek made notations on his assignment sheet. "You'll be going to Augusta."

"And, hey," hollered Lorberg to the guards still standing behind the formation, "be sure to tell Whitcomb that he's going, too."

The one nearest Lorberg raised his eyebrows, puzzled at this decision.

"Sir?" asked the guard.

"Why the hell not?" asked Lorberg, irritated at being questioned. Whitcomb had been there before with no problems as far as John knew. Why send somebody new?

"So what if he's nuts?" added Lorberg. "Seems like all you guys are, one way or another."

Chapter 23

Katherine gripped the wheel tightly and tried to keep her mind only on the passing scenery as she made the long drive back to Augusta. She hadn't thought of Robert Whitcomb for a long time—repressed memories maybe—but seeing him today brought that string of unpleasant events from last year rushing right back.

"God," she said aloud, shaking her head as she drove, "what a mess."

But then she smiled again, thinking of the time with her brother. The unhappy coincidence of seeing Whitcomb had done little to dampen the joy of being with John again.

The family had been thrilled when he was transferred to Fort Leonard Wood eight months ago, thanks to Walter's calls to a few well-placed connections in the War Department.

In reality, however, the change hadn't made much difference. He'd only been out to the farm once on a three-day Christmas leave. Them going to see him was not any easier. Fort Leonard Wood was still more than four hours away; with rationed tires and gasoline it was hard to justify that type of trip.

Plus Katherine had a lot going on with the farm, too. It wasn't like she was just sitting around looking for stuff to do. Regardless, having him there did mean he was closer, and she was grateful for the chance to see him, even if it was just for a short time like today.

As Katherine approached the house, her father's black sedan was parked out front. She smiled, surprised and happy. He had been in Jeff City all week and wasn't expected back until the day after tomorrow. She knew he'd be pleased to hear the arrangements she had made for the POWs to return. Little did

Katherine know that he had even bigger news for her.

"Hello, Dad," said Katherine as she stepped into the warm kitchen. The smell of frying pork chops filled the room. Caroline stood at the stove while her father perched on the edge of one of the kitchen chairs. He was leaned over with his elbows on his knees, playing dolls with a little girl who sat on the floor next to the table.

"Hello, hon," Walter replied, looking up. "How was the trip?"

"Great," she called as she hung her coat in the anteroom. "Very successful. Nailed down the agreement to have the POWs back. Looks like they'll arrive middle of next week."

"Wait," her father told the little girl, holding up an index finger. It was John's daughter, Ellen. He tucked a floppy bear under the little blanket bed they had made on the floor, smiled at her and stood.

"That's great, Kat. Good for you," he said, holding out his arms. Katherine wrapped herself in his big hug and gave him a peck on the cheek as he continued. "Good for us, actually. We'd be in a damned fine mess here without those workers. Looks like those calls to General Archer paid off."

Katherine crouched next to the little girl still playing on the floor and gave her a kiss. "I saw your daddy today," said Katherine, pointing to the black-and-white photo on the mantle. The girl smiled. This separation from Ellen was one of the unspoken frustrations of having John so relatively close, yet so far away.

"You saw John?" asked Walter.

"Only for a couple of minutes," said Katherine, standing again. "But it was still nice."

She looked again to Ellen, engrossed in her dolls.

"I wish we could see more of him," she sighed, knowing that having him even here in Missouri had been a fabulous stroke of luck. During his first two years of his service, he'd been stationed at remote posts – first Texas, then Washington and they hadn't seen him at all.

"It looks like we might get that chance." Walter offered, smiling at his daughter. "He didn't say anything?"

Katherine looked at him sharply. "What are you talking about?"

"He might not even know yet himself. Remember Lieutenant Bray? The one here last year with the POWs? I was on the phone with Col. Whiteside this afternoon and told him that since this was an even bigger group coming out, more guards, more prisoners, he'd probably want a captain to be in charge."

Katherine began to nod excitedly.

"I told Whiteside that, sure, there were some good ones at Fort Leonard Wood," continued Walt, "but it made sense if he had someone who already knew the area, the local farmers. There might be slack time when we'd have extra workers and could hire the POWs out. More income for the government. It'd make him look really good."

"Oh, daddy," said Katherine. "You think there's a chance?"

"More than a chance," said her father. "Sounds like a done deal. Whiteside's pretty dense though, and at first didn't get what I was hinting at. Must be from Arkansas. I nearly had to come right out and ask him."

Walt began to imitate Col. Whiteside, putting on a heavy southern twang.

"'Well, Lorberg,' he croaked to me, 'you're asking me to put my ass over a barrel here. Truth is, don't matter to me. We've got a couple larger groups going out, and your boy has got to go somewhere with one of them. So it's either there or to Atherton to dig potatoes. And I figure the Army ain't gonna mind if a side benefit of an assignment includes placing a man with his only daughter.'"

"That's so wonderful of him," said Katherine.

"Yes, but he had a strong warning, too. Any hint of problems and John gets pulled back."

Walt slipped back into his accent.

"'I know John, and I know you, Walt, and I don't believe this arrangement's gonna cause any problems. But I'm very concerned about this getting out. The boys in D.C. will have their panties in a bunch if they thought I was playing favorites or had some damn politician—no offense, Walt—pulling strings. So I'm telling you straight. I'll do this, but if there is a whiff of trouble, anything at all that could draw the least bit of attention, I'm pulling John back.'"

"Does she know?" asked Katherine, nodding toward Ellen.

"No," said Walter. "Things can change right up to the last minute, so I'm not saying anything until I see him in the driveway. Just in case it doesn't go through, you know. It'd break her heart. She's doing remarkably well, all things considered. We just don't need to give her any upset. It's hard enough as it is. Last thing we want is her to get all excited about her daddy being here, then have it all go poof."

Katherine smiled as the girl on the floor glanced at her again.

"Daddy," she said, pointing to the photo again. "Daddy."

Chapter 24

The night before the POWs were to leave for Augusta, Robert Whitcomb stood in the darkness, tucked in the shadows of the barracks. With a second figure lurking behind him, they waited and watched the street in front of the mess hall, eyeing the POWs who passed as they returned from dinner. They were quiet until Karl Leider emerged from the mess hall, the last one through the line.

"That's him," hissed the man behind him as Leider came out the door. Whitcomb said nothing until Leider was almost past him.

"Hey," he said in broken German, taking a step from the darkness, "Come over here a minute."

Leider paused, unsure of what to think. He was wary of this American guard who wanted to talk with him in an obviously unofficial conversation. He had seen Whitcomb around the camp, remembered him from the parade grounds that morning he went berserk.

"It's okay," said Whitcomb. "Just want to talk for a bit."

Leider tried to shrug casually and followed Whitcomb around the corner of the building. There in the darkness between the two barracks, he froze when he spotted the second figure waiting, seeing a set-up for sure. The other man stepped forward, letting a bit of light fall on his face.

"Hey Karl," he chuckled.

It took but a moment for Leider to recognize the man.

"Gieseke! That you?" asked Leider, amazed.

"It is indeed," said Herman Gieseke. He slapped Leider fondly on the arm and smiled broadly. "I can't believe how long it's been."

"Last time I saw you was when you left for artillery school," said Leider. "Heard you had a hell of a time on the Eastern front."

"That's right," said Gieseke, eyeing the private's tab in Leider's collar. He winked, knowing better than to ask about the missing SS insignia and major's rank. "And you! I always knew you'd do great."

"Hey, you two can reminisce all you want later," interrupted Whitcomb. "We've got shit to figure out." He leaned in, talking confidentially to Leider. "Him and me got a little arrangement going, and you may be able to help us with it."

Gieseke nodded and Whitcomb continued.

"You know how the Red Cross is always sending goodies to you? Cigarettes and chocolate and other humanitarian bullshit. One of you Germans always has to sign for it. I direct the deliveries straight to him for signature, and then we split the goods."

Whitcomb glanced at Gieseke, nodded for him to continue.

"About half of what I get, maybe less, goes to the POW canteen," said the German." "I keep the rest, use it to pay for favors, things like that. Works real well in maintaining control. You know how people are. They'll do anything for that stuff."

"What do you do with your part?"

"I resell to the people stuck in the crappy little towns around here," said Whitcomb. "There's nothing else available for miles. You know what a guy'll pay for black market smokes when he can't get them anywhere else?"

Gieseke nodded. "He's making a bunch of money. For us the power is in controlling the camp supply."

"It's a beautiful thing," said Whitcomb. "We make a killing, you get to keep order and everybody's happy, especially the smokers. It's like we're doing a good deed for society."

Gieseke nodded again.

"So why are you telling me this?" asked Leider.

"A fair question," asked Whitcomb. He was stamping his foot in excitement and the glass eye bulged. "Gieseke and me have been working together for a long time. When he figured out that you were here, he told me about you. Said he's known you for years and that he'd trust you with his wife and his wallet. That's saying something."

Whitcomb stopped for a second and glanced around again. He was rubbing his hands together.

"About a hundred and fifty of you are getting ready to go work at a side camp," said Whitcomb. "It's a big farm, a place we were last year, Augusta. Looks like it's going to be a long term deal."

Whitcomb paused, looked at Leider to see if he was getting it.

"This new camp offers the chance to expand the operation," said Whitcomb. "But I need someone to work from your side of the wire. We think that could be you. You decide if you're in, and you get added to the list to go to Augusta. Easy as that."

"You should see how much money this generates, Karl," added Gieseke.

"We were out there for just a month and a half last year. Too short to really get much started, though we did make some dough stealing fuel," Whitcomb continued. "Being out there longer with a much larger group, this could be a lucrative operation. You'll be a very powerful person in the camp."

Leider frowned inwardly. The power this offered was undeniable. But he wasn't sure he wanted to get drawn into this filthy business. What he really couldn't understand was why a guard would collaborate with prisoners like this.

Whitcomb smiled. "I know what you're thinking. Listen. I'm not eager to help you Nazis," he said. "But what you believe and how you handle your people is your business so long as nobody runs off and the camp stays quiet. I just know that it's a chance for me to make some big honkin' bucks, a whole lot more than Uncle Sam is payin' me. That's what I'm all about. If us working together is what it takes, I'm fine with that."

It was quiet for a moment.

"So what do you think?"

Leider glanced at Gieseke, who nodded slowly.

"It's been a good arrangement, Karl," he said. "I wouldn't have brought you in if I didn't think so."

Leider looked back at Whitcomb, remembering his ranting as he was pulled from the fight on the parade grounds. But he trusted Gieseke. Always had. And if Gieseke was okay with Whitcomb and their arrangement, then Karl could make it work as well. And when it came down to it, this would provide some very effective tools to point things in the camp in the right direction.

Leider nodded. He was in, too.

"All right," said Whitcomb. "Pack your shit. We leave tomorrow."

Chapter 25

A big crowd buzzed around the string of army trucks the next morning, cramming them full of equipment needed at the side camp. In the hubbub, no one noticed the German with the jet-black hair make his way in. With his duffel bag and work clothes, he blended just fine with the departing group.

The guard checking the roster to Augusta saw the man's name as a late addition to the list. Nothing unusual there. Last minute shuffling meant probably a dozen changes in personnel for various reasons. He didn't question those and he thought nothing of this one either. Before long, the wheels were turning and the men were on their way to Augusta.

"So long," thought Stefan, as they rolled out of the gates of the POW camp. He and Otto sat in the back of a truck, peering out the canvas. He could see the envy on the faces of the Germans left behind, nothing better for them to do than watch as the trucks departed.

"It'll be nice being out in the country," said Otto as they bounced along the gravel road, trailing a dusty plume behind them. "Glad to be leaving?"

"Yeah." Stefan watched the camp grow smaller and smaller out the back gate of the truck. "Glad to be getting the hell away from Karl Leider."

He exhaled forcefully, feeling relief seep through his body, something he hadn't experienced in a long time.

The trip was a chilly all-day ride in army trucks that maxed out at 35 mph. What took Katherine just four hours in her black sedan turned out to be a ten-hour, sputtering, start and stop affair. A couple of breaks along the way to hit the john or eat a sandwich did little to ease the discomfort of riding in the back of the truck that long.

Relief finally came at dusk when the trucks drove through the main gate of the farm, below a soaring white arc that read *Lorberg Farms and Orchards*. Approaching the large complex of buildings clustered at the end of the lane, the trucks came to a halt and the POWs spilled from the back and shuffled into formation, getting their first exposure to their new home.

"Look at this place," whistled Otto. "It's huge."

They stood in the middle of the broad courtyard, fencing and farm buildings on each side. The barns and grain elevator loomed above them, but Otto's eyes were drawn to the buildings full of tractors and farm implements of every sort, literally dozens of pieces of powerful machinery used to work the farm.

"You could mount an invasion with all that equipment," said Otto.

Set back at a short distance along one edge was the big white house. A broad porch faced the courtyard, and the three-story structure was bounded by a white picket fence that enclosed dormant flowerbeds and a large but immaculately kept yard, even in January.

As the sergeants called the men to order, counting noses with the guards to make sure they hadn't lost anyone on the trip, Captain Lorberg climbed from his perch in the cab of the second truck. He looked around and smiled. He started for the house, pausing for a big yawning stretch, arms reaching high as he tried to work out the kinks that the miles had knotted into his body.

"What's his problem? He had a cushioned seat at least," groused Otto. "But you know, the greasy wheel gets the squeak."

Stefan looked at him. "Huh?"

"You know what I mean."

Lorberg strode across the courtyard and to the fence fronting the broad house. He had barely opened the gate to let himself in when the front door of the house flew open with a terrific bang. A little blond-haired streak shot down the steps and rocketed across the yard to fly into his arms.

John Lorberg held the girl pressed against him for a long time, finally moving again to cross the yard and climb the steps to the front porch. Still carrying the little girl, arms tightly wrapped around his neck, Lorberg crossed the porch and went inside the house, pulling the door shut behind him.

Stefan watched this happy reunion until Otto nudged him with his elbow. "Look over there," Otto muttered.

A few rows in front of them in the formation stood Karl Leider. He turned, staring at Stefan. Their eyes met, and he nodded once, narrowing his eyes, and turned back to face forward.

Stefan cursed silently. His joy at going to Augusta had just vanished. He shook his head and frowned, wishing this specter to disappear.

It hadn't been easy to avoid Leider at the big camp. Being in different barracks and work details had helped, but Stefan had still worried. And here he was in Augusta. It would be much more difficult to dodge the man here, given the smaller numbers, fewer guards and closer quarters. He could never relax, never let his guard down.

Satisfied that they had everyone, the guards released the formation and got the men fed, laying out a late supper. Stefan's appetite, though, was gone.

They worked late that night, both guards and prisoners, transferring equipment from the trucks into their new quarters, two long but low-slung structures that had previously served as brooding houses for chicken and turkeys. Long and narrow, the white wooden buildings took one entire side of the courtyard and were at least 200 feet long.

Otto and Stefan carried equipment into the guards' building. Their first trip was to help drag a heavy wooden desk into a large room that John Lorberg would use for an office. Back and forth they went, carrying boxes, typewriters, chairs.

"I think he brought most of Fort Leonard Wood with him," said Otto, plopping himself on the desk. He mopped at his brow, having just rolled a second heavy metal filing cabinet into the room. Two more waited outside on the trucks. "Anybody have any idea where he wants these?"

Lorberg himself stuck his head in the room as if in answer to the question. He frowned momentarily seeing the man sitting on his desk, all sweaty and breathing heavily. But he laughed as Otto's eyes grew big and he shot up off the desk to stand at attention.

"It's okay," he said. "Just put them over here," he said, pointing to an interior wall next to a large closet. Though it had windows to let in light, Stefan could see the little room had been fitted with iron bars and a heavy wooden door. It was a secure storage spot for things like rifles for the guards or cash for the payroll.

"Sheesh," said Otto. "Looks like a jail."

"Could be," smiled Lorberg. "Use it for locking up the bad guys."

He winked at the pair, but he wasn't kidding. Stefan knew the captain would happily use it as a holding pen if need be.

"And those filing cabinets?" offered Lorberg before moving on. "They slide pretty easy if you take the drawers out. You'll just have to make another trip or two."

When finished setting up the office, Stefan and Otto grabbed their duffel bags off the truck and headed for the other building set aside for the POWs. It had

been segmented into a half-dozen medium-sized rooms, each with space to bunk about 25 POWs.

The two lingered just inside the front door, watching for Leider. They hadn't seen him since formation. Though Stefan and Otto hadn't talked about him while they worked, both had tried to process just what it meant to find him there.

"There he goes," said Otto, scowling at the man's back as he walked down the hall. Leider found a spot in the second room to bunk in, and the pair hustled past to the far end of the building. They plopped their stuff in the very last room, as distant from him as possible. It had been a long day and they were bushed. Before long the cots were assembled and the weary prisoners stretched out their bedrolls, some snoring even before the lights went off.

"How did he end up here?" Stefan spoke softly in the darkness. He lay on his back, with his arms behind his head, staring at the ceiling. "His group wasn't one of the ones sent along."

"Who knows?" said Otto. "Must have got added at the last minute."

Otto was quiet for a minute then spoke again.

"I'm sure he'll leave us alone though." Otto tried to sound optimistic. "If he really wanted to do something, it would have happened back at Leonard Wood."

"Yeah. We just have to be careful and stay away from him," said Stefan. "Nothing's going to happen."

Both were silent in the darkness.

"Stefan?" said Otto, after a time. "You know it's coming, right."

Stefan sighed grimly. "I know."

He rolled on his side and for a very long time tried to sleep, never turning his back to the door.

Chapter 26

"What the hell!?"

The words came flying out of Katherine's mouth before she could stop them. Her mother gasped from the kitchen and turned pale.

"Katherine!" she hollered. "How dare you speak like that in this house!"

Katherine stood at the front window, holding back the curtains just enough to peek outside. The newly arrived Germans were spilling out of the mess hall into a loose formation at the center of the courtyard. Some guards stood together at the back, and there he was — Robert Whitcomb, again at the farm.

As if he could feel her presence, Whitcomb eyed the house, thumbs in his belt loops, seemingly staring straight at the window. Katherine let the curtains drop back quickly and slumped to the couch, feeling disgust welling in her stomach.

"I should have said something to John while I was there," thought Katherine, pacing back and forth. "John could have kept Whitcomb back. It would have been easy to do. Swap him out, simple as that."

Katherine put her hands to her head. The possibility of Whitcomb coming back hadn't even occurred to her until she had been confronted by him and the accompanying wave of bad memories that morning on the parade ground.

"Why am I so damned stupid?" she muttered, rocking back and forth. "Why didn't I tell him what happened?"

Katherine knew why, of course. She didn't want to ruin those few minutes with her brother. Didn't want him to know that she had been out with that horrible man. Didn't want to endure the humiliation of recounting the details of that dreadful night and how she had been such a dope to say yes in the first place.

She sighed and peeked between the curtains. There was Whitcomb, still ogling the house.

What were the odds against Whitcomb's ever coming back? With 5,000 Germans at Fort Leonard Wood, there had to be 500 guards to draw from. Given the sheer number of GIs and the dozens of branch camps across the state, she had reckoned that there was no way in the world he'd be back in Augusta. But that had backfired and here he was. She felt trapped in her own house.

"What's the matter, dear?" her mother asked from the doorway.

"Nothing."

She couldn't tell her what was wrong, couldn't tell John either. He wouldn't be able to do anything about it. She knew what they had said. Absolutely no troubles at the camp. Not a hint of anything or John would be replaced. She wasn't going to lay that on him. She'd just have to deal with it herself.

"Doesn't sound like nothing. The last time I heard that kind of language was when your father fell down the stairs."

"It's nothing." Katherine crossed her arms. She remained facing the window and did not look at her mother.

The clock in the hall chimed nine. It was time to go to the office. A salesman was calling soon and she'd have to walk across the courtyard to meet him.

Turning from the window, Katherine took a deep breath and stepped slowly to the front door. She paused there before turning the cold knob in her hand. She'd have to see Whitcomb eventually. Now was as good a time as any to get it over with.

Walking across the courtyard, she felt the eyes on her. It was everyone, it seemed—the guards, the POWs, the farmhands. They all stopped what they were doing, and heads turned to follow her path, staring at her without restraint.

Katherine's route took her past the group of guards but she didn't hesitate as she passed, not even when Whitcomb muttered something to them, and they bawled out their bawdy laughter in response.

He leaped out when she drew near, just like before, just like she figured he would. She would not let herself be caught off guard again.

"Hello, dear Katherine," he said, bowing deeply. "How much I've looked forward to seeing you again." He reached to take her hand, clearly intending to kiss it. She slapped it away.

"Listen." She said, loud enough for everyone to hear. "Don't talk to me again. Else you'll regret it."

The words came too quick. She hadn't meant to make a threat, but her emotions were running high.

"Wow," said Whitcomb, looking hurt and surprised as the guards' laughter washed over him. He turned red first, and then the purple shade rolled across his face too.

He leaned toward her and whispered, softly enough that only she could hear.

"You're not such a big deal," he said. Though he carried a sweet smile, his voice dripped with scorn. "Don't let yourself get carried away."

Katherine glared at him. He stepped back.

"Remember what I said," she replied, then strode quickly past him to the office.

"Well then, you just let me know when we're getting back together, sweetie," responded Whitcomb, so all could hear. "I sure enjoyed last year."

He blew a kiss as she went past.

The salesman ended up being almost twenty minutes late, and Katherine was glad. By the time he got there, only a little bit of red remained around her eyes, not enough to really show how hard she had cried behind the office door.

Chapter 27

"I do say I've lost a good bit of my capacity for worrying about that guy," said Otto standing in line for dinner one night about two months into their stay. Since their arrival, they had watched and remained wary of Leider but so far nothing had happened.

Leider had already finished eating and they watched him leave the cramped dining hall. The men ate in shifts due to limited seating and though occasions like this offered frequent passing encounters, they had little interaction with Leider aside from his usual sneer.

"Maybe that's just the way he looks," said Otto after Leider smirked his way past them as he crossed the courtyard. "Maybe he was born that way and can't help it."

Though Stefan was still not sleeping very well, their conclusion was finally that Leider was nothing more than a big talker and a mailroom sneak, and that's how he got the information about Dr. Goetz.

"You see," said Otto, lying on his bunk one rainy Sunday afternoon after lunch. "He's like a school yard bully. He talks big with all of his buddies around, but you get him on his own, and all of a sudden he wants to wave the hot flag of white air."

"Huh?" Stefan glanced at his friend, eyebrows raised.

"You know what I'm trying to say."

It was now pushing into March 1945, and Stefan found that, other than the ongoing tension with Leider, the peaceful country routine of work-eat-sleep agreed with him. He relished outdoor labor, especially compared with the chemicals and steam that surrounded him working the press in the laundry back at Fort Leonard Wood.

Though a few prisoners tended livestock, helped fix barns or took care of machinery, the majority worked in the fields. They planted acres of cucumber, squash and watermelon. Other prisoners crisscrossed the rows, working fertilizer into the rich soil, bright green and lush with new sprouts.

On most days the GIs dropped the POWs off in the morning in a section of fields with a farmhand who knew what needed to be done and then they'd disappear. A guard would return again at lunchtime to bring food and check on them. Sometimes they'd be out in the evening to bring them back; other times, depending on the distance back to the farm, the prisoners simply returned on their own.

"Isn't this amazing," Stefan said to Otto one evening as they took themselves back to the camp. The pair had walked for ten minutes and had ten more minutes yet to go. "Completely by ourselves, not a guard in sight."

Even after eight weeks of this he couldn't get over it. The one guy supposed to be watching them, Robert Whitcomb, was just waking up in the cab of an Army truck parked by the river. He had spent the day trying to sleep off a hang-over. What the army had figured out, and what really made these side camps possible, was the low level of supervision the POWs actually required. On that particular evening, almost a hundred POWs strolled back by themselves. From the first Germans just arriving at the courtyard to the slowest bringing up the rear, they were stretched over a mile of Missouri countryside.

"You know," said Otto. "It's really something. There are plenty of chances for a fellow to run, but what's the use?"

"True," agreed Stefan. "You'd just be right back in uniform if you ever actually made it home."

It was nice to be with Otto. It was already Friday, and only the first day that week his friend had been out in the fields. Most of Otto's time had been tied up on other jobs around the farm.

It took just a couple of weeks at the Augusta camp for Otto to endear himself to the farmhands, who used him whenever they could for any odd jobs. They loved him for lots of reasons but none better than the mangled English he spoke.

"Should I throw the cows over the fence some hay?" he asked one day early on as he stood outside a pen. The delighted hands laughed uproariously. Otto did, too, without knowing why, and they were won over. They loved to take him along to help on errands around the farm or when they had to go to town.

Otto found himself helping a lot with the trucks that came to the farm's busy front office to pick up or drop off loads. He liked keeping track of things and talking to the drivers.

"Yeah, working up front is a pretty good deal," said Otto. "The best part is getting to see that family."

"And who in the family might you be talking about?" Stefan was kidding Otto now. "There's the dad and he's gone a lot. And the mother, too, she mostly stays inside."

He figured Otto was talking about Katherine for sure. The woman was every bit the knockout that the POWs remembered, and when she walked by, everything stopped. But she seemed distant, different from what Stefan remembered from their first meeting. She was intimidating, an ice queen. Even the guards knew better than to try and talk with her. All but Whitcomb.

"Yeah. Katherine's around," Otto smiled. He hadn't missed Stefan's riff. "But there's the little girl, Captain Lorberg's daughter. I've seen her a couple of times. Absolutely adorable. Reminds me of my own."

"Helene or Margarite?"

"Helene. The six-year-old. They look like each other."

"Yeah?"

"Yeah. Even the same laugh." Stefan could hear his friend's voice go soft.

Just the day before, Otto had been up front at the office with one of the farmhands and three or four other POWs. They stood by the receiving dock, waiting to unload a truck with a big seed delivery. The driver hopped from the cab and handed over the invoice, and Otto and the farmhand began to check the shipment against the order before it came off the truck.

While they chatted, Lorberg came through, making his rounds like he did every morning, checking to make sure everything was in order. Nothing unusual there, but what stood out to the men was the little girl that walked with him hand in hand. It was Ellen, John's daughter.

Charmed by the child, and thinking about their own little ones back home, the men were drawn irresistibly to her, speaking to her and smiling at the girl as she passed. They could not help it.

"Good morning," said one, crouching to look at her at eye level.

"Out for a walk with dad?" asked another.

Ellen said nothing in return. She only smiled shyly back at them, holding her daddy's hand tighter and pressing herself a little closer against his leg when they paused to talk.

Otto stood transfixed as they approached. He was still at the front of the truck, checking the shipping list with the driver. He watched as the pair lingered for another minute with the POWs. One of the Germans pulled a stick of gum out of his pocket and gave it to Ellen, then folded the foil wrapper into a sailboat.

Otto still stared, captured by her, forgetting completely about the load of seed and the shipping list.

"Hey Otto," said one of the farm hands, "need your help here."

He was jerked back to the task at hand, and after a couple minutes more, John Lorberg moved on and took the little girl with him. Otto watched until they finally moved out of sight. Then he closed his eyes and thought of his own little Helene back home, and tried to ignore the aching in his heart.

Chapter 28

With the weather growing warmer, Ellen played outside more, adding a new happiness for everyone. All day she roamed around in the barns and around the front office while a whole crew of farmhands and prisoners kept an eye on her. Caroline monitored things too from the window or the yard, where she worked tending her flowers in the morning, and so the happy girl had a whole host of people looking out for her.

Otto in particular took a shine to the girl. Even though his English was coming along well, talking with Ellen was easier and more fun than conversing with the drivers who still sometimes struggled with his accent. He stacked some crates and pallets off to one side of the dock one day, building a marvelous little structure that could be a stage, a castle or a playhouse all depending on her mood.

Walter Lorberg was the only member of the family the POWs really hadn't seen much. With the fighting in full swing around the world, Walt basically lived in Jeff City and Washington D.C. these days, drumming up government contracts for Missouri agriculture to help support the war effort.

Otto and Stefan stood in the courtyard one morning after breakfast, chatting idly with the other prisoners who milled about, waiting to begin the day's work.

"Psst," said Otto. "Who is that?"

He nodded toward the fence where someone new stood, an older man, nicely dressed in slacks and open-collar shirt. He had the look of someone used to being respected, used to being in charge.

"Huh," said Stefan. "I think that might be the senator."

Walt intended it to look like he had come out to make an inspection, to observe the men working on his farm. Really he was waiting to intercept a delivery. He kept glancing at the lane, hoping to spot the truck before Katherine did. But as the group noticed him, he felt warmed by their curious and friendly faces and just couldn't resist. He smiled broadly at this group of prisoners, came over, started shaking hands with them, introducing himself, always the politician.

"Howdy," he said, "glad you're here. I'm Walt Lorberg." He waded through the crowd, greeting them individually. "Nice to see you. Welcome." It was genuine and the prisoners could feel it.

While this continued, Stefan heard a motor in the distance. He watched as a small flat-bed truck pulled into the gate at the far end of the lane, worked its way toward the house. Pulling into the yard, the driver stopped the truck at the dock and Otto went to meet him. Walt Lorberg saw the arriving truck, too, and hot-footed it to where the man was climbing out of the cab.

"Walter Lorberg?" the man asked Otto.

Surprised, Otto shook his head no. Out of the dozens of shipments he had handled, none had ever come with the big man personally named.

"That's me," Walt said, stepping next to them.

"Special delivery, sir," said the driver. "It's your grapevines."

The driver went to the side of the truck with Otto following. The two hefted trunk-sized wooden crates off the back and stacked them in a single pile. Walter, flushed and eager, pulled out a pair of pliers and pried the top off the first crate.

Sensing his excitement, all watched as he lifted the lid with a dramatic flourish and handed it to Otto. Walt reached slowly inside to pull out a grapevine to show them his new inspiration. All gasped as he held it high, for it was a disappointing little sprout, dried-up, brown and wispy. He looked crestfallen.

"These look okay to you?" said Walter, looking worriedly at Otto.

Otto just smiled and shrugged.

The whole thing had started several months back. While sniffing around for more business opportunities for Missouri agriculture, Walter learned that the government was providing big subsidies to establish domestic vineyards. For the last five years, the pipeline to the European growers had been busted from the war, and stateside grape growers and wineries had not been able to keep up with demand. Walt saw an opportunity to branch out in a new and lucrative direction.

"No, Dad, absolutely not," Katherine had told him, firmly, when he mentioned it to her.

Normally she gave him some latitude with these experiments, but with the expense of acquiring quality vines and the way the farm was already overstretched, it just wasn't a good idea.

"Now is not the right time," she said. "We don't know anything about grapes, don't have people to tend to them and are plenty busy with what we have."

"You're right, dear," Walt had told her, honestly resigning himself to taking a pass on the grape-growing. But then his mouth went into high gear in a Jeff City bar while talking with a grower who had pushed for the subsidy, and he ended up ordering a bunch from the man anyway.

Walter knew that his daughter was right, again, that he had no idea what to do with these crates of very expensive grapevines now sitting in his yard. That made him even more determined that they were going to be successful.

"Sir, I don't know anything about grapes," said Otto, "but my friend there happens to be an expert." He pointed to Stefan, among the crowd of the POWs.

Stefan's eyebrows shot up, wondering what sort of snare Otto had created for him.

"Can you come here, son?" called Walt.

Stefan walked to them hesitantly, worried what he was getting into.

"You know something about grapes?" he demanded excitedly as Stefan approached.

Stefan nodded. "Sure. A bit."

"I've always thought this area would be good for grape growing," said Walter. "But we've got no experience growing them around here, even on a small scale."

Walter glanced around nervously and lowered his voice.

"Plus I've sunk a whole bunch of money into these damn things. My daughter will have my ass if flops."

"Dad, what is this?" It was Katherine. She pointed accusingly at the crates, GRAPEVINES stamped on the sides in big letters.

"Ah, Katherine, dear," Walter laughed. "Those grapevines I was telling you about? Well, I went ahead and got some. The deal was too good to pass up and I think we're really on to something here."

"Dad! We talked about this," Katherine muttered, gritting her teeth. "We weren't going to order any grapevines. We're sending them back."

"We can't send them back. No returns unfortunately," said Walt, grinning nervously. He was trying to think of something quick. "And anyway, that conversation was before we knew that the POW group included an expert in viticulture."

Stefan had been standing awkwardly off to the side, but suddenly found Walt taking him by the arm and pulling him forward for support in the face of his daughter's wrath. "And here he is," said Walter triumphantly.

"Hello," said Katherine, looking at Stefan suspiciously. He couldn't tell if she remembered him but he sure felt a thrill just being this close to her again. He had almost forgotten how beautiful she was.

"What's your name, son?" asked Walter, drawing him away. "We got to talking and I didn't even have a chance to find out."

"Biermann. Stefan Biermann."

"Stefan here knows everything there is to know about growing grapes, and I say we put him in charge of this whole deal."

"Is that right?" Katherine frowned skeptically. "How do you know so much about grape growing?"

"When I was a kid, I spent a lot of time at my grandparents' vineyard. I worked there for many years."

"But can he be spared from his regular work?" asked Katherine. "We don't have extra people just sitting around. And Dad? Just where the hell are we going to plant these things?"

Walt said nothing.

"No idea, huh? I thought not. I'm going to call the dealer. I don't care what he says. He's going to take these damn grapevines back."

She glanced at Stefan still standing there.

"Thank you," she said, dismissing him. "We'll let you know."

"Thank you, son," said Walt, smiling gratefully.

Katherine turned and launched into her father before Stefan even began to walk away.

"Now, damn it, Dad, if we say we're not going to do something, it means we're not going to do it. You take care of the outside business and I handle things here. You've been out of the farming side too long. You don't know how things operate around here."

"Katherine, you've got to take a risk once in a while," Walt interjected. He was irritated because he knew she was right. He wasn't going to give in though. "We'll make these grapes work, even if I have to plant them myself."

As Stefan returned to the group, he saw John Lorberg talking with Otto. Little Ellen played nearby, running back and forth waving a long stick she had picked up from somewhere.

"I've been thinking about putting you in charge of the front office," Lorberg was saying. "You know the routine here, how to talk with the drivers and handle the paperwork. We've just got so much going on that I don't need to leave these other guys," Lorberg hooked a thumb at a couple of farmhands leaning against the fence, "tied up here idle, waiting for trucks to come in. There's too much else they could be doing."

Lorberg didn't say it, but both knew that having Otto there permanently would be a great thing for Ellen. She was happiest in the sunshine of the courtyard, whether following Otto around or just entertaining herself with make-believe play somewhere close.

"Having you handle the loading dock and front office could be a good arrangement. Plus, Caroline's usually nearby in case you got stuck," said John, looking over to where she worked in the front yard flowerbed.

Ellen tugged at the hem of his uniform blouse while he talked, wanting to be picked up.

"You'll find it mighty enjoyable. Just enough trucks coming and going each day that you won't get bored," said Lorberg, lifting the girl to his hip. "You'll be the envy of all the other POWs busting their asses in the fields, that's for sure."

"Good for him," Stefan thought. The job was ideal for Otto. Stefan noticed a new happiness in his friend when he talked about the little girl. Though it would never be a substitute for time spent with his own daughters, Stefan knew that being with Ellen helped Otto ease some of the loneliness he felt.

And Stefan smiled as he thought of this interesting new development that had opened for him. Might not go anywhere with the grapes, but if it did, it would be work he enjoyed. If nothing else it offered him the unexpected chance to get a good close look at Katherine Lorberg once again.

Chapter 29

"Dad," said Katherine. She was in the living room standing over him in the recliner. She repeated it, louder this time. "Dad!"

He snorted once and woke with a start from his nap. It was a week later, a Tuesday afternoon about two p.m., and he had lain down briefly after lunch.

"Dad. I finally talked to the grower. He's not going to take the vines back. Said you knew it, too, that he told you that when you ordered them."

Walt was irritated. He sat up and rubbed his eyes. This was the third time she had bugged him about these vines since they arrived. He would have no peace until things were resolved.

"Dad," Katherine was insistent. "What are you going to do with them? The grower said we've got to get them in the ground soon or else it'll be too late."

"Damn it, Katherine," he sighed. "I'll plant them, okay?" Dragging himself out of the chair, Walt shuffled toward the stairway to find his work clothes, muttering all the way about the indignities forced upon him by these infernal Lorberg women.

※

Katherine watched from the porch with arms crossed as her father grabbed a shovel and headed toward the dock where the crates of grapevines were still stacked.

"I'll show them," he muttered, carrying a shovel. In truth, he couldn't remember the last time he had worked in the fields. It had been some years, going back before he had gone into politics full-time and John was not yet old enough to supervise the hands. But no matter. You can't forget how to farm. It's like riding a bike.

With everyone else out working in the fields, the courtyard was quiet and warm in the midday sun. Katherine frowned as Walt wrestled the heavy crates onto a wagon, struggling to heft them by himself. Her frown deepened as Walt walked to the big shed and climbed on the old tractor and tried to fire it up. It was the one he was most used to driving, but for the past fifteen years it had been a back-up to their newer machines.

The tractor lurched and sputtered as he tried to back it out of the barn and hitch it to the wagon. Walt struggled to control the tractor; it bucked each time he engaged gears to change direction. Just lining up the hitch with the tongue of the wagon proved to be harder than expected. He'd move forward, try again, fight with the steering wheel and the clutch only to find himself either too close or too far away. After ten minutes of trying to get the wagon hitched, he was no closer than when he started.

When Walt finally stopped the tractor long enough to mop the sweat from his head and plot his next move, he saw Katherine watching him from the porch. Walt scowled at her so fiercely she laughed out loud. Seeing the absurdity of the situation, Walt cut the engine.

"Well," he called out. "Hate to admit it, but you're right. I can't even back the damn thing up anymore."

Katherine smiled with satisfaction, and he fired up the tractor again and drove it back to the barn. Katherine stepped from the porch and back inside. She'd ask John tonight about getting that German who knew so much about grapes to lead a crew of POW workers in planting the vines.

※

"No, Kat, past your one grape-growing expert, you don't want to use any more men on this," said John, chewing on a mouthful of roasted chicken. He tried to come in for dinner when he could. Otherwise he ate with his men. "The others are already tied up. You take them for grapes, something else doesn't get done."

"John, you think it's wise to put complete responsibility on him for this?"

"Why not?" asked John, jabbing at the air with his fork to make his point. "Most of the work is going to be in the planning, and that's not a team job."

"What do you mean?"

"Well for starters, you've got to identify possible locations, test the soil, and plot out how the vines will be planted. That right there will take a couple weeks or more, I bet. You ever see fields full of grapevines? They don't just throw those things out there willy-nilly. They probably have to pay attention to a whole bunch of stuff that we know nothing about."

He put his elbows on the table, wiped his mouth with a napkin.

"Kat, it'll work fine to put that one guy in charge. He can get others to help when he needs it, but for now let him work on his own doing all that initial stuff."

"Who's going to supervise him? Gus?"

"Supervise him? Ha!" said John. "Nobody. He'll be working by himself. He can come to you if he has questions."

"Me? Good Lord, John. I can't watch him. What's to keep him from running off?"

"Kat, nobody watches any of them and you know it. They could run off a dozen times a day if they wanted to. These guards, they don't give a sh—." John caught himself and looked sheepishly at Caroline. "These guards don't care. Usually one guy is supposed to watch a hundred POWs spread over 40 acres. And is he actually paying attention? Hell, no. He's off sleeping under a tree somewhere."

"What about me, John? What if I have to go out to the field? Won't it be dangerous to be alone with the man?"

"Are you kidding? I looked as his file. He was a professor back in Germany. The guy'll probably be scared of you. Anyway, you ever think twice about getting into a truck with one of the hands?"

"No, but. . ."

"Well, just look at it like that. The army's already weeded out the bad characters. You'd probably be in more danger with one of the guards. Those are the nut cases."

You can say that again, thought Katherine.

"At any rate, we've got dad's old .22 pistol around somewhere. I can put it under the driver's seat of the truck. How's that sound?"

"Well, I don't know," said Katherine, thinking about the pistol, a teeny silver thing that would have fit in her purse. It was about two steps up from a BB gun. They used to shoot it down by the river, plinking at soda cans turning lazy circles out in the slow-moving water. She was comfortable handling it, and supposed it would come in handy in case of emergency, but Katherine didn't want to think about things even getting to that point.

"Okay. But listen, John." She paused. "If I get any sort of bad feeling from this man, we're doing something else. Deal?"

"Deal."

Ж

The next morning as the POWs waited to go to the fields, John came out of his office and mentioned something to the lead American guard.

"Okay," said the guard, then turned back to the formation. "Stefan Biermann, you stay behind," he called out. There was a murmur among the POWs. "Everyone else, head out."

Stefan looked at Otto when he heard himself singled out, but Otto shrugged his shoulders.

"Captain wants to see you," said the guard as the other POWs moved to the fields. He pointed to the office. Stefan went and rapped lightly on Lorberg's door, and he heard the man's voice from within.

"Come in," called Lorberg.

Lorberg was behind the heavy wooden desk that Otto and Stefan had hauled in their first night. Katherine was there, too, sitting in one of the wooden straight-backed chairs in front of his desk. The other stood empty next to her.

"Morning," Lorberg said, rising cordially as Stefan entered. He gestured toward the vacant seat and the two men sat simultaneously.

"You know my sister, Katherine, I believe?"

Stefan nodded. "We have met."

"You and I talked about the grapes we ordered," said Katherine. "You said you have experience with them?"

"Yes ma'am. That's correct."

"There was a slight miscommunication here at the farm and we may have gotten into this business prematurely." Katherine glanced at John. "But what's important now is that the vines are here and we need to make a go of it."

"Yes, I understand."

"We thought you could be in charge of getting these grapevines established," said John.

"This project has to be successful because of the investment that's in it. We don't want to stick somebody on the job who would rather be somewhere else," added Katherine.

"You following all this?" asked Lorberg. He thought Stefan was fairly fluent, but it never hurt to check.

"Yes."

"You'd have a lot of flexibility in this work," said John. "Not necessarily even the same hours as the others. Whatever it takes to get the job done, as long as you're not abusing it."

"Okay," said Stefan.

"Okay what?"

"I'll do it." He didn't know if he was supposed to think about it but there wasn't anything to consider. It was work he loved. And he'd be on his own. Sounded great in every respect. And he knew it would beat the hell out of hoeing every day.

"Well, fine then." John looked at his sister as Stefan stood to leave. "Why don't you go ahead and take him out now, Kat? No sense in waiting to get started."

Katherine glanced sharply at John, scowling at him for putting her on the spot. It certainly hadn't taken long for Katherine to be confronted with her concerns about being in the car with a strange man.

"Um, sure," she said, standing, too. She wasn't going to be rude to the man, even if he was a German. "I've already been thinking about some possible sites for the grapes. You can tell me what you think."

Stefan stepped aside and allowed her to go first out of the office. He glanced back, gave a farewell nod to John, who remained behind his desk.

Stepping out into the bright daylight, Katherine went to the pickup parked next to the office and got in. She started it as Stefan opened the passenger door.

The days of labor in the field had agreed with him, and she noticed the combination of power and grace in his suntanned limbs as he stepped smoothly into the cab and eased into the seat. Putting the truck in gear, Katherine slowly drove from the courtyard, pointing the vehicle toward the fields.

The silence in the cab was awkward. Both sat stiffly, like people on the first ten minutes of a blind date. Neither knew what to say, and Stefan wasn't sure if it was his place to ask her questions or just be silent. Katherine figured that if the guy sitting next to her was interested in agriculture, she'd tell him how Lorberg Farms operated. She tried to keep it simple so that he'd understand.

"This field has cows," said Katherine as they passed the first set of pastures

"Cows?"

"Cows," nodded Stefan.

"Or we grow hay here," she said, pointing to another field full of alfalfa.
"Cow food." She felt like she was talking to a four-year-old.

"Cow food," replied Stefan.

"You have cows in Germany?" She looked at him sideways, waiting for his response.

"Yes," he replied, then paused. Katherine figured he was stumbling with the words, but Stefan was trying to recall the breeds. He knew grapes, not cattle.

"In Germany, we have many of the same breeds that you do. Holstein and Brown Swiss are the most common dairy cattle," said Stefan. "Most beef are Simmenthal, though some farmers have tried crossing Angus bulls with the Simmenthal. They're trying for no horns and leaner meat than pure Angus."

Stefan tried to lean back casually, arm on the edge of the open window. He hadn't intended to sound like a professor, but it had just come out. He glanced at Katherine. Her mouth had dropped open.

"Wow, your English is great," said Katherine. She hardly knew what to say. "Better even than most of the people who live here."

"Yeah, well, I spent some time in the States," he said. "Just long enough to pick up a bit." He smiled at Katherine.

She shook her head, still astonished.

"You should have seen the group here last summer. Hardly any of them could speak or understand English. We had to rely on a translator, and he was completely worthless."

"How did you communicate?"

"Mostly gestures at first," Katherine laughed at the memory. It wasn't hard to explain hoeing, but she recalled Gus Davis on the first day, demonstrating the work to be done. He was stooped over in the courtyard in front of the POWs chopping at imaginary weeds in the courtyard with an imaginary hoe, hollering "Johnson grass! Johnson grass!" The Germans had watched in bewilderment. "But it did get better in time."

"Nobody else could speak German?"

"A few of the hands knew a little, which helped. And they picked some up in the process."

"How about you?" Stefan asked.

"Well," said Katherine, "I still know a bit of German from high school, but it's pretty weak. I wish I could speak it better. It would sure be handy."

They rode on, a bit more comfortable now, as the truck bumped and jostled through a seemingly endless procession of fields interspersed with thick swaths of woods. They could have turned around at any point, but Katherine found herself driving farther than she had planned. She talked crops and farming techniques used in the different fields and Stefan asked questions here and there in return.

As they went on, Stefan suddenly realized that they were well beyond any place he had been with the work crews. He knew the farm was big, but it was only now, seeing it all first-hand, that Stefan got a sense for just how sprawling it really was.

The truck gradually descended toward the river, and Katherine pointed out the transformation to row crops. The air grew cooler as the property approached the water, still farther in the distance. She eased the truck to a stop in the middle of the lane, and they both got out, stepping from the truck into the twin dirt tracks that ran along the lane. Corn was planted on one side, soybeans on the other. Their little sprouts bursting through the soil covered the fields surrounding them with a lush, vibrant green carpet.

"Let me show you something," said Katherine. As he came around the side of the truck, Stefan's eyes were drawn past her into the cab to the silvery grip of the pistol barely protruding from beneath the seat.

"That's the Gasconade, way up there," Katherine pointed toward the river about a half mile ahead.

It was quiet there in the bottoms. A hawk circled overhead. The truck motor ticked softly as it sat cooling. The smell of honeysuckle filled the air, and it combined with the rich green of the crops and the cool dampness of the bottoms. A slight breeze rustled the plants on either side of them.

"The soil here is really rich," Katherine said, testing him. She leaned over and scooped some of the damp dark dirt and let it run through her hands. "What do you think?"

He crouched next to hear and did the same with the dirt.

What do I think? I think you are absolutely beautiful, mused Stefan, staring at her dark eyes. She was talking about the location of the vineyard, of course, but Stefan couldn't help what came into his mind.

"Actually some of the higher ground would be better," said Stefan, trying to keep a rein on his thoughts. "This is good soil for these row crops, sure. But I bet it stays damp down here, all summer."

"Yep. Even when everything else is all dried up."

"Grapes don't do well sitting in wet soil. You want somewhere that drains well. Loose, light soil, more sandy than this. Plus you want them somewhere that gets full sun in the mornings. Best is a slope facing southeast."

Katherine smiled. She wanted to test this prisoner her father had declared an expert in grapes and had read up on grape growing in the past week.

According to the book from the county agriculture office, he was right on.

Driving here with him wasn't part of the original plan, though. Everything she read had said clearly that trying to grow grapes in the bottoms wouldn't work. But they needed to tack on the extra portion of the trip just to be sure. Or so she told herself.

Suddenly Katherine looked at her watch. They had been gone for almost an hour and a half. She needed to get back to the farm.

"So higher is better?" asked Katherine. She stood, went to the cab, made like she was going to climb in, signaling it was time to leave.

"Yes. Before we go, may I look around for just a bit more?" asked Stefan. "This reminds me of my home."

He closed his eyes and breathed in the cool heavy air of the bottoms, the distant smell of the river and the richness of things growing all around.

"What's it like?" Katherine asked suddenly. This man she was driving around the farm, all the people and places he knew best, things that she had never seen, were thousands of miles away.

Stefan opened his eyes and turned to her. "What do you mean?"

"The people, the landscape. Everything. It must be very different."

"Actually it seems quite similar so far."

"I wouldn't have thought that. I figured it would be a completely different world."

"Well, America is bigger," said Stefan. "But where I'm from, the landscape actually looks a lot like this. And people are people, right? No matter where they live."

"I'm not sure I'd agree," Katherine said, frowning. She tried to choose her words carefully. "Don't take this the wrong way, but I think of your people as different. More . . . should I say it? Warlike. Angry. Something. You seem decent enough, but let's face it – collectively you Germans don't have a shining record."

"No, that's not how it is at all," Stefan protested. "People are the same, no matter where they live. Little kids laugh and play in Germany, just like here. And the families raising them only want a future full of opportunity for them, just like here."

"How can you say that? Happy families?" snapped Katherine. She thought of Michael off fighting in Europe and John, gone from his little girl for the last two years because of these "nice" Germans. "All the misery and trouble you've caused for the world? Doesn't exactly seem to go together, does it?"

A cloud crossed Stefan's face.

"There are a lot of us who think what happened is wrong," he said, speaking slowly. "Don't assume that we all wanted the war."

She frowned further, a deep crease furrowing her brow. *These sneaky Germans will say anything*, she thought.

"No question that Hitler is a madman and the whole war was a mistake. But I couldn't say that publicly. The Nazis would have come for me. And Germany will be ruined when this is over. Why would anyone want that?"

"You think it was all wrong?" demanded Katherine, her voice rising. "Are you saying you didn't support your country? You were in the army yourself."

She had liked this Stefan, wanted to believe him, but thought again of her brothers off to war, of a little girl crying herself to sleep because her daddy was gone. She thought of Walt and Caroline praying at dinner each night with bowed heads and folded hands, a simple line for Michael's safety added to the end of the table prayer.

"No," Stefan protested. "That's not it at all."

"You know what really happened? You've changed your tune," she said. "You got captured, got sent to America, and now you want to get in good."

He shook his head fiercely but Katherine continued.

"Hitler ist bad. Germany ist bad," she mimicked him. "That's all crap and I'm not buying it."

"No, listen, Katherine," he pleaded, using her name for the first time. "It's true. I was a professor until last year. I was in the classroom. But then I got drafted. They're taking everybody. It was that or a work camp. What was my choice?"

"Hmmph." she scowled.

"Just think about it," he said. "I speak English. Had they known that, or had I volunteered for the army, I would have been in at least two or three years earlier. And I sure would have been something more that a private in some nothing unit in France where we got captured."

"My brother's over in France right now," said Katherine, looking at him. "It's hard for me to see all of you and somehow forget that. I'm just so worried about him . . ." Her voice trailed to a whisper, her chin quivering slightly.

"I'm sorry," he said.

He was looking right at her, and she believed him, but the tears still came. He took a step closer to her, felt like he should hold her and comfort her. Katherine looked up at him, and just for a second it seemed as though she would fold herself into him and accept his embrace, a natural reaction, one person comforting another. But she realized what was happening, just how close she was, and she stiffened, straightened up and pulled away.

She turned back toward the truck and climbed quickly into the cab, wiping her eyes, thinking he wouldn't see.

"Come on," she said to him curtly over her shoulder. "We've got to get back."

⋊

Late that night, lying in bed, Katherine thought of Stefan again. What was it about that man? This morning before he climbed in her truck, Katherine had been ready to dislike him, just like all the other Germans. They were the enemy. But there seemed to be something about him. She shook her head in the darkness, trying to clear it, trying to counter this nonsense. This Stefan was just like the rest of them, Katherine told herself. Still what she feared most wasn't him, she realized, but the faintest of stirrings in a heart she thought was long dead.

Across the way, Stefan, too, lay awake in his bunk. And he couldn't blame it on the stuffiness of the barracks. He stared into the silent darkness, thinking of Katherine, how she looked, how she smelled that day as she had sat by him in the truck.

"It's been so long since I've been around a woman," Stefan tried to tell himself. "It's only natural to dwell on it a little bit."

Trying again to find sleep, he worked with little success to point his heart back to Maria and home.

Chapter 30

First thing the next morning Stefan began prepping the grapevines for planting. He trimmed the dead leaves and exposed the roots, readying them for the soil. He felt great working in the sunshine, excited about the new assignment. Katherine had said that when he was done, she'd take him and the crates of grapevines to the fields. They still needed to make a final determination on the site, then they'd unload the boxes and he'd get started planting.

The POWs assembled in the courtyard as he worked, getting ready to go into the fields for the day's labors. He smiled at the thought of riding around the farm again with Katherine, just being with her. But that smile froze on his face when he saw Karl Leider standing with the guard, Robert Whitcomb. Both leaned against the fence looking at him with dead, cold stares.

"What's with those two," wondered Stefan, chuckling nervously to himself.

Though he had little contact with Leider these days, he still got shook when he saw the man. And him with Whitcomb? What kind of strange pair was that?

Stefan went back to his work and soon the prisoners departed for the fields. The time went quickly and before he knew it a couple of hours had passed. Stefan was almost ready for the last bundle of grapevines when he heard the truck engine. He smiled and set down his shears. Pulling off his work gloves, he tossed them on the crate and walked toward the passenger side of the truck, stopping alongside as it rolled next to him.

"Why don't you get in," she said. "We'll go pick that spot for the vineyard."

He climbed into the cab and they pulled from the courtyard, pausing for John, who flagged them down on their way out.

"Hey Kat," he said, standing next to the truck door. "I'm on my way to

Leonard Wood. Colonel called and I've got to take care of something there."

"When'll you be back?"

"Tomorrow afternoon." Lorberg bent, looked through the window at Stefan.

"Getting started on those grapes, Biermann?"

"Yes sir."

"Well, good luck," he said. "Watch out for your boss. She's a tyrant." He winked at Katherine as she eased the clutch and the truck rolled forward.

"Be safe, John," she said and left the barnyard, looking back at him in the mirror as he waved goodbye.

Touring the locations they had identified before, they soon settled on the final spot that, though more distant from the main part of the farm, seemed ideal because of its soil and the way the ground was situated. They drove toward it through the fields until Katherine spotted an old ramshackle barn that marked the turnoff sitting weedy and decrepit alongside the road.

"This once was another farm," murmured Katherine. Broad pastures framed by rusty old wire fences spread on either side of them. The fields were overgrown with waist-high weeds. "A family lived here years and years ago. That barn there by the road, the one that looks like it's about to fall down? All that's left."

She parked the truck and they stepped out to take a final walk around the site. The hillside was broad where the upper pastureland began its gradual slide into the bottoms. Set back a couple of hundred yards from the road, the ground was smooth and fertile, with just the right combination of soil and sunshine, south-facing and well-drained.

Stefan had known it was an ideal spot when they checked it out yesterday, couldn't imagine that they'd find another better than this. But he hadn't said anything, content to let Katherine drive on.

"You feeling any better today about us Germans?" he asked as they walked. He was smiling a bit, kidding her, but they both knew the question was serious. And they both knew that it wasn't just a question about Germans in general.

"Well, I'll never be happy about the war or with the Nazis for causing it," said Katherine. "It's had a hell of an impact on our family."

She looked at him. Their eyes met for a moment, then she looked away quickly.

"But I believe you told me the truth yesterday," said Katherine. She paused, then spoke again slowly. "And Stefan? When I think of Michael, I don't see you as one of the people trying to kill him any longer."

She turned from him and kept walking. He followed and caught up with her, and they were silent as they continued their loop around the site. Before long they were back at the truck.

"So this place looks good to you?" she asked.

"I think it will be great," Stefan said. He smiled. "We've chosen well."

Katherine climbed into the truck. He started around the other side.

"Where you going?" she said.

Stefan stopped, puzzled.

"You've got work to do here. Next step is to survey the plot, right?"

"Yes, but . . ."

"Well, there's a box of stakes and flags for marking," she said, hooking her thumb toward the truck bed. "And Gus had the cooks make you up some sandwiches. They're there, too."

He got the stuff out of the back and stepped back. Smiling, Katherine revved the motor, dropped it in gear and roared off in a cloud of dust, leaving him in the field. He stood for a few minutes, watching the truck get smaller until it disappeared over the hill and its dusty plume drifted slowly away.

It was quiet out there after she left. As Stefan walked the ground, marking in his mind its boundaries and how the rows of grapes might flow, he thought about her, thought about their conversation. He was glad that Katherine was convinced that he wasn't part of the Nazi gang out to rule the world.

"But why do I care what she thinks?" he asked himself. It was important to him, he realized suddenly, because he was finding himself attracted to her. She was smart and tough, and not afraid to challenge something she didn't think was right. And he liked that.

Stefan stopped to think about this a moment. It was warm in the sun, and he pulled out a handkerchief to mop his brow. As soon as he saw the embroidered initials on the white linen, he thought of Maria.

"Good Lord," he said to himself. "What am I doing?"

He felt sudden shame at this disloyalty to Maria, and tried once again to push Katherine from his mind.

X

Stefan worked into the early evening, pacing off the distance, driving stakes, laying out what would be the vineyard. The time passed quickly, for he was absorbed in the labor, lost in thought.

167

Stefan looked at his watch. 6:30 already. He hadn't realized it was so late. He hustled around wrapping things up, trying to finish in time to catch dinner, when the sound of a truck rolling slowly down the main path through the fields caught his attention.

"Who could that be?" he wondered casually. It was later than you'd normally see anyone out still working. Stefan figured it was just one of the farm hands heading in. Then the truck went silent and he looked again.

The truck was an army truck, not one of the farm vehicles, and it had backed in next to the old abandoned barn that Katherine pointed out alongside the road that marked the turn-off. It was a curious place to stop, because the building was so dilapidated that it couldn't possibly have any current use. The driver was carefully maneuvering the vehicle under the barn's low-hanging eaves, tucking it nearly out of sight.

"What the hell are they doing?" he muttered.

Stefan watched, still unobserved. He was far enough back from the main road that unless he jumped up and down, flapping his arms and hollering, he wouldn't be noticed in the growing twilight. Whoever was with the truck assumed they were alone in the empty fields.

The doors opened and two men emerged. It was Whitcomb and Leider! And when they disappeared around the far side of the building, he couldn't resist. He had to find out what they were up to, better judgment be damned.

Stefan hustled to the edge of the field, hopped over one of the old fences and crept closer. Heart pounding, he scuttled quickly across the wide pasture toward the shed, concealed by the scrubby brush that filled the space. He worked his way rapidly closer, coming around the back of the barn, near enough now to see and hear what they were doing.

"Holy shit," Stefan whispered softly, astonished by what he saw. Under its green canvas cover, the back of the truck was stuffed with boxes, each stenciled with a Red Cross logo and *tobacco* or *chocolate* in big black letters. Whitcomb and Leider worked quickly to unload the boxes, piling them nearby in a long row of waist-high stacks against the outer wall of the barn. Another green tarp, this one older and half-rotten, lay on the ground, ready to cover the goods when the truck was empty.

"Amazing, ain't it, how much they send?" said Whitcomb, looking over at Leider. "Ten cigarettes a day for each of you. Plus a chocolate bar, too."

They paused in their work for a moment as Whitcomb quickly counted the boxes.

"That's enough for now," he said, gesturing to the pile. "The rest is your share and goes back to the camp. Your people will think they've died and gone to heaven. Just imagine if they knew what they were supposed to have."

"When you gonna sell this stuff?" asked Leider, nodding toward the stack.

"Later this week," said Whitcomb, taking a small flask from his pocket. He raised it to his lips and pulled several deep swallows. He stopped to wipe his mouth with his sleeve and gestured toward a dozen five-gallon gas cans also piled nearby. "Still gotta fill these from the big fuel tank. The gas truck from town comes out every Wednesday to refill it. And nobody's tracking how much gets used. Unbelievable."

He paused, took another drink.

"Sometimes, we'll just siphon it straight from the tractors too, when they're parked in the fields. In the little bit we were here last summer, we swiped almost 150 gallons. Make just as much money selling that as you can the smokes."

Stefan had seen the big elevated tank in the barnyard used to fill the tanks on the farm's equipment. So Whitcomb and Lieder were stealing fuel, too. People'd pay a fortune for gas on the black market.

Still crouching, partially hidden by a stunted black locust tree, Stefan leaned closer to listen and look. A stick snapped beneath his foot, loud as a gunshot in the still evening air.

"What was that?" said Whitcomb. He took a few quick steps from the barn, squinting into the pasture, trying to locate the source of the sound. He seemed to look right at Stefan, who froze behind the scrawny tree. As Whitcomb peered into the growing twilight, Leider hurried behind him to unload the last few cartons of cigarettes from the truck.

"Hurry up!" called Whitcomb over his shoulder, still looking nervously out into the evening. Just then from off in the distance came the sound of another truck headed toward them.

Whitcomb glanced toward the headlights cutting through the dusk, still a half mile away. It was the black Lorberg Farms truck Katherine always drove. "What the hell's she doing here?"

He raced back to the barn with Leider to get the old rotten tarp pulled over their booty. They worked remarkably fast and when she pulled up just a minute later, the stuff was well hidden, covered by the tarp and a layer of branches.

Katherine hit the brakes when she saw the army truck. She swung off the road and pulled up into the lane next to them. Whitcomb and Leider stood awkwardly nearby.

"What are you doing?" She frowned as she looked out the window at them. "Is there something wrong?"

"Nope, nothing wrong," said Whitcomb. "Me and him was checking to see that everyone was in from the fields."

Katherine frowned at that, but he smiled in return, a leering, open-mouthed gape.

"Glad to know you were concerned about us," Whitcomb continued, snickering. "Must have missed me. Wanted to come out and see me. That it?"

Katherine's face flashed red for a second, embarrassed and angry, but she was not about to allow herself to be intimidated nor put down by him. She threw open the cab door and climbed out, stomping quickly toward him.

"Hey, Whitcomb, I don't know what you're up to, but you're obviously clueless about who's in charge around here."

He laughed, but she went on, her voice getting louder. Standing close enough to poke Whitcomb in the chest, she pointed at him with each word to punctuate her meaning.

"Listen here," she snarled. "You mess with me, you'll be back at Fort Leonard Wood peeling carrots in the chow hall before you even know what hit you. Don't think I can't make it happen."

She didn't normally talk so fiercely, but it was needed now. Stefan crouched in the bushes, awed by her angry eloquence.

"Yeah, well," retorted Whitcomb, "after a year alone out here with nothing but me to think about, I figured you'd be about ready to peel my carrot by now. If you know what I mean."

He glanced at Leider, laughing at his comment. Suddenly Katherine slapped him hard, right across the face. Whitcomb turned purple with shock and rage and instinctively, his fists shot up. For a split second, it seemed certain he would strike her.

"Wow, baby," he said, smiling at Katherine despite the red handprint on his cheek. "Love hurts." He couldn't win by acting rashly here, he knew and slowly he lowered his hands to his sides, the anger melting away.

"You better not touch me, Sgt. Whitcomb," she said coldly. "Or you'll regret it as long as you live."

Katherine walked toward the truck. She turned and spoke before she climbed into the cab.

"Get back to camp right now. And I better not see you anywhere you're not supposed to be."

She started the motor and waited until Leider and Whitcomb were in the army truck and headed to camp before pulling in behind to follow them back.

Stefan remained in the pasture until the dust from the trucks in the lane settled again. It was almost dark, and though he hadn't eaten since noon, his appetite had left him again.

He began walking back to the camp, thinking over what had happened, trying to decide what to do. What he had seen at the barn could put him in grave danger. Yet he realized it could also be very useful. John Lorberg was still gone to Fort Leonard Wood, but would be back tomorrow.

"I'll tell him about this soon as he gets back," Stefan thought. He'd be rid of Leider once and for all, and also wipe out that lunatic Whitcomb in the process. And that was sure to make Katherine happy. He smiled at the thought and kept walking.

Chapter 31

Katherine leaned over her brother's desk the next morning and pounded on it with her fists.

"Gone, John! I want him gone!"

John sighed. He hated when his sister got like this.

"Again, what exactly is it about Whitcomb that bothers you so much?"

He leaned back in the wooden chair with his hands interlocked behind his head.

"It's the way he looks at me. The things he says."

John tried to act interested, he really did, but he was having a hard time seeing what she was so riled up about.

"And what sorts of things has he said?"

"Offensive things."

"Tell me exactly."

She paused.

"John, he said I wanted to peel his carrots."

John raised his eyebrows at his sister. Katherine looked back at him and scowled, biting her lip. She knew she sounded foolish.

"Listen, it's not what he says, but how he says it. Damn it, I just want him out of here."

"We just can't send him back unless there is an awfully good reason. And him looking at you funny is not it."

John leaned forward, trying to explain.

"Listen Kat, I know he's a crude, obnoxious man, a first-rate pain-in-the-ass. The colonel cannot stand him. And that's why Whitcomb's here. It gets him out of his hair."

Katherine frowned, and sat in a chair at the end of his desk. She drummed her fingers on the wood, trying to think of what to say. There had to be some way to get rid of that horrible man.

"You know we've got a good thing going with me being here," her brother continued. "Whiteside really bent the rules to make it possible. And sticking Whitcomb out with us was a big part of the deal."

John had a tray on the corner of his desk for mail, and while he talked, Katherine flipped idly through a stack of outgoing letters from the POWs. The envelopes were unsealed, waiting for the censors' approval.

"If I send him back, saying he's a problem, Whiteside's gonna question the whole arrangement. And I will not jeopardize being with Ellen. You know that. You're just going to have to find a way to ignore him."

Katherine wasn't listening. One of the envelopes had *Biermann* in the return address, and was directed to a woman named Maria. She sucked in her breath and tucked it back into the pile.

A light tapping on the door interrupted their discussion, and Katherine looked to see Stefan standing at the door. She smiled, but then stopped, thinking of this Maria back home that obviously held sway in the German's heart.

"May I come in, sir?" he said in his softly accented English.

"Please do." Katherine stood as if to leave but John glanced at her. "You can stay," he said to his sister. "What can I help you with?"

Stefan hesitated for a moment. What he was about to say would set things in motion from which there could be no turning back.

"There is wrongdoing in the camp you should know about, sir."

"What do you mean?"

Stefan took a deep breath.

"Last night I saw a POW and a guard in a truck. They were in the fields. I watched as they unloaded a truck filled with stolen cigarettes at an old barn. I heard them talk about stealing fuel and reselling it."

Katherine's mouth fell open and John frowned as Stefan went on in detail. He described how Whitcomb and Leider stashed the goods at the barn and recounted the confrontation between Whitcomb and Katherine Lorberg, including the slap.

"Hah! See there John!? He did say I should peel his carrot," Katherine proclaimed triumphantly.

"Yes sir," said Stefan. "The man did suggest carrot-peeling to her."

"And you hit him, Kat?"

"John, he deserved it."

He nodded and then glanced again on Stefan. "These are serious allegations. They never saw you?"

Stefan shook his head no.

"Why didn't you say something?"

"It all happened so fast."

"Time for a little trip." said John.

Together they exited his office and climbed into the truck parked nearby. They drove to the barn and Stefan led them to the back, ready to show them the contraband he described.

"Here it is," he said, and went to the old rotting tarp and pulled it back. But there was nothing. No cigarettes, no chocolates, no gasoline cans. The place looked like it always had, overgrown and weedy, without the first lick of proof to support his story.

"But it was all right here," exclaimed Stefan, not believing it could all disappear so quickly.

John said nothing, just shook his head and got back into the truck. Stefan followed him back helplessly, still protesting as he and Katherine joined him in the cab.

"I swear it was all right there . . ." said Stefan, pointing to the barn.

John Lorberg turned to him, even as he stepped on the gas and turned the wheel to take them back out on the road.

"I don't know what to think. Seems you're telling the truth, but how could the stuff just vanish?" He paused, glanced over, a bit of skepticism crossing his face. "This tied to some dispute you've got with Leider?"

"But I saw them out here, too," Katherine protested.

"Kat, they told you they were making sure everyone was in from the fields. And wasn't the headcount at dinner actually one short with him out here working? Sounds reasonable to me. Listen," said John, stopping the truck abruptly in the middle of the lane. "Maybe there is mischief going on. There always is in these camps. But unless we have proof of some serious wrongdoing, I am not going to the colonel."

"But John. . ."

"Kat," said John firmly, We'll keep watching them. But I will not jeopardize being here with my daughter based on nothing more than flimsy allegations from some German hiding in the bushes and my pissed-off sister who didn't actually see anything anyway."

He jammed the truck back in gear and they continued the short distance back to the farm in silence. As they rolled back into the barnyard, Stefan saw Whitcomb and Leider leaning against the fence, frowning as they spied him with John and Katherine in the truck.

Chapter 32

"I don't know what's going on," said Whitcomb, leaning against the wall of the barracks. He took another hit from his flask. "Odd that she's with him all the time. And now Captain Lorberg is in the mix, too."

"You think they're on to us?" asked Leider.

"Ha," snorted Whitcomb. "Don't be silly. You signed the Red Cross receipt on behalf of the prisoners. I hauled the stuff in and out of here. Who could know?"

"Nah," he continued, pacing. "Our plan is perfect. Loaded up the truck this morning with the smokes and the gas and off we went. Sold it all in Rolla for five hundred bucks. Easy as pie. Often as I go back and forth to Leonard Wood, we can get rid of the stuff quick, within a day or two. It's almost foolproof."

Whitcomb had no idea that Lorberg's visit to the barn came just 15 minutes after he left.

"No, it's something else. The way the two of them look at each other. Now that makes me nuts. You'd think Biermann was back in grade school, the way he stares, making googly-eyes at her all the time."

Whitcomb fiddled with his own eye and continued.

"But you know what really burns me up, Karl?" Whitcomb looked at the German. He knew Leider didn't like it when he called him by his first name. "That she don't seem to mind at all when he starts looking at her like that. You'd think she was sweet on him."

Leider frowned but said nothing. This man was insufferable.

"Yep, she missed the boat when she turned cold on me. Ain't that right, Karl?"

"You're right about Biermann," said Leider ignoring the question. "He never says much, but he's always looking, always around. Then you'll see him later with Lorberg and his sister."

"We should send him some kind of message," said Whitcomb, voice rising, stamping his foot with excitement. "You and a couple of your Nazi pals could set on him in the night. Give him a little pain, yeah, get him to back off some."

Grinning manically, he looked at Leider and continued, talking faster and faster. He liked the thought of somebody getting hurt.

"It'll work great. He'll get sent back to the big camp. For his own safety, you know," said Whitcomb. "And that'll be the end of this little Valentine dream they got going. She don't know this yet, but we're getting back together. Her and me. She can't resist the Whitcomb charm. Nobody can."

Leider sighed. What a loon. But they were linked together now.

"All right," sighed Leider. "We'll pay him a visit in the barracks. I've got a couple of men who'll take care of this. One way or the other, he'll be out of the way."

※

It was later that week, four nights later, when Leider set his plan in motion.

Stefan was only lightly asleep, even though it was after 2 a.m. The sound of soft footsteps shuffling in the night nudged him awake. He opened his eyes but didn't move. Probably just someone taking a piss. But then he made out not one, but two figures creeping in the darkness. They moved stealthily, sliding silently between the rows of bunks holding the sleeping men.

"Psst," hissed one man. "Fifth one down?"

"Yeah," said the other, and they passed two more beds and then stopped, just past Stefan and Otto. The man in the bunk closest to them was sound asleep, snoring softly. "This is it."

The first man quietly straddled the sleeping prisoner, using his knees to pin his arms. He jammed his forearm into the sleeping man's windpipe while the other man pressed a pillowcase over his face.

"Stay the hell away from the Lorbergs," he hissed, close in his ear. "You're a German. Don't be a traitor."

Both began punching him in the face, hard and fast, seven or eight times.

"Hey!" Stefan shouted, bolting upright. "Get off him!"

The two men vaulted over the bunk and ran out the door into the darkness. Somebody found the switch, and bright lights flooded the room. Stefan went to help the man they attacked. He sat stunned in his bed, unable to stop the blood gushing from his broken nose.

Chapter 33

The next morning, Katherine drove to the fields for her daily check of the properties and work crews. Along the way, Gus Davis waved at her as she passed. He was fuelling one of the tractors from the farm's massive fuel tank. Shaped like a thick sausage, the tank was mounted on a head-high frame and held 500 gallons of gasoline.

Seeing it made her think yet again about Stefan, probably the twelfth time today. Still puzzled by the episode with the black market cigarettes and pilfered gasoline, she recalled the stunned surprise on his face when he threw back the old tarp only to find nothing there.

It was a mystery, that was sure, and she vowed to watch the fuel supplies more closely. Tracking usage was a tough job though. Sometimes a dozen vehicles gassed at the tank each day. She sighed. If fuel was missing, she'd have a hell of a time trying to figure it out.

She didn't know what to make of Stefan's story. He seemed so certain of what he saw, but she still couldn't believe that she had missed what he described. She was especially annoyed with herself for not looking around more closely. Whitcomb and Leider stopped at a rickety, long-unused barn should have made her suspicious.

All this turned though her mind as she made her way across the courtyard. After their sour parting yesterday, she decided she'd stop by John's office to see where his mood stood.

The dark circles under his eyes were the first thing she noticed when she came into his office.

"Good Lord," she said, trying to keep the mood light. "You look like you didn't sleep a wink."

"Kat, there was an attack in the barracks last night," he said grimly.

"What?"

"One of the men was roughed up pretty good while he was asleep. He's got a broken nose."

"Oh John, who was it?" Fear and worry filled her voice.

He looked at her sharply, surprised that she'd be so anxious. It was just one of the prisoners.

"It's not Biermann, if that's who you're asking about."

Katherine exhaled, relieved. Her own sudden concern had shocked her, too, even as the words leaped out.

"But he's mixed up in this, too. He was 'somehow' awake to witness the attack that 'somehow' happened two bunks down from him. Two men in the dark. That's all he knows."

"Katherine," he said, rubbing his eyes. "I'm going to send him back to Fort Leonard Wood. Seems like he's always involved somehow whenever there's trouble. The other guy has to go back regardless to get his nose patched up, and Biermann can go with him. We'll get two new ones who won't give us these problems."

"But you said we can't—"

"We can't send Whitcomb back because the colonel can't stand him. The prisoners are a different story. One guy needs to go to the clinic. Another one just isn't suited for life on the farm. No big story. Whether you've realized it or not, we've had Germans coming and going all along."

"But John," she pleaded.

He glanced sharply at his sister again. This wasn't like her.

"What's up with you?" he asked.

Think about business, she told herself. It's about the farm.

"John, we need to keep him here because of the grapes. He's just now getting started and it's almost time to plant," Katherine said, trying to sound rational. "We need more time from him to get the vineyard established else we're going to lose all of the vines. He's the only one who knows how to do it."

John looked at her skeptically.

"Please, John," she said, trying not to sound like she was begging. "Please let him stay."

"I've got a bad feeling about this," he sighed, shaking his head. "How long is the work going to take?"

"Two weeks."

"I'll give you two weeks," he said. "But he's gone after that."

"Thank you, John." She turned to go. She didn't know if getting only two weeks more was good news or bad.

"And Kat?"

She paused at the door.

"Any more bullshit in the meantime and he's gone at once."

Katherine nodded and left the office.

"But Stefan can't leave," thought Katherine as she drove. She gripped the wheel tighter. All week long she had tried not to think of him, tried not to think of reasons to check on the progress of the vineyard yet again. "Not now. Not two weeks from now."

She bumped over the ruts of the lane, turning into the field where she knew Stefan would be working. He had finished marking the rows and was now readying the soil for planting, preparing the holes where the grapevines would go.

Katherine could see the lines of the vineyard taking shape in the distance. The rows curved gently, following the slope of the land, reflecting his years of expertise growing grapes in Europe.

"This is really turning out to be something," she whispered to herself. Stefan's knowledge was a thousand miles beyond the information she gleaned from the books at the county agriculture office. It was almost as if fate had sent this man to salvage her father's folly.

As Katherine drew nearer she found Stefan stripped to the waist, for it was warm in the sun. She sucked in her breath sharply as she saw the sweat-glistened muscles rippling on his back as he worked the shovel.

She eased the truck in next to the plot and killed the motor. Stefan stopped, put his shovel down and smiled. He pulled his white handkerchief from his pocket and used it to mop his brow. He looked forward to her frequent visits, but wondered too if she was checking on him so frequently out of more than just curiosity about grape growing.

"Hello," she said, walking to him. "How's it going today?"

He smiled at her, and she felt her heart flutter.

"Quite well, thanks," said Stefan. "And you?"

"John told me there was trouble in the barracks."

The smile disappeared from Stefan's face.

"Yes. A man was attacked in the night."

"He said you saw it."

"It happened somewhat close to me."

"Do you know what it was about?"

Stefan hesitated.

"You know, just the normal disputes in the camp."

Katherine was blunt.

"John thinks you're somehow involved in this, Stefan. He wants to send you back."

"No," he gasped.

"No? What does that mean?" Katherine asked. "No, you're not involved in this, or no, don't send me back."

"No, don't send me back."

She smiled.

"I've worked it with him for you to stay, at least for a while. I had to plead though, so be straight with me, do you know anything more about the attack?"

"Katherine, it's meant for me, and I know Leider was behind it. He's the one who was with Whitcomb out at that shed. He's one of Nazis I told you about. He's never liked me."

"How come?"

"He thinks I'm disloyal. He thinks I'm not a good German because I won't go for all that Nazi propaganda."

"But it was somebody else that got hurt. I don't get it."

"They got the wrong guy in the dark." Stefan said. "And now since they bungled it, they'll have to lay low for a while. It'll be fine."

"Stefan, what can we do? I don't want you to get hurt," she paused for a moment and then looked at him. "We could send you back if it meant you'd be safe."

Both of them knew neither wanted that.

"What we do is keep watch for the proof that your brother needs. They get busted and sent on and I get to stay here." Stefan paused. "With you."

There. It was out. The strength of these feelings for Katherine had surprised him, but he was no longer able to squelch them.

She fought with these emotions, too, this longing for him that was rising to the surface.

"I'd like that very much," she said, acknowledging what they both felt, but what both needed to deny.

She tried to douse this fire by picturing her brother dodging German bullets in some lonely foxhole.

"Here," said Stefan quickly, trying to turn them to a topic that was safe. "Let me show you what I'm doing."

He led her to the row of holes he had dug. A grapevine lay ready by each for planting. The damp, rich soil steamed in the midday sun, and the vines he had stretched out beside the holes almost ached to be sunk in their moist darkness.

"We're ready to plant now," said Stefan. "You should know how it's done."

He crouched at the edge of the first hole and picked up a vine. It was a dry, brown root, with a few tiny dots of green at the top, long and slender, nearly eighteen inches from root to tip. Taking the vine gently in one hand, he placed the root end in the ground, just barely brushing the bottom of the hole. With the other hand, he gently scooped the soil around the root, filling it loosely until only the top six inches of the grapevine stretched from the lightly packed soil.

"There," he said. "The Lorbergs are officially grape growers. It's only proper if you plant some, too, madame. You'll forever have a direct connection with these plants and the soil."

"You're right," said Katherine, and she bent over to place the next vine into its new home. She smiled as she dropped the wispy little vine into the hole and began scooping dirt in after it.

"Wait," he said. "The vine should just barely touch the bottom, and it needs to remain straight as you fill in the soil. Here, let me show you."

Stefan leaned in behind her, wrapping his arms around to help with the vine. His hands were rough and dirty from digging in the soil, but he took her soft, smooth hands into his own as he guided the vine back toward the hole. He pressed lightly against her back, and she could feel his breath on her cheek.

"Let's lift it just a bit," he said softly, close to her ear. "That'll allow it to stand taller, and let the roots shoot out straight."

Slowly, slowly they scooped the soil into the hole. The plant stood tall as they held it at the right height. She could feel him pressing against her more firmly now, and she allowed herself to sink back a bit, leaning into him in return.

"That's perfect. That's beautiful," he murmured, allowing his cheek to brush gently against hers. At the same time, almost without realizing what was happening, he interlocked his fingers with hers.

Katherine turned her head toward him and stared into his eyes. He looked at her for a long moment, reading what she was feeling until they moved slowly toward each other, eyes closing as their lips came together. It was just a moment, and then Stefan pulled away. He said nothing, just smiled at Katherine as she opened her eyes and gave her a gentle squeeze with his arms still wrapped around her. It happened so fast she could scarcely take it in. Yet it also felt right, and she wanted nothing more than to kiss him again. But her head was spinning and she didn't want to lose control.

"Well," she said, pulling herself loose from him and standing upright. Her legs had fallen asleep under her. She wobbled and Stefan offered her his arm.

"I can't believe that happened," she said, smiling. It had been a long time since she had kissed anyone. Her heart was pounding and she was still addled by the power of their embrace.

"Are you okay?" Stefan smiled at her.

"I've got to get back to the farm," Katherine stammered, not knowing what else to say. Her brain buzzed with desire, attraction, confusion, excitement. She rose on her toes and kissed him again quickly. "Don't you dare tell anyone about this."

She fled to the truck and gave him a quick wave from the window, spinning the tires as she tore out of the field, doing a joyous 180 and throwing gravel and dust into the air. She wasn't sure she was ready for this, and especially not with a German. She felt exhilarated, yet torn and confused all at the same time.

Stefan watched as the truck disappeared, his heart feeling the same conflict. He pulled out his handkerchief to mop his face with it again.

At that same moment, somewhere in Germany a man with a withered hand slept beside Maria, having made love to her yet again. She was still awake. As she lay there, head on the pillow, she saw the wastebasket in her bedroom, nearly full with letters from Stefan, all unopened.

Chapter 34

A vein stood out on Karl Leider's temple as he looked on the courtyard through the barracks window. A GI was helping the battered POW, still hunched and clutching his nose, into an army truck to return to the main camp at Fort Leonard Wood. Leider clenched and unclenched his fists, pacing back and forth.

"You got the wrong man!" he raged at the two men who were supposed to take care of Stefan. "Only a dozen guys in the room and you get the wrong one? Worthless. You're absolutely worthless."

Leider burst out the door and stomped across the yard to Whitcomb, who was watching Stefan talk to Katherine by the main office. She stood framed by the doorway; he leaned against the wall outside. They tried with their posture and stance to give the impression that they were talking about farm business, but it was hard to maintain the formality and distance between them.

"Look at them," Whitcomb muttered, tapping on the face of his watch. "Biermann stopped by the office after breakfast and they've been going on like that ever since. Somethin' funny going on, I'm telling you." He glanced at Leider and frowned. "So when are you gonna get him?"

Leider cringed at the smell of stale alcohol and body odor that oozed from Whitcomb as he spoke. He must have gone on a hell of a bender last night. Whitcomb's hangovers only magnified his normal foul temperament. He scowled at the pair some more, his glass eye bulging.

"Didn't you hear?" said Leider, uneasy about provoking the man further. Whitcomb craned his head around to gape at Leider with his good eye. "They got the wrong guy."

Whitcomb stared at Leider for a minute, then screwed his head back around to look at Stefan and Katherine again. He shook his head with disgust.

"You'll just have to try again," he muttered. "Think you can maybe get it right this time?"

Leider glanced at him. He didn't like being mocked.

"And this time, please make it serious," said Whitcomb. "No more of this pansy-ass bullshit, where you pop a guy in the nose. I want you to take him out."

Leider nodded. He knew what Whitcomb meant. He left Whitcomb leaning on the fence, still staring and scowling at Stefan and Katherine who were happily chatting away.

Chapter 35

At dinner that night, Otto looked at his friend across the table. The light chatter and laughter of the other POWs surrounded them, but Stefan stared off dreamily, smiling in some other world. His mouth hung open, and he held a sandwich halfway to his mouth, as if his thoughts were so powerful and inviting that they had carried him away in mid-bite.

"Hey, Stefan," said Otto, trying to draw him back to the present. He was burning to know what was going on. His friend had dumped his normal moodiness and brooding for something altogether different.

"Hey, Stefan," said Otto, more persistently. Stefan finally snapped awake, suddenly back in reality. Otto stood, tray in hand. "I'm finished. You ready? I think we should take a little walk."

Together they carried their metal trays to the big trash can, scraped off the scraps, then stepped outside into the evening.

With Stefan busy at the vineyard the past couple of days and Otto either tied up at the front office it had been a while since they had been able to talk.

"Seems like you've got a lot going on," said Otto, as they strolled the perimeter of the courtyard in the twilight. "New girlfriend, maybe?" Otto was joking. Though Stefan spent a lot of time with Katherine, it was too far-fetched to consider seriously.

Stefan smiled, not sure where to begin.

"A lot going on," he paused, "That's one way to put it. Both good and bad. What do you want first?"

"Give me the good stuff."

"Okay, well, I think this is the good stuff. I can't decide."

"Huh?"

"You mentioned a girlfriend. . ." he let his voice trail off.

Otto stopped in his tracks.

"What?" asked Otto. "Come on."

"Yeah," said Stefan. "It's probably nothing. But Katherine comes every day to see how I'm doing with the grapes. And then we'll sit and talk." He paused, thinking of her again. "She doesn't have to come nearly as much as she does. But it's like she can't stay away. And, Otto, I think about her all the time, too."

"Let me get this straight," said Otto, slapping his forehead. "Lorberg's sister? The boss of this whole place?"

Stefan didn't say anything, just nodded in acknowledgement.

"And what about Maria?" continued Otto, still staggered by what he had just heard. "That just vanishes all of a sudden?"

"That's just it, Otto," said Stefan. "In Katherine, I'm seeing everything Maria is not. And that I'm not. And that I can be. That make any sense?"

Otto nodded, amazed. He had never heard Stefan talk like this.

"So what are you gonna do?"

"Don't know." Stefan shook his head somberly. "Any ideas?"

Otto wanted to grab his friend by the collar and tell him exactly what to do. Ditch the wretched girl back home.

"What is your heart saying?" he asked, hoping Stefan would come to his own conclusion.

Stefan sighed, stood silently for a moment.

"I'm realizing that regardless of what happens here, Maria may not be the best thing for me."

Otto wanted to throw his hands in the air, to let his feet do a wild happy dance. His stupid friend might finally be seeing the light.

"Stefan, that's terrific insight."

"I've had the chance now to look from a distance at things she's said, things she's done," said Stefan, quite seriously.

"Like what? Getting only one letter from her in response to the three hundred or so you've written?" said Otto. "And having it say she was spending her free time with another man?"

vom SEPT. 44
bis JUNI 45

Die Lagerstraße
Camp Clark /Missouri

Otto covered his mouth with his hands and feigned shock at what had popped out.

"She has been really horrible, hasn't she?" said Stefan.

"Yes," said Otto. "So what are you going to do?"

"I might write her, tell her that we're through," he paused. "Wish I could say it in person."

"You are a sensitive man, thoughtful for her feelings. That's nice," said Otto.

Stefan nodded somberly.

"Wonder if she'll read it before or after she's done rolling with that other guy," Otto thought. But this time he managed to keep the words to himself.

"I know it's not ideal to do it that way," said Stefan, "but it's only right to her to allow her to move on." He paused, and turned to look at Otto.

"I've finally realized that I stayed with Maria because I didn't know any better. I had no reason to move on."

"But now you do," offered Otto. "So don't beat yourself up over this. She had plenty of areas for improvement. And you also deserve better."

Stefan and Otto walked on while Otto digested what his friend had said. He was still elated that Stefan had finally understood about that wretched girl and the way she abused him. But then his face fell. Stefan had mentioned other things going on.

"Okay," said Otto, "so that's the good news?"

"Yeah," said Stefan, "the downside is just as complicated. Seems I've made myself some enemies."

"Yeah, Leider," said Otto. "That's not new. He hasn't liked us since France. Someone else?"

"Well, there's Whitcomb too. He's got a thing for Katherine. Tried to date her last year but she ditched him quick," said Stefan. "Remember that big fight on the parade ground at the main camp? That's what that was about."

"Ahhh," said Otto, remembering.

"But Whitcomb and Leider are working together, stealing tobacco and gasoline to sell on the black market."

He continued, filling in Otto on what had happened, including the missing contraband and what was behind the attack that night in the barracks.

"And now Lorberg's wondering if I'm the problem, that all this is mainly just trouble among the POWs. He wants to send me back, but Katherine convinced him to keep me here.

"Why don't you go back, Stefan? Might be the smartest course, given the threat from Leider."

"I want to be here," said Stefan, "because of her."

Otto made a choking noise. Admiring a girl from afar was one thing. Getting involved with her was another.

"Well, Stefan, if you don't want to go back to the main camp, then how about the prison where they send POWs who engage in this sort of romance. And they wouldn't just take you. They'd also take your darling Katherine. For her this is TREASON. She's a cutie, I agree, but stripes are not her thing."

"I hear you, Otto, but I can't just walk away."

Otto grabbed his friend by the shoulders and looked him in the eye.

"This involves me, too, Stefan. They know we're friends. If Lorberg sends you away, he'd get rid of me, too."

Stefan nodded. He thought he understood, but his friend went on.

"I've really grown close to Ellen. She's getting to be like a daughter to me. . ." Otto's voice trailed away. "It'll be hard enough when the time comes to leave, but hopefully we'll be able to prepare and not just get ripped away."

Stefan stood, quiet for a time before he spoke.

"I never realized this could cause you any problems, Otto, and I'm sorry for that." Stefan spoke softly in the darkness. "But, I was weak before, content to just float along with Maria. Now I know a whole lot more about who I am and what I want. I want to be with Katherine. And I want to nail these bastards."

"Well, I can't stop you, of course," said Otto. He paused for a moment. "She's really got you, hasn't she?"

Stefan nodded, smiling slightly.

"I thought so. You talk different about her than you ever talked about Maria."

"It feels different," agreed Stefan.

"Nothing else like it, is there?" said Otto, thinking of Elise back home.

"I know there could be consequences, but it would be worth it to be loved by a woman like that."

"How will you sustain this? We still have to go back to Germany, you know." said Otto. He wasn't used be being the pragmatic one. "And it'll be sooner rather than later. The Allies are almost to Berlin."

"Don't know how we can continue. But it's got to work somehow. And anyway, all we've got is the present."

The two had circled the perimeter of the courtyard and were walking along the last stretch of buildings. They would be back to the barracks in just a minute.

"Stefan?"

"Yeah?"

"You are going to tell Maria?" It was part question, part statement. Otto still wondered if Stefan was strong enough to break things off, of if he'd go back to her out of guilt or habit.

They stood on the threshold to the barracks.

"Yes," said Stefan. "I'm going to write her now."

Chapter 36

Stefan lay on his stomach, his tablet in front of him on the bunk.

"Dear Maria," he scratched on the lined paper.

You're used to getting a lot of letters from me. Well, this is unlike the others. It's difficult to write, but necessary. I am bound by my honor to be truthful with you.

The words flowed from his pen, his smooth script belying the pain it would carry. Here came the words he knew would break her heart.

Ich liebe dich nicht mehr. Ich habe eine andere gefunden.

"I don't love you any more," wrote Stefan. "I have found another."

He thought back to a Sunday afternoon in the summer, shortly before he left to go into the army. They took a picnic basket and a blanket, and walked together deep into a forest outside of Heidelberg where the trees opened onto a meadow, dotted with daisies and other wildflowers. They made love in the sunshine, and when they were done, Maria laid her head on his chest.

"Do you love me, Maria?"

She said nothing.

"Do you love me?" he asked again, and then yet again, still more persistently when she didn't respond.

"Sure," she uttered, resentful, knowing she couldn't ignore him any longer.

She was ambivalent toward his feelings, he now knew, wanted to be rid of his pathetic pleading. Still extracting that begrudging "yes" made him happier than he had ever been and had carried him through many long days of the war.

He shook away the memory and continued the letter.

I know that you will be hurt, but finally I am certain of my own feelings. You will probably have questions and perhaps someday we will be able to talk about this if you wish. At least it would give you the answers I cannot provide to you now.
Good-bye, dear Maria. I will always think of you and the time we spent together with fondness.

Yours,
Stefan

Stefan folded the letter in thirds, and tucked it into an envelope. Writing Maria's name and address on the front, he set it on the window sill next to his bed, ready to be mailed tomorrow. At peace with himself, Stefan turned in for the night.

Chapter 37

The next morning, Otto leaned against the wooden wall of the office in the shade of the overhang on the dock and watched the men depart for the fields. A couple minutes later, Stefan emerged from the barracks and strolled to the truck in front of the Lorbergs' house. Otto gave him a lazy wave as Katherine came from the house and the two climbed into the truck and started toward the fields.

Otto shook his head, smiling, now understanding the real reason for the interest Katherine took in the vineyard. He was glad for his friend's new happiness but that still couldn't push aside his concern for the danger the relationship brought.

Otto yawned, leaned forward in the rocking chair and rested his elbows on his knees. Ellen sat at his feet, playing with one of her dolls on the broad wooden floor of the dock. It was only 9 o'clock and shaping up to be a slow morning.

Standing, Otto shuffled over to the logbook. Tracing the day's schedule with his finger, he saw there were no deliveries expected until 11 a.m. It was a perfect opportunity for a stroll.

"Be right back," he said to Ellen. Glancing toward the house, Otto saw Caroline's broad straw hat bobbing over the flower beds and he ambled over to clear things with her across the fence.

"That sounds like a wonderful idea," she said from her knees, waving a dirty trowel at him with her gloved hand. "You two go and have fun."

"Want to go on a walk?" Otto asked.

"Yes, yes, yes!" Ellen bounced up and danced around him. The pair set off down the lane toward the fields where the POWs were working. Several times along the way they paused, including a stop to look at a bluebird's nest built into a fence post and another to roll over an old log in a ditch to see what sorts of bugs made their home underneath. Farther along, they came to the old barn that Stefan had told him about. From the road, it looked to Otto like it hadn't been used in a decade. Ellen noticed it, too.

"Can we look in?"

"I don't know" said Otto, doubtfully, but Ellen was already running off ahead, following the tire tracks through the weeds. It probably wasn't a good idea, but there was nobody else around. What was the harm in just taking a peek? Maybe they'd find something to help validate Stefan's story.

Ellen reached the barn and tugged heavily at an old wooden door. It creaked loudly on rusty hinges as it opened. Stepping into the quiet of the barn, they paused for a moment until their eyes adjusted to the darkness. The dust kicked up by their footsteps rose lazily through the narrow sunbeams slicing through gaps in the outside wall. Not much to be seen in the dim interior of the barn except some moldy old hay bales, a long idle harrow and a leather harness, stiff and brittle, hanging from a nail on the wall.

Walking the length of the barn's interior, the two came to the rear door, opened it and stepped outside. Nothing back there but the weedy pasture. Ellen skipped around the side of the barn where the overhang stood and Otto followed. Swallows flitted and whirled overhead as the pair circled around and came to an old tarp. It was bunched against the wall, draped over something, probably some old boards or other junk.

It sure didn't look like much, couldn't possibly be what Stefan was talking about. But still Otto took hold of one corner and raised the tarp to peek underneath and there it was: a store of gas cans and cigarette cartons stacked neatly underneath. His mouth fell open.

"Well, I'll be damned," whistled Otto. "Stefan was right."

Standing next to the barn, neither of them heard the army truck until it was too late. They glanced up as it drove slowly past, Whitcomb at the wheel, staring blackly at Otto holding the corner of the tarp.

Chapter 38

"He was just standing there looking at it, I tell you." Whitcomb paced, fiddling with his eye. He was sweating and trembling. "Just holding the tarp up, taking it all in."

"Who—Biermann?" asked Leider.

"No. Biermann's friend. The fat one with the red hair."

"Great," murmured Leider. "He's got the biggest yap of all. We're screwed."

"I'm the one who's screwed. They'll send me to the pen at Leavenworth. You just get a ticket back to the main camp and then on to knackwurst land after the war is done."

His pacing increased.

"There's no way to get that stuff out until the day after tomorrow, earliest, cause Lorberg changed the schedule for the trucks again. We've got to do something to get rid of the problem."

Whitcomb stopped suddenly, and a slow smile crept across his face.

"I think I've got the answer," he said, then laughed softly.

Leider laughed, too, though he wasn't sure what Whitcomb had in mind. Moving the smokes to hide them somewhere else, maybe.

"And this will also solve our other problem with Biermann, take that little turd out of the picture," Whitcomb was standing legs spread, arms held wide, thrilled with his solution to the dilemma. "Yes."

"Yes," said Leider back, nodding. He didn't get it. "What are you talking about?"

"Simple. We bump off Otto and frame Biermann for the murder. Make it look like he's the only one who could have done it."

"Huh?" said Leider. "That doesn't make any sense. Everyone knows they're friends."

"Yeah, well, maybe there was drinking involved, and tempers got hot. They fought. Sometimes people get a little nuts, know what I mean?"

"Only too well," said Leider.

"Or maybe it was an accident. I know it's not perfect, but we can make it work," said Leider.

"I don't know about this."

"Listen, we've got no choice. You saw Otto standing there looking at all the shit. You think he's gonna keep quiet? We've gotta move on this quick, or we're busted," said Whitcomb.

"Okay," said Leider. "Whatever we've got to do. But you're taking the lead on this."

"We'll be fine. Just trust me." And then Whitcomb laughed again.

Chapter 39

Katherine smiled at Stefan as he climbed into the truck beside her. She drove out into the fields for a couple of minutes, then stopped the truck, letting it idle in the lane.

Before she turned to him, she checked to make sure they weren't being observed. A farmhand on a tractor, cutting hay in a distant field, was the only person they could see. He was nothing more than a little black dot slowly working his way across the pasture.

"I'm glad to see you," she said, "I've been thinking about what happened the other day in the vineyard."

Stefan nodded, understanding completely. After writing the letter to Maria, he had dreamed of Katherine constantly and without restraint. In replaying that scene in his mind, he feared that he had overstepped the boundaries with the kiss and prayed he had not misread her affection.

"It kinda surprised me," she continued, turning forward, looking distantly through the windshield at nothing in particular. She had rehearsed this in her mind, going over it again and again so that it would come out right.

"It's a bit of an odd situation, you know," she said, "you being you and me being me..."

"Yes," said Stefan, as tongue-tied as he had ever been. Was she now backing away? Telling him it couldn't happen again? He was afraid this dream had ended too soon.

She looked at him as if to say, "Well?"

"I understand if it puts you in a difficult position here..." Stefan tried to hedge, but she looked hurt. She wasn't concerned about a conflict with her role at the farm.

"...but I, too, was very surprised and very happy about what happened," said Stefan, trying to rescue the moment.

She smiled.

"Stefan?" She paused, gripping the steering wheel, still looking straight ahead. She couldn't believe what she was saying. "Do you want this to continue?"

Stefan looked at her in surprise and then smiled. His heart nearly leaped from his chest.

"Yes," he said. "Very much."

He had no more words. Katherine pressed her hand onto his and leaned across the seat to give him a quick peck on the corner of the mouth. She looked at him closely for a moment, then slid back behind the wheel.

Putting the truck in gear, they continued through the fields, but did not stop when they came to the vineyard. Stefan glanced over at Katherine and raised a questioning eyebrow.

"Just wait," she said, "I told them I had to go into town today to take care of business. That means we've got some time, so I'm going to show you a very special place."

The truck rolled into the valley toward the river where they had walked together that first day. As they approached the water, Katherine turned left into a barely visible lane, just a gap in the trees. It ran into the woods, parallel to the river bank, just wide enough for a single vehicle to pass. Tree branches brushed the side of the truck as they followed the track through the woods.

They continued slowly for about ten minutes, the woods cool and shady. Then tall bluffs, at least a hundred feet straight up, drew close on the left, the river close on the right. Finally, Katherine cut the engine and rolled to a stop when they could go no farther.

"Okay," she said, "we're here." She smiled at him and took his hand, and gave it a squeeze. "My grandfather showed me this place."

As they got out of the truck, Stefan could hear the sound of rushing water. A waterfall plunged from the bluffs directly ahead, splashing into a deep, clear pool before joining the river. They walked to the base of the waterfall and stood among the ferns and mossy rocks that surrounded the deep pool. The water was so clear Stefan could see bluegill and trout swimming against the dark bottom far below.

"Isn't this great?" Katherine asked. She smiled and took his hand again. "It's my favorite place in the whole world."

"Really beautiful," murmured Stefan, looking at her.

Katherine led him to the base of the bluff, to a point where a steep path led up the hill.

"And up there's the best part," she said. "Come on. It's not as difficult as it looks."

She turned and led him up a zigzag path between the boulders. The two of them quickly ascended thirty or forty feet. The waterfall tumbled by, sending a refreshing mist wafting over them as the path wound up the bluff.

"We're almost there," she said as they neared the top. "The best part of all."

Another few feet up and Katherine was standing on a broad flat ledge. Stefan scrambled behind her and saw that the path lead to an extraordinary place. The waterfall, formed by a huge spring that flowed from the side of the bluff, cascaded over a rock ledge jutting from the cliff, leaving a large open space behind the curtain of water. She led him inside and onto the smooth rock floor of the dry and warm space behind the waterfall.

"What do you think?" Katherine asked.

"Simply amazing," said Stefan.

Bright sunshine sparkled through the curtain of rushing water, its rays illuminating the space with a million points of brilliant light that danced around them like diamonds

Katherine faced him, and taking both of his hands into hers, she looked deeply into his eyes.

"You don't know how long I have waited for this," Katherine said. Rising up onto her toes, she pressed her lips against his. Stefan felt her mouth open and her tongue against his, probing and greedy. He pressed back, feeling the desire that welled within her.

They continued the embrace, longing for each other, feeling emotions so powerful that they forgot everything, concentrating only on each other as the rest of the world was swept aside.

Chapter 40

Otto was tired. He set his clipboard on the chair and leaned against one of the supports of the loading dock. It had turned out to be a busy day after all, and he hoped this would be the last truck. The driver was finally finished unloading thirty-five bags of alfalfa seed, and had climbed back into the cab. A friendly wave in the mirror and he was off. Otto watched as he headed toward the main road.

So far he had stayed mum about what he had seen at the barn. What he really wanted to do was to talk with Stefan, to tell him about it. Then they could both go to John Lorberg and provide him with the evidence he needed.

Otto would have gone talk to him directly, but of course the captain was away again on some important errand, and all the guards were out in the field. And who knows which of them might be involved, too? Well, he'd just tell somebody the first chance he got.

Ellen was off by herself at the edge of the courtyard between the big barn and the machine shed. Earlier she and Otto had been inside the barn playing in the hay bales, her favorite game of all. She never grew tired of having Otto stack the bales into various configurations, and over the past couple of weeks they had created an intricate network of rooms and tunnels going up and into the massive pile of bales that filled the airy barn from floor to ceiling. Ellen could spend hours playing castle, either by herself or with Otto, laughing and climbing and crawling throughout.

Otto thought he should probably check on her, but first wanted to take a look at the schedule to see if he needed to watch for any more trucks. He had just started toward the office when he picked up the sound of another engine, this one a vehicle coming from the fields. It was getting toward the end of the day and the POWs would be returning soon.

Otto turned to look at the truck as it entered the courtyard. It was a single vehicle, an Army truck with a canvas top, and Robert Whitcomb was at the wheel. He waved to Otto as the truck wheezed and snorted to a stop. "Hey, Otto," said Whitcomb. "Help me unload the truck. There are planks in the back old man Lorberg wanted hauled."

Otto was wary of Whitcomb, especially now with what he had seen, but what could happen out here in broad daylight, in the middle of the barnyard? Had Whitcomb actually recognized him looking at the stuff? He gave no indication that anything was wrong. Maybe they'd both just pretend everything was normal and play along on this.

"Hop on up there in the back," said Whitcomb, as natural and easy as could be. He ambled off into the yard, calling back as he went. "I'll get a cart to haul the stuff, and you can hand it down to me."

Otto thought about this some more as he walked to the rear of the truck. If there was an attack, it would come tonight in the barracks, he was sure of it. Seizing hold of the handle on the tailgate of the truck, he took a deep breath and heaved himself into the back. Rising to his feet under the canvas, he suddenly found himself face to face with Karl Leider, who hafted a thick wooden ax handle in his hand.

Leider whacked him at once on the side of the head, knocking him to his knees, and then a second time more savagely to render him unconscious. Otto didn't even have time to cry out. It was the most merciful aspect of what he was about to experience.

Otto lay sprawled out face down, and Leider grabbed him by the back of his shirt and yanked him farther into the truck. He paused for just a moment as Whitcomb climbed into the truck to join in pummeling him with fists, feet, and the ax handle, their sole aim to kill him.

In their intensity, the pair missed the small girl watching from the corner of the barn. Ellen didn't know for sure what happened to her friend Otto, but she realized it must be something horrible when she saw Whitcomb climb out of the back, face red, breathless and blood-spattered.

He hurried around the front of the truck, climbed into the cab and cranked the starter, trying to wake its sluggish engine. Finally it fired, and hand over hand Whitcomb cranked the wheel hard until the truck pointed toward the field again.

As he jammed the truck back into gear and mashed down hard on the gas, out of the corner of his eye, he caught just a flash of the girl's white shirt as she threw herself back behind the barn, screaming a horrible silent scream at the dark blood slowly dripping down from the truck bed into the dust of the barnyard. He shook his head grimly, knowing there was now another detail to attend to.

As the truck sped off into the fields, Leider chucked a pilfered handkerchief out into the weeds growing up at the edge of the road. Swiping the handkerchief had been his idea, another piece of evidence to point to Stefan in this sketchy plan. Now the cloth was no longer white; the blood that soaked it nearly covered the letters SMB in testament to the savageness of the beating Otto absorbed.

Chapter 41

After they climbed from their warm and sunny perch, Katherine took him back to the truck. Leaning over the side of the truck bed, she pulled out another surprise.

"*Voila!*" she said, presenting a picnic basket she had brought stuffed full of wine and cheese, sandwiches and fruit.

"Wow," Stefan whistled, shaking his head, astonished by her thoughtfulness.

"Better than army food?" she asked.

"Oh, yeah," he grinned.

He took the basket and together they walked to the river. They threw down a blanket and sat, then dug into the basket, enjoying the food and each other, trying to delay as long as possible the return to the farm. As they sat, she nestled against him, their fingers intertwined.

"I have to confess that this all feels a bit odd," Katherine said. "I've never done this sort of thing before."

"I bet you say that to every prisoner who comes to town," Stefan replied, winking at her.

"Ha. Not true," she laughed, pausing to look at him. "But I'm sure you never expected anything like this to happen when you came to America, either, did you?"

She was joking with him, too, but there was a serious edge to it as well. Katherine thought about the letter she saw that day in her brother's office; the one from Stefan to some woman in Germany. Katherine desperately wanted it to be a sister or someone else like that. Please, God, not a girlfriend.

"You're right about that," Stefan said. "How to handle an unexpected romance was never a part of any of our army training."

"I'm serious, Stefan," she said. "This is a big risk for me. There hasn't been anyone for me in a long, long time because of being out here and the complexities of running this place."

"I understand. It would be bad for your father and the business if this got out." said Stefan. "You don't have to worry about me giving away our secret."

"Come on, professor," she said with exasperation. "For being so smart you sure are slow sometimes."

He smiled, took no offense. He knew he wasn't always the best at reading women.

"Stefan, I don't just give my heart away to anyone who happens along," she said. "I want to know something."

He nodded as she paused and took both of his hands into hers. She felt the words coming and knew that she, the pessimist who believed she would never again find love, was willing to risk everything for him.

"Do you have anyone back home?"

She was trembling slightly.

"There is no other," Stefan said. He had already made that break with Maria, knowing that he wanted to be fully, always, only with Katherine.

She squeezed his hands, held them tightly.

"Stefan, do you see a future for us?"

He looked deeply in her eyes, knew what she wanted to hear.

"No matter what it takes, Katherine," he said, "no matter what happens, I want to be with you."

She bit her lower lip, felt her eyes fill as she listened to him, and believed him with all her heart.

"Oh, Stefan," she said, and she hugged him deeply, wrapping her softness into him. He returned the embrace, holding her completely, and kissed the top of her head.

Chapter 42

"No, no. We can't hurt the girl," pleaded Leider, as they pushed Otto's motionless body off the back of the truck in the woods by the river. It hit the ground with a thud. He was frightened by this irrational man.

"She's the only one who can tie us to him," panted Whitcomb, wiping his bloody hands on his pants. He jumped down and rolled the battered body face down in a shallow ditch. "Leave this to me if you can't handle it."

Whitcomb gestured at their clothes. Both looked like they worked in a butcher shop.

"Besides, you've got other stuff to do. We've got to get some new uniforms. You'll have to take these to the burn pit."

Leider glanced up at Whitcomb. "Now how in the hell am I supposed to do that without anyone seeing me like this?"

"You figure it out," said Whitcomb. "Now get in the truck."

X

Too soon it was time for Stefan and Katherine to collect their things and return to the truck. They dawdled as long as they could, trying their best to delay the inevitable. But it was getting late, approaching four o'clock. Returning together, they replaced the basket in the truck bed and climbed into the cab. Katherine still had to drive and he sat next to her in the middle of the bench seat. They cuddled like teenagers as they returned through the thick woods down the isolated narrow lane, laughing and talking as they made their way back.

They were almost to the hidden gap in the trees, just ready to make the turn onto the main road when an army truck screamed by in front of them. It was going very fast and took just a split-second to flash past the gap, much too quick for them to see Whitcomb at the wheel, still sweating and bloody.

"Whoa," said Stefan. "Who was that?"

"Just some of the GI's messing around," said Katherine. "Don't worry about it."

Stefan raised his eyebrows questioningly.

"They didn't see us," she reassured him. "Besides they're always racing here in the bottoms after they've dropped off the prisoners. Doesn't bother me when they do that as long as they're not tearing up any crops."

They sat in comfortable silence on the drive back, Stefan's arm draped around her shoulders. He scooted back to his side when the truck began to climb from the bottoms. Too soon they were back at the vineyard.

"Remember that no matter how we feel, we can't let it get out," said Katherine. "The end of the war will be here soon enough, but for now, we've got to keep things under wraps."

She stopped the truck.

"So get out," she smiled. "I'm still your boss."

She kissed him again and he stepped from the truck.

"You'll have to walk back to camp," she said, looking at her watch. "It's after five o'clock and you'll be late for dinner. But I know Otto'll save you a plate."

He swung the door closed and watched Katherine leave, shaking his head in wonderment over what had just happened.

Ж

John Lorberg circled the side of the office, headed across the courtyard to the barn. He needed to make one more stop to check in with Gus before calling it quits. He was glad it was the end of another work day. He was hungry and he knew Caroline was making a big roast with mashed potatoes. The prisoners too had finished their work and were headed for dinner. All in all it had been a good day.

Passing the guard's quarters, suddenly he noticed a POW inside, rooting through one of the soldier's trunks.

"Hey," he hollered through the door. "What the hell are you doing?" He moved in quickly, certain he had interrupted one of the petty thefts that occurred from time to time, usually somebody's wallet getting nicked.

"Hello, sir," said the POW, cordially and unruffled. It was Leider. A neatly folded GI uniform sat on the bed next to the open trunk.

"I hope you can explain this, because it doesn't look good."

"Oh yes, sir. Sgt. Whitcomb and I were working on one of the trucks. He was lying underneath, trying to get at the transmission when a gasket came loose and sprayed him with fluid. He got soaked and he asked me to come get him a new uniform. I am here with his permission."

John Lorberg scowled. "I'm going to have to talk with him. You and he both know this isn't proper."

"I understand sir."

"And what's in that bag?" Leider held a burlap sack at his side.

"That's his old one, sir. I'm afraid it might be ruined. It's going to be turned in at supply."

"It'll come out of his pay, if that's the case," said Lorberg. "Now get out of here. You're not allowed in here again, no matter what he says."

"Thank you, sir." Leider took the new uniform from the bed and tucked it carefully under his arm. He left the guards' quarters, taking the burlap bag with him.

"Something odd about that," thought Lorberg. He made a note to speak to Whitcomb about it. Surely he ought to know better than to send POWs into the guard barracks to retrieve things for him.

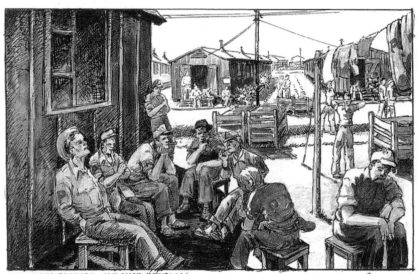

IM KRIEGSGEFANGENENLAGER CAMP CLARK / MISSOURI U.S.A.

Chapter 43

After dropping Stefan off, Katherine followed a circular route through the fields instead of going back directly. Taking this way brought her around to the main road and allowed her to return to the house via the front drive as if she had really had been in town.

She stopped at the farm's big mailbox on the county road just before she turned into the drive. Looking toward the house, she saw the POWs milling around the barnyard before dinner. John walked with Walter across the courtyard, and John held the door for the older man as they went into John's office.

Katherine felt a twinge of guilt and shame. But as she thought of Stefan, his eyes, the warmth of his embrace and his gentle touch, she knew it had to be right.

Katherine swung the wheels straight again and drove on about a mile farther. She parked the truck off the gravel away from the road beneath a huge oak tree in one of the fields, shielded from view. She didn't plan to tell them about Stefan, of course, but didn't like being deceitful either.

"I'll wait until everyone goes in for dinner," thought Katherine. "Then I can head straight to the office and settle in without having to see anyone."

Any small talk could be dangerous. A simple question about her day could mean getting tangled up in some small detail that would trip her up. She would have to be careful.

Walking around to the truck bed, she dug again in the back for the picnic basket and rooted around inside for another sandwich. This day had made Katherine ravenously hungry and utterly happy.

※

After a half-hour lingering around the vineyard, replaying the afternoon in his mind, Stefan knew Katherine had plenty of time to return to the farm. He started walking back when suddenly he heard the wail of the siren rise from the camp.

"Wonder what that's about?" he mused, trudging on. The only time the siren was used was for an escape or a serious emergency. It had been blown a time or two for test or when somebody accidently bumped the switch, but never for real that he knew.

Stefan figured his own absence surely hadn't excited anyone. A couple of times already he had missed the nightly head count, but that had never been a big deal. There was always a foreman or one of the guards who knew he was finishing up in the vineyard. He hadn't cleared today's rendezvous with anybody, of course, but he couldn't imagine that his being gone would cause that much of a stir. He shrugged and kept walking.

Back at the camp, the place was being slammed into lockdown. Rumors of an escape – started by Whitcomb of course – had swept through the guard corps. A quick headcount uncovered two missing POWs, Otto and Stefan, and suddenly John Lorberg thought he had a situation on his hands, given all the odd events lately at the camp.

"Damn it!" he shouted, rising from behind his desk. "I want the POWs confined to their barracks. And you other guards, start searching for those two."

The men sprang into action, pushing the stunned Germans into their quarters and starting the hunt for the two escapees. All the while, the siren continued screaming.

As Lorberg scrambled to the courtyard, he saw Whitcomb climbing into a truck.

"They were headed for the river," shouted Whitcomb. "That's what the POWs are saying."

Whitcomb slid behind the wheel and jammed the truck into gear. Three more guards with automatic weapons jumped in the cab and on the back as he gunned the motor. The vehicle roared down the road toward the bottoms, barreling past Stefan who had crouched down in the weeds just in time, confounded by what was happening. Had he and Katherine been found out?

"They couldn't possibly know about us already," he thought, panicking, trying to figure out what to do.

With Whitcomb in the lead, the guards criss-crossed the woods and bottomland fields. He barely made a pretense of searching before guiding the men to the ditch where he knew Otto lay. It would only be a minute before the searchers found his body.

Not twenty minutes later, a second group of guards spotted Stefan alongside the road as they passed. The truck stopped abruptly, wheels sliding in the dust as GIs spilled from every door.

Though Stefan stood, hands high, offering no resistance, two GI's flew at him, knocking him to the ground. They pinned him there, binding his hands and feet tightly while a third struggled to restrain the fierce Doberman that snarled and snapped at Stefan, just inches from his face.

"What is this about?" pleaded Stefan, his face in the dust.

They offered no explanation, just picked him up and threw him roughly into the back of the truck.

Down the road a third group of soldiers found another piece of the puzzle when they stumbled upon a bloody handkerchief, wadded in the dust. It was a sad reminder of the violence that had taken place, and a clear sign pointing to who had done it.

Back at the camp, the guards dragged Stefan from the truck and pitched him into John's office. Moments later, the captain paced in front of Stefan, interrogating him as he lay on the floor.

"Where were you today? Why were you by the river?" he asked over and over.

Stefan said nothing. He had promised Katherine he would not give their secret away.

"Sir," said a guard from the door, holding up the bloody handkerchief. "We found this outside."

Stefan frowned at the dark red stains, but did not recognize the crumpled cloth as his own. John saw the questioning look on his face.

"Don't act like you don't know what this is about," said John Lorberg. "Was there a fight? I thought he was your friend."

John shook his head in frustration. How could this German just sit there and say nothing?

"Sir," said another GI, poking his head into the room. "They're coming in with the body right now."

'I'll ask you again. What did you do to Otto Haertling?" Lorberg demanded.

A horrible realization began to sink in. Something had happened to Otto. They thought he did it. His head began to buzz and he found it hard to focus. Though Lorberg continued to question him, Stefan would not tell him what had taken place that day. Blackness crept over him and he remained silent, unable to offer any proof of his innocence, unwilling to betray Katherine.

"John, have you seen Ellen or Katherine?"

It was Walt Lorberg now standing at the door. He was pale and trembling, concern obvious in his face.

"No, I haven't."

John's breath came in short gasps and he began to panic. He tried to steel himself, to think rationally. If Stefan had so savagely killed his best friend, what more could he have done to Ellen and Katherine?

"Ellen was with Otto Haertling the last time anyone saw her," said Walt slowly. "And that was earlier this afternoon."

"I thought Katherine was going into town?" asked John.

"That was the plan," replied Walt, "but one of the laborers out on the tractor said she picked up the German and then drove toward the vineyards. No one has seen her since."

"My God, they're missing!" An icy bolt of terror shot down his spine. He went to the door, shouted frantic orders to the guards gathered in the courtyard. "Katherine and Ellen are gone. Back into the fields!"

The guards raced to the trucks, scrambled aboard even as the vehicles were leaving. They tore down the lane, back to the river, back to the vineyard and pastures and woods, back to search the hundreds of acres on the sprawling farm, hoping desperately to find the two, and hoping just as desperately that they wouldn't.

Only two GIs remained behind, directed by John to stand guard over the other Germans inside the POW barracks. They watched with rifles ready, blocking the exit doors on either end, glaring fiercely at the frightened POWs.

John stepped back to Stefan. It didn't make sense. Stefan didn't seem like the type of person who could do this. But who knew? He had always been suspicious of him. He should have sent Stefan back when he had the chance. But he didn't, and now his daughter and sister may have paid the price.

"Where are they?" He screamed, bending over the prisoner bound on the floor. "What did you do to them?"

Stefan said nothing, still lost, unresponsive as before.

"You bastard," John lowered his voice, whispering now, his face contorted with rage. "Tell me what you did with them."

Stefan saw fists flying toward him in slow motion. He heard the crunching of the bones around his eye socket and cheek but felt no pain, only a wet warmth as the blood flowed down his shattered face.

"Tell me," John screamed. "Tell me what you did to them."

John continued to thrash and kick at Stefan's limp body with manic fury until he was exhausted and his knuckles and boots were covered with Stefan's blood. John stood, breathing hard, knowing he was getting nothing from this man, knowing that he himself was losing it, too. He had to confine Stefan, join the search.

But he couldn't move Biermann into the barracks all beaten and bleeding. The prisoners would riot if they saw him like that. The secure office closet would have to suffice. Besides, in Biermann's condition, he wasn't likely to go anywhere.

John rolled Stefan's limp body into the storage closet behind his heavy desk. With Stefan inside, Lorberg slammed the door shut, locking it securely from the outside. Seizing the knob, he rattled it hard. He gripped it tighter, trying to force it open. It wouldn't budge. John checked the padlock again, rammed his shoulder against the door. It was firm and plenty secure.

Stefan lay motionless inside, still bound tightly, almost unconscious. He didn't hear the truck tearing by outside with his friend Otto in the back, barely alive, on his way to the military hospital at Fort Leonard Wood. It was doubtful he would hang on, but the GIs drove like hell the whole way, hoping desperately he could make it.

John grabbed his heavy service revolver and started outside where Walt was waiting.

"Aren't you going to keep a guard on him?" Walt asked.

"He's not going anywhere," John said. "And I'm not having somebody sit there staring at that door when they could be out searching. There's something terrible that's happened, and we've got to find Katherine and Ellen."

Chapter 44

When Katherine finally returned to the farm, the courtyard was oddly quiet. The only sound came from her tires crunching across the gravel as she idled slowly toward the office.

Bringing the truck to a stop, Katherine climbed out of the cab and looked around in puzzlement at the deserted barnyard. This time of day the space was usually crowded with POWs after dinner, laughing and talking and smoking. But the place was empty and eerily silent.

"Where in the world is everyone?"

Katherine went inside John's office to see if he was there. It was empty, too, like her brother had stepped away for just a moment. His half-filled coffee cup sat on the desk and his jacket was draped over the chair.

Katherine scanned his office once more, trying to figure out what the hell might be going on. A stack of outgoing mail sat in the tray on his desk, and Katherine saw a letter on top. It was from Stefan and addressed to this same Maria. It was unsealed, a requirement for the censors. Her hand trembled with anger and confusion as she reached for it. Who was this girl really? Why was he writing her? She held her breath as she pulled the paper from the envelope.

The letter was in German, and she struggled to make out what he wrote, digging through her brain for the rusty words and phrases she'd learned so long ago in high school. Nearly all of it was unintelligible, but she remembered enough to pick out words here and there. Her eyes scanned the page until she spotted "*Ich liebe dich . . .*"

She didn't know what the rest said but "*Ich liebe dich*" was clear enough. They had learned it the second week of class.

"I love you?" she said angrily. "What the hell is this?!"

She clutched the letter. This was no sister or mother or friend. Her hands trembled uncontrollably now. He had lied to her.

Her eyes stinging with tears, Katherine stumbled out of the office. She staggered to the truck and leaned against it, utterly lost as to what to do next. Strong Katherine had vanished and this Katherine felt completely helpless and out of control.

She pulled open the door and climbed behind the wheel, contemplating just driving and driving and never coming back.

"Damn it," she cried, pounding the steering wheel. "Why am I so dumb?" She should have known from the start it was a mistake to get involved with him. Silently Katherine sat for several minutes with her head on the cool rim of the wheel, feeling its gentle ridges press into her forehead.

Suddenly, off in the distance Katherine heard the sound of crying on the breeze, soft sobbing carrying over her own. Distant and muffled, it was hard to tell exactly from where it came.

She sat upright and listened. After a moment she recognized it.

"Ellen!"

She sprang from the truck and listened closely.

"Where are you? What's wrong?"

Wiping her tears, she circled the courtyard, slowly at first, then faster, desperately trying to pinpoint the source of the sound. She hunted in one building, and then in another, never getting closer. Finally, entering the dusty darkness of the big barn, she heard the sobbing grow louder. She ventured deeper inside to try to find the girl.

Chapter 45

"Gotta get some spotlights," shouted Whitcomb to the other searchers in the growing darkness. "I'm going back to the farm."

He climbed in the truck, testing the limits of the engine as he tore back to the farm alone. The other guards and farm workers stayed behind, still searching in the bottoms, scouring the woods and the riverbank near where Otto had been found, desperate for any trace of Katherine or the little girl.

"Gotta find her, gotta find her," Whitcomb muttered, gripping the steering wheel tighter as he raced through the fields. He didn't want to hurt the little girl, but now he had no choice.

Whitcomb figured she was still hiding somewhere around the barn and that he'd have no problem dispatching her once he found her. That would get pinned on Biermann, too. After all it was obvious that not only had the man gone berserk and killed Otto, but that in the process he also murdered the little girl who so adored his friend, the one who was with him almost every waking moment. He grinned to himself. This frame-up was working even better than he hoped.

Whitcomb pulled into the courtyard and stopped for a moment, looking carefully around the courtyard. He needed to be certain he was alone. A farm truck was parked by the office, its door open. Probably just left there in the hubbub. Walt Lorberg sometimes used it, but Whitcomb had seen the old man in another truck with his son, out riding through the fields, helping direct the search.

Approaching the office, Whitecomb saw the door standing partway open. He pushed it the rest of the way and let himself in.

"Poor Captain Lorberg," he chuckled, as he saw the man's empty desk. "First a dead wife, next a dead daughter. How sad."

His gaze fell to a folded sheet of paper on Lorberg's desk lying next to an opened envelope. It was the letter that Stefan had written to Maria.

"And poor Biermann, too." he laughed as he saw the name on the envelope. He knew he didn't have time to snoop, but couldn't resist just a peek. "What's your little fraulein back home going to think when she hears about how you went nuts and killed all these people?"

Whitcomb picked up the paper and started to read, eyes scanning the lines quickly.

Ich liebe dich nicht mehr, read Whitcomb. He knew enough scraps from being around the POWs to get what it said.

"'I love you no more.' Hmmm... sounds like a Dear Johanna letter to me." He laughed at his own joke. "What kind of asshole does that to his girl back home with a letter? Not like he's got any possibilities here..."

His mind began to turn. Unless... Whitcomb thought of all the times he saw Biermann talking to Katherine. Not possible. He read further.

Ich habe eine andere gefunden. I have found another.

"That bastard," he snapped, crumpling the letter, face turning purple with fury. "Him and Katherine."

He wasn't sorry for what would happen to Ellen now. That would be Stefan's fault. But now he knew he had to get Katherine, too. He clutched at his head, trying to keep the blackness from taking control.

"First the little girl," said Whitcomb, reminding himself of the plan, trying not to get derailed by the rage that filled his brain. "Then we'll get her, too."

Whitcomb spun on his heel and headed for the barn. He would begin where he had last seen little Ellen. As he left, he didn't hear the slight stirring now coming from the locked closet behind him.

Chapter 46

"Ellen?" Katherine called out to the dim interior of the barn. She stood silently, letting her eyes adjust to the dusty darkness. The soft crying came again, seeming to arise from somewhere within the massive pile of hay. At its base, Katherine spotted the opening to the hay fort tunnel and headed inside.

The entry was only shoulder high, and she had to duck to go in. It was even darker there than in the barn itself, and she used her hands to follow the walls. The tunnel made a turn to the right and then went straight again, opening into a small room.

Otto, who'd had great fun when he built these tunnels for his little friend, had gapped the walls to allow in a bit of light. The first little room in the hay tunnel was empty, but Katherine heard the sound of sobbing grow stronger, and she knew Ellen was just ahead.

Katherine continued on in the tunnel where it left the other side of the room. First came a sharp turn, then she climbed four or five layers of bales that carried her closer to the ceiling of the barn. The hay scratched her hands and the dust tickled her throat but she pushed on.

The light grew brighter as she continued, and suddenly Katherine found herself in a much larger room that Otto had constructed atop the pile of bales. It was as big as their living room and tall enough for a man to stand upright. Otto had built it against the back wall of the barn, incorporating a window there to allow light from the outside.

After the deep black of the tunnel, the brightness of the room temporarily blinded Katherine. She squinted through the backlight from the window and saw Ellen curled against the wall on a pile of loose hay.

"Oh God," cried Katherine, and she rushed to her and threw her arms around the little girl. Ellen jumped, startled at her touch, and looked at Katherine, her face puffy and red from crying and from the hay. Her eyes grew wildly panicked, and she threw herself at Katherine, trying to bury herself in Katherine's chest.

"Where were you? Where were you?" sobbed Ellen. Katherine sat holding her, rocking her, trying to comfort Ellen, to calm the girl.

"What is it?" Katherine asked. She couldn't imagine what had happened. Maybe something had happened to her father. "Is it Grandpa? Is he sick?"

Ellen's eyes were wild. "Otto got hurt," she barely got out the words. And she began to tremble violently and wail again.

Now Katherine was really confused.

"Otto hurt? Here, in the barn?"

She wondered if the portly man had had a heart attack climbing around in the hay pile. That would traumatize the young girl, especially if the body of her friend was still lying somewhere nearby.

"No, no, no." She was shaking, pale, eyes wide. "They were fighting. Otto hurt. Where were you? I was scared."

"Otto was fighting?" asked Katherine. This made no sense to her.

"Yes."

"Who was he fighting with? A soldier?" asked Katherine, and Ellen nodded.

"Who was it?" asked Katherine. "Which one?"

There were only a dozen guards there at the farm. Ellen knew each one well. They gave her candy, thinking of their own little girls at home, and loved to watch her as she played in the sunshine of the courtyard, following Otto around as he worked each day.

"It was Sgt. Whitcomb."

Chapter 47

The cool concrete floor felt good on Stefan's throbbing head. It took him a moment to make sense of where he was, but as Stefan gradually returned to consciousness, the taste of blood in his mouth and his bound arms and legs provided all the reminder he needed.

It was quiet in the office outside, but Stefan recalled the intimation that something very bad had happened to Otto, and that they thought he was responsible. A sick sense of disbelief crushed down on his chest. He had to do something. But what? Suddenly, he heard shuffling outside and muffled speech drifting through the door.

"Poor Captain Lorberg. . ." said the voice. It was Whitcomb! Stefan could hear him in the office, muttering to himself. The only words he heard clearly were those punctuated by the hatred in Whitcomb's rising voice.

"First the little girl," continued Whitcomb. "Then we'll get her, too."

"Oh, God," muttered Stefan. Fear and panic coursed through his veins as he processed what he had heard. Whitcomb had found out about him and Katherine. And he intended to kill both her and little Ellen.

Whitcomb's heavy boots thudded across the floor and the door slammed as he rushed from the office. The man was gone.

Stefan struggled against the ropes binding his wrists and ankles, wriggling desperately to free himself. The tight cords cut into his flesh, but ignoring the pain, Stefan continued working at the ropes. The minutes passed as he frantically pulled and tugged, the coarse fibers shredding his skin. Finally, lubricated by his sweat and blood they began to loosen until Stefan was able to slip them from his wrists and then untie the ropes from his legs.

He stood quickly, but his legs were wobbly and the blood rushing to his head made it throb painfully. He leaned against the wall, trying to calm the swirling in his head. Fighting against pain and dizziness, he staggered to the door and shook the knob. Locked!

"Let me out!" he shouted.

Nothing.

"Somebody! Let me out!"

Still no response. No one was around.

Stefan rattled the knob again, then pushed weakly against the door with his shoulder. It did not budge. Taking two steps back, he slammed himself into it harder. The door shook in the frame a bit but did not come loose. He backed up again, getting as far back from the door as possible and threw himself at it again. A bolt of pain shot down his arm. The door shuddered again in the frame but still held.

He looked around the room. The only other fixtures were the metal filing cabinets they had helped drag in the day they had arrived at the farm. God, it seemed like such a long time ago.

Suddenly he remembered what John Lorberg had said as Otto sweated and wrested with the damn heavy things.

"They slide pretty easy if you just take the drawers out," he had told them.

Stefan hurried to the biggest one and started yanking the drawers out, letting them crash to the floor. Papers and file folders spilled everywhere and the cabinet was quickly empty. Its metal bottom grated loudly on the floor as Stefan grabbed the empty frame and lined it up with the door.

"This is it," thought Stefan. He paused for just a moment, then lowered himself to brace against it with his shoulder. He took a deep breath and started to push, driving the cabinet as hard and as fast as he could, trying to fight through the painful throbbing in his head.

Accelerating quickly, Stefan drove the cabinet toward the wooden door, barreling at it like a battering ram. He gave a final thrust at the last second just before the heavy cabinet smashed into the door, expending nearly all his strength with the effort. The crash and cracking of the wood frame made a deafening din as the filing cabinet smashed through the door. Stefan followed behind it, falling underneath a shower of splinters raining from the demolished door and onto the floor of John Lorberg's office.

Slowly rising to his feet, Stefan staggered to the door. He couldn't see Whitcomb anywhere. Katherine's truck sat next to him at the side of the office, its door standing open. He went to the truck and reached under the seat, feeling for the cold metal of the pistol he knew she had placed there. Grabbing it, he started circling the courtyard, checking the buildings one-by-one, frantically hoping to find Ellen in time.

Chapter 48

"Whitcomb hurt Otto?" asked Katherine. Suddenly it was all too clear what had happened. In order to take out Stefan they had gone after his friend. "Oh God. Oh no."

Ellen nodded her head frantically, weeping now and nearly beside herself. "He hurt Otto bad. Where were you? I was so scared. And you were gone so long."

"It's okay, honey," said Katherine, holding the girl, rocking her, trying to think of what might comfort her. He mind raced and she talked aloud, anything to calm the little girl, anything to calm herself. "Shhh, shhh. It's okay. I was with Stefan. But shhh shhh. I'm back now, it's okay."

Then Katherine heard the cold metallic click of a revolver being cocked. She looked up at the sound. Ellen followed her gaze and saw the man standing in the hayloft with them.

"And I'm back now, too," said Whitcomb. He had crept to the hayloft, following the voices. Whitcomb raised a pistol and pointed it at the Katherine. "Surprised?"

Katherine gasped.

"I heard everything you said," said Whitcomb. The hand holding the heavy pistol trembled as he pointed it at them.

"Oh God, no," begged Katherine. She pulled Ellen in close to her chest. They were both weeping.

"I'm sorry to have to do this to her. She and Otto just saw something they shouldn't have out at the old barn," said Whitcomb, gesturing at Ellen with the gun. "But you, Katherine. You deserve it. You defiled yourself with that Kraut."

His voice grew low, bitter, snarling.

"I'm not good enough for you, but you're fine with giving yourself to the enemy." His words dripped with contempt and hatred. "You filthy whore."

Whitcomb swung the pistol down and pointed it squarely at her face.

"Goodbye, bitch," he said, and a gunshot roared through the hayloft. Ellen screamed at the concussion and buried herself in Katherine's chest and Katherine's ears rang so loudly she could hear nothing else. Everything went into slow motion.

"So this is what it feels like to be shot," she thought.

Katherine reached to touch her face, expecting to feel a gaping hole. As she did, Whitcomb lurched forward instead, the pistol falling from his hand unfired, surprise and shock on his face. As his knees buckled beneath him, Whitcomb looked behind him where Stefan stood holding the little .22 pistol, a thin curl of smoke rising from its barrel.

"You . . ." choked Whitcomb, then was silent. He fell face first on the hay, a stain spreading quickly across his back where the bullet entered.

Stefan dropped the pistol and stepped over Whitcomb's body to Katherine and Ellen and he wrapped his arms around them, holding them tightly.

Then the click of another pistol being cocked sounded through the hayloft.

"Back up!" screamed John Lorberg, his heavy service revolver pointed squarely at Stefan. "Put your hands up and move to the wall!"

In shock and surprise, Stefan looked up. "But . . ," he stammered.

"I said move," raged John, finger tensing on the trigger. Stefan stood quickly, arms to the ceiling and followed his directions. They could hear the shouting of other guards now entering the barn. Two more followed behind John, their rifles trained on Stefan.

Lorberg threw himself on his sister and daughter as the other men moved in to seize Stefan.

"Thank God I made it in time," he said, now crying himself. "I came back from the river and heard you in here."

As the guards dragged him out, Stefan tried to look back at Katherine. But as they pulled him from the barn, he saw a hurt and hatred in Katherine's eyes that he could not understand.

They hustled him from the hayloft and out of the barn. Katherine looked at her brother.

"John," she said softly, but nothing more followed. He lifted Ellen from her lap into his own arms. Katherine stood numbly and followed John out of the barn on rubbery legs as she tried to process what had just happened.

Chapter 49

Stefan sat, bound again hand and foot on the hard concrete floor in the next room down from John's office. This time one of the guards watched him intently, his rifle slung across his lap.

"I'm not making the same mistake twice," muttered John from the hallway. "Not with that bastard."

Criminy, he thought to himself. A dead camp guard plus a badly-injured prisoner who probably wouldn't pull through. And all on account of this one sick man. What had made him snap? He'd probably never know. He shuddered as he thought how close Biermann had come to also killing Ellen and Katherine, and offered another silent prayer of thanks.

In the hallway, Lorberg looked at his watch. It was almost 9 p.m. He needed to ring the main camp. It was a task he did not relish. He picked up the phone, pressing the cool black earpiece against his head.

"Fort Leonard Wood, please," he said quietly when the operator picked up. "I need to speak with the commander of the POW camp."

From the next room, Stefan could hear Lorberg talking.

"Sir, Captain Lorberg. There's been trouble here," he said in a grim voice. "Sgt. Whitcomb is dead and there is a POW on the way to the hospital. He probably won't make it."

Lorberg paused, listening to the commander.

"Yes sir, in custody." He paused. "Another prisoner. Biermann."

Stefan stiffened against the ropes, finally realizing what was happening.

"I didn't do anything!" he shouted. "Otto was my friend!"

Lorberg cupped his hand over the mouthpiece, frowning against the ranting coming from the next room.

"Shut him up, will you?" he hissed to the guard in the hall.

"Whitcomb was going to kill them!" shouted Stefan hoarsely. "I saved their lives!"

His eyes were wild as he struggled and jerked, bucking against the ropes that bound him tightly. The guard slammed the door to the hall and approached with a dirty rag in hand. He rolled Stefan over, still struggling and shouting, and knelt on his back. His knee drilling into Stefan's spine, the guard worked quickly to tie the cloth around his mouth.

All was quiet again and Lorberg returned to the conversation. "Sorry about that," he said, then paused as the colonel spoke.

"No, sir. Everything's under control," said Lorberg.

He was silent for a moment, listening to the man on the other end of the line.

"You'll be here in the morning? Yes, sir. Understood. I'll have all the details for you then."

John Lorberg hung up the phone and rubbed his eyes wearily.

"John."

He glanced up. His sister stood in the doorway.

"You can let him go," she said flatly. "What he's saying is true."

John looked at his sister, puzzled.

"What are you talking about?"

"John, he saved our lives."

"Saved your lives? I don't understand. First he attacked Otto, then he killed Whitcomb in the hayloft. You two were next."

"Listen, John. Stefan didn't kill Otto. What he told us about the smuggling was true. Leider and Whitcomb were trying to kill Otto, and frame Stefan for it because they had been found out."

A look of skepticism crossed John's face. But he listened.

"Ellen saw them go after him, so he was going to kill her too. That's what he was about to do when Stefan shot him."

She paused, and took a deep breath, trying to stifle a sob. She had to see Stefan, even if it was just for a moment. He had saved her life and deserved her thanks, yes, but she needed also to confront him about his lies. She had trusted him with her heart and he had deceived her.

"Where is he? I need to see him."

"He's next door. You can talk to him, Kat, but I'm keeping the guard on him. There's too much that doesn't make sense. And I gotta go find Leider."

She stood up, and walked to the room where Stefan was held.

"I need to talk to this man," she said. "Would you please loosen those bindings, and then give us some privacy?"

From inside the room, Stefan was overjoyed to hear her voice. Still reeling himself, he longed to try and make sense of what had happened to Otto.

"Katherine," he croaked, smiling at her as she came to the doorway. She gasped silently, her hand over her mouth, recoiling as she saw his swollen crooked nose, and the deep purple rings around both eyes that testified to the way he had been beaten. Katherine wanted to run to him, to hold him tight but again she pictured his letter to Maria on the table, and she restrained herself, using everything she had. She entered the small room and sat stiffly in the chair that the guard had occupied. She did not approach him, did not return his smile.

"Katherine, thank God you're here" said Stefan. He was still on the floor, though sitting up now against the wall, rubbing his wrists where they had been bound. "Something happened to Otto yesterday and they think I did it."

"I want to thank you for saving my life," she said first. "Yes, Otto has been badly hurt, but I told them you were not responsible. It was Leider and Whitcomb, trying to make it look like you."

She said nothing further. Stefan was puzzled by her coldness.

"Katherine, what's the matter? I didn't say a word about us. Do they know?"

She couldn't keep it in any longer.

"You said you had no one else," she said, her anger and sadness at being betrayed boiling over.

"And that's true!"

"Stefan, I saw your letter. The one you wrote two days ago," she said accusingly. "*Ich liebe dich*? I love you? Stefan, I saw it. You lied to me."

Stefan struggled, trying to figure out what she was talking about, trying to remember what he had written. "I don't . . . Katherine, I can't . . ." His head throbbed and the stammering just made it worse.

"I'm sorry I ever trusted you," she said. She shook her head sadly, hating herself for opening herself to him. "How could I have been so foolish?"

She stood, turned toward the door and left, not once looking back.

"Katherine," he called hoarsely as she headed down the hall. His head throbbed, and he felt as if he might vomit. "Katherine, wait! I don't understand."

"You can go back in," she told the guard in the hall. She looked away as she passed, but the man still saw the tears running down Katherine's cheeks as she rushed outside into the dark night.

Chapter 50

The next morning, John sat in the kitchen with his daughter in his lap. She was in her pajamas and still sleepy, but perked up as Caroline slid a plate full of pancakes in front of her and drizzled them with syrup.

Katherine stood silently, looking out the front window at the colonel's black staff car and another automobile parked by John's office. The investigators from Fort Leonard Wood had arrived early, but after a couple hours their work was nearly done and they stood next to the vehicles ready to depart.

Her heart felt cold and empty. She supposed she was glad that the true story had come out and that they no longer suspected Stefan of being a murderer, but she hated him, hated herself for what had happened between them. She couldn't believe she had been so completely taken in by him. He seemed so honest, so good. She felt a connection with him that she believed she'd never know again. And it was all a lie.

Suddenly she saw Stefan being marched from the barracks. They guided him into the back seat of one of the cars and slammed the door shut behind him.

"John, what are they doing?"

"Kat," he said slowly. "I told you this already. They're still taking him back. Even if he is innocent, he's been in the middle of too many things to stay here. It'll be too much of a disruption."

John lifted the little girl from his lap and slid out from underneath. She was so busy working on the pancakes that she hardly noticed. He went out the front door with Katherine behind him and crossed over to the cars, while Katherine remained on the porch. From there she could see Stefan slumped in the back seat of the sedan.

"You getting ready to leave, sir?"

Colonel Whiteside nodded. "But I need to talk to you, Lorberg. The whole arrangement is over. I'm shutting down the camp."

"But sir . . . ," protested John.

"Lorberg," snapped Whiteside. "It's not open for discussion. I'm giving you a week to get these men back to Fort Leonard Wood."

He nodded. He had expected this ever since calling the colonel last night.

They stepped back into the courtyard and an aide opened the car door for Colonel Whiteside.

"One more thing," said the colonel, standing with one foot in the idling car. "We talked with the hospital just now. You can tell your daughter that it seems likely the German will pull through. She's pretty close to him?"

"Yes, sir."

He nodded a farewell and climbed in the car. The vehicles idled for a minute, waiting for Leider to be brought out. Katherine crossed the courtyard to stand next to John by his office.

"What'd he say?"

John sighed. "Looks like Otto may make it. At least they've got him stabilized."

"Oh, thank God," she whispered. If the blood that soaked the truck bed was any indication of how badly he had been injured, she just didn't see how anyone could have survived.

John turned to look at her.

"And Kat, the camp is being shut down."

"No," she gasped. "We still have work to do!"

"Maybe so, but we wouldn't have had these men that much longer anyway. Our boys are in Berlin right now and the Germans can't hang on for more than a couple weeks. It's not the end of the world."

But to Katherine's heart, that's exactly how it seemed.

As they talked, Gus Davis came past with two farm hands, ready to repair John's office. They shoved the heavy desk out of the way, and picked up pieces of the broken door, long splinters that covered the floor.

Katherine glanced over at Stefan's silhouette, still motionless in the back seat of the second car. One of the men in the front jumped out and opened the rear door of the vehicle. The guards were bringing Leider from the barracks. They held him by the arms, dragging him across the courtyard.

"I didn't do it," shouted the Nazi. "I was never involved, had nothing to do with what happened to that man."

They tossed him in the back seat next to Stefan and slammed the door. With that, the vehicles slowly began the long trip back to Fort Leonard Wood.

"Hey, John," hollered Gus, poking his head from the office. He had picked up some crumpled sheets of paper from the floor. "You need this?"

He and Katherine turned to look.

"Don't know," said John. "What is it?"

"Looks like a letter. It's from that Biermann."

"What's it say?" laughed John bitterly. He was realizing that all this meant he would have to leave Ellen again soon.

"It's to some girl back home." He held up the paper in his thick fingers, lips moving slowly as he read. "Sounds like he's breaking up with her."

He read on.

"*Ich liebe dich nicht mehr.* I don't love you any more. *Ich habe eine andere gefunden.* I have found another."

Gus lowered the paper.

"What do you think of that?" He shrugged, tossing the paper in the trash and getting back to work.

His words hung in the air and Katherine stood frozen. She watched the long black automobile drive down the lane. Just before it reached the main road, Katherine saw Stefan slowly look back at her through the rear window. The sedan paused for a moment, then turned the corner and disappeared.

Chapter 51

The chatter between Gus and his helpers continued behind her as Katherine numbly turned and walked to the house. She felt like she was moving underwater. Entering the yard, Katherine saw little Ellen waiting for her on the porch. The girl was still in her pajamas, fuzzy flannel things with footies. She stood blinking at her in the bright sunlight. A well-worn teddy bear was tucked in the crook of her arm.

"Where's Otto?" she asked as Katherine approached, climbing the steps.

"Not here," Katherine replied, shaking her head. She didn't know what she could tell the girl.

"Is he still hurt?" She started to cry, big tears rolling down her cheeks and took two steps toward Katherine. Katherine swept her up, and held the little girl tightly in her arms. Ellen buried her head in Katherine's neck, and her small body convulsed again with sobbing, the trauma of what she had seen yesterday too fresh in her mind.

Still holding the girl, Katherine heard the heavy clump of John's boots on the wooden steps behind her. She turned to him for help.

"She wants to know about Otto," said Katherine.

"Don't know what to tell her." John frowned. "Just say that he'll be okay, I guess."

"Honey," Katherine tapped Ellen on the shoulder. The little girl sniffed and looked up. Her eyes were red and puffy. "Otto's gonna be just fine."

The girl looked at Katherine and then to her father. She smiled hopefully, still unsure.

"I want to see him."

Katherine and John looked at each other, eyebrows raised.

"I want to see him," she said again, more insistently.

"Oh honey, I don't know," said Katherine, shaking her head slowly.

"I want to see him," she becoming frantic again, starting to breathe hard and shake, burying her face again in Katherine's neck. She needed proof that her friend really was okay.

"What are we going to do?" Katherine asked John.

He got where he could look Ellen in the eyes. "Yes, honey," he said, "you can see Otto." Still looking into her eyes, he nodded, affirming what he said.

"What?" said Katherine, turning to look at him. "Now how are we going to do that?"

"Easy enough, Kat." John replied. "I'll be back and forth a bunch to Fort Leonard Wood as we shut things down here. We'll find a time for Ellen to go along. She can visit him in the hospital."

"Are you sure?" Katherine frowned. "The worst thing would be to get her hopes up by promising something that won't happen."

"Well, we may have to give him a couple of days to heal, but I'm certain it will work."

Katherine took hold of the girl's shoulders and pulled her back a bit so she could look her in the eyes.

"Yes, Ellen, you'll get to see Otto," said Katherine. "He's not here, so it won't be today or tomorrow, but in a few days.

Ellen smiled. "Soon?"

"Soon," said Katherine, trying to smile for the little girl.

Chapter 52

Stefan slumped against the door as the black sedan carried him back to Fort Leonard Wood. They had already traveled two hours since leaving the farm, and the green of the countryside was just a blur through his swollen eyes. A terrible throbbing pounded in his head, and Stefan felt like someone with long jagged fingernails had seized the cover of his brain and was trying to rip it in two.

From the front seat of the car, he could hear the two officers talking. Their voices sounded faint and tinny, and an echo of their words rolled through his head.

"What'd Whiteside say we're doing with these two?" asked the driver.

"Well, we're taking the SS man straight to the stockade," said the man from the passenger seat. He leaned back casually to look at Leider, who glowered back at him. "The other, I guess he's just going back to the barracks."

The man turned in his seat to look at Stefan, whose face had turned the color of ashes. Stefan's breathing came in shallow gasps, and small drops of clear fluid dripped slowly from his nose, soaking the front of his shirt.

"Cripes, Martin, will you look at him?" muttered the man to the driver. "He's not doing so good."

As the captain behind the wheel turned to look at Stefan, he saw a thin line of saliva hanging from the German's lips, trailing to his shirt. Suddenly, Stefan's chest began to heave, then he vomited a great stream of blood and bile on the fancy leather upholstery of the sleek black staff car.

"You better step on it," said the major, sitting bolt upright in the passenger seat. "We need to get him to a doctor."

The captain pressed the gas pedal hard, watching the thin white needle on the speedometer climb until it hit the top of the dial. The car shimmied and shuddered on the curvy roads but he kept the accelerator floored until they finally reached the gates of Fort Leonard Wood.

The private manning the front entrance to the post stepped from his guard shack and saluted the staff car as it approached.

"We need to get this man to the hospital," shouted the major through the window, the car barely stopping as it weaved through the gates. "Call ahead and tell them we're coming."

The guard turned and scrambled back inside. As he picked up the handset to ring the hospital, the car accelerated as it sped onward, winding through the streets of the post.

Stefan moaned as the car approached the post hospital. He could no longer see, and a crushing blackness pressed on his brain. Screeching to a stop at the front entrance, the driver ran inside to fetch a doctor, while the other man jumped out of the passenger seat and threw open the rear door. He pulled Stefan from the car, his head flopping limply forward onto his chest.

Stefan heard faint voices, felt hands lifting him from the vehicle as two orderlies transferred him to a stretcher, then rushed him inside. They took him straight to the main operating room where a surgeon waited.

Behind them, the sleek black staff car sat in the circular drive in front of the hospital's main doors. Left alone in the back seat, Karl Leider opened the car door and casually climbed out. Looking first left and then right, Leider stuck his hands in his pockets, and soon disappeared among the people coming and going around the streets of the busy post.

Chapter 53

A week passed, and Katherine tried her best to forget about Stefan. She tried to tell herself that yes, it had been a sad mistake, but she would soon get over it.

"It was like a crush," she said aloud one morning in her bedroom, trying her best to convince the woman in the mirror that things would be okay. "How can those feelings be that strong? We were together for such a short time."

Katherine let her hands drop limply to her side as the tears started to fall again. She stared at herself like she was a stranger, knowing her words had betrayed her. "*We were together.*" That said everything, and now she had lost it all.

Katherine thought back to that day she last saw Stefan. Gus and his crew had worked most of the morning repairing John's battered office. As Katherine lingered near the courtyard, it seemed that they'd never be finished.

Finally, after lunch the hammering stopped. Katherine stared dully from the front windows of the house, pulling aside the curtains to watch as the men swept sawdust from the doorway into the courtyard, dawdling in the warm sunshine.

When at last the men departed, Katherine hustled for the front door. Throwing it open, she hopped down the porch steps two-by-two, trying hard not to break into a run as she went for the office. She had to see if what Gus had read was true.

Inside it took a moment for her eyes to adjust to the darkness. The crisp smell of the sawdust hung in the air and tickled her throat. Katherine went straight for the trash can, where just a corner of the letter poked from under a pile of sawdust and wood shavings. She pulled out the sheets and shook them, trying to get rid of the sawdust that stuck stubbornly to the pages.

Her hands trembled as she unfolded the paper and read what Stefan was really telling Maria.

"Dear Maria," his tight script crossed the lined paper. Her eyes followed Stefan's message:

It's difficult for me to write . . . I'm sorry that this has to be this way, but I have to tell you something. *Ich liebe dich nicht mehr. Ich habe eine andere gefunden.* "I don't love you any more," wrote Stefan. Finally, Katherine saw it correctly, her lips moving slightly, mouthing the words as her eyes followed them on the page. "I have found another."

Her heart swelled with emotion for this man as she read, yet it ached, too, like it would burst apart completely—for she knew she had lost him forever.

"I would do anything to get him back," Katherine had murmured. She'd stood inside John's small office, the letter clutched to her chest, tears streaming down her face.

Still staring at the mirror, she was drawn back to the present by the sound of little Ellen padding in. The girl was in her pajamas, rubbing the sleep from her eyes, carrying her bear. Katherine sat on her bed and scooped the girl up in her lap, wrapping her arms tightly around her.

"Are we gonna see Otto today?"

Katherine shook her head sadly. The little girl wasn't doing so well either. She asked about Otto constantly, wandering around the house aimlessly, saying little, eating little. Katherine heard her again last night, crying in her sleep. It was the third night in a row.

It didn't help that everywhere they looked were reminders of what they had lost. Each army truck and soldier, each prisoner in his work uniform, each time they looked across the courtyard and saw the great barn – they all tore open again the wounds that had barely begun to heal.

Katherine heard heavy footsteps coming up the stairs. John appeared in the doorway in his uniform. He had been so busy the past few days with getting the camp packed and the prisoners ready to go that she had barely seen him.

John crossed the room and knelt next to Katherine and Ellen. He stroked the girl's blond hair with the back of his fingers, pushing the long locks off her cheek.

"Hello, sweetie," he said softly. The girl looked away from him, turned her face into Katherine's neck and hugged her even tighter.

John leaned back a bit and looked now to his sister.

"I have to run back to Fort Leonard Wood tomorrow morning," he said. "It's just a day trip."

John paused.

"This will be the last time before we move everyone out of here for good," he said.

Katherine knew what he was getting at. If Ellen was going to go see Otto, this was it.

"How is he?"

"They said it's going okay. He still looks pretty bad now, but he should be fine soon enough."

"And you think this is a good idea?"

"Kat, we promised her. And you've seen how she is." John stood. "I think it would be a good thing—probably even necessary—for her to see that her friend. And this will be their chance to say good-bye."

Katherine knew that she shouldn't ask about Stefan, but couldn't contain herself.

"And whatever happened to Biermann?" She tried to sound casual, but John's head snapped around. She avoided his eyes.

"Just curious," she said, briefly glancing up. "He saved our lives, you know."

"I haven't heard anything about him," he said slowly, deliberately. "I expect he's back among the prisoners, probably working in the laundry again."

John's eyes narrowed, thinking back to that day. He decided it was time to ask the question that had been on his mind.

"How was it Kat, that you were both gone at the same time? They said that you were the last person to be seen with him. But neither of you were at the vineyard."

Katherine said nothing, didn't look at her brother. The silence hung between them.

"Well," he said. He had his answer. "What's done is done."

John crossed to the door of her bedroom, then stopped one last time at the threshold as he turned to her again.

"You'll be coming along too, right?"

Katherine nodded, drawing in her breath, thinking about what this might mean. She paused for just a moment to compose herself, then raised the little girl's face from her neck.

"Tomorrow," said Katherine. "We'll see Otto tomorrow."

The little girl's eyes lit up suddenly as she understood. She squealed with delight, throwing her arms tightly around Katherine's neck again.

"And maybe Stefan, too," Katherine murmured to herself. She knew that this was foolish, that she was setting herself up for devastation once again. The chances of somehow seeing her Stefan among that crowd of 5,000 POWs sequestered at the camp and being able to talk to him were few. But even that slight possibility was enough to give her hope that somehow she'd be able to tell him that she'd been wrong and that she was sorry. She smiled at the little girl and hugged her tightly again.

Chapter 54

For a long time Stefan was only barely aware of muffled talking and a bright unfocused light that hurt his eyes. He tried to concentrate on one voice, and then another, but he lost track before he could make sense of what was being said.

He tried to lift his head to look at the people who came and went from the room. But each time he did, a rush of blackness came over him and he was gone again, for how long he did not know.

After a while, he heard a voice speaking to him softly, but insistently, saying his name again and again.

"Stefan."

It was a man's voice, calm and soothing.

"Stefan. Stefan, can you hear me?"

Stefan tried to open his eyes, to focus them on the source of the sound. A man in white stood over him framed by the light coming in from the window.

"I think he's finally waking up," the man said.

Stefan tried to raise his head from the pillow and bring his eyes in on the speaker. The man had dark hair and the metal glint of a stethoscope around his neck. That much he could see.

"Don't strain yourself," said the man. Stefan sank back on the pillow.

"That's good," he said, stepping closer. The man pressed the back of his hand against Stefan's forehead. His fingers felt cool against his flesh.

"How are you doing?"

Stefan nodded faintly, weakly. He felt very thirsty.

"I'm Dr. Behnke," he said. "I'm the one who operated on you yesterday afternoon."

Operated on? Stefan tried to speak. He wanted to ask what had happened to him. His head was beginning to throb again.

"Don't," said Dr. Behnke. "You're still very weak. Somebody really did a number on you. You were hemorrhaging in the brain when you arrived. We had to operate right away to relieve the pressure inside your skull."

The pounding in his head was increasing by the minute, and Stefan couldn't bear to keep his eyes open to look at the doctor.

"The fact that you're conscious is a good sign. If we can keep your signs stable, we'll be in good shape."

The doctor continued to talk, but Stefan heard no more as it all faded to blackness again, and he went away for a long time.

IN DER BARACKE

CAMP CLARK, MISSOURI, U.S.A.

Chapter 55

Nobody said much for the first two hours of the drive to Fort Leonard Wood. John was making a mental list of all he had yet to do to get things tied up, while Katherine's insides churned with anxiety. Ellen simply gazed out the window in wonder at all the new things that lay beyond Augusta.

After a time, John looked at his sister. She held the accordion-folded state highway map tightly in her hands. She had nearly torn the thing to shreds, ripping off one tiny piece of paper after another.

"What's eating you, Kat?" he asked, watching her hands attack the map.

His sister glanced down, surprised and embarrassed, and tried to quickly brush away the bits of paper that covered her lap. She hadn't even realized what she had done.

"Hmm," she said, "hope you still know how to get there." Katherine tried to force a laugh that convinced no one.

John looked at her.

"Seriously, sis, you all right?"

Eyes big, she nodded her head at him too fast.

"Really?" pressed John. "I mean, since this all shook out you haven't been the same."

He looked sideways at Katherine.

"You're still jumpy from the trauma, maybe," he offered.

"I guess," said Katherine, happy to have an out.

"Well, maybe this will be a good trip for you, too," said John. She glanced at him, wondering what he was getting at. John said nothing more, just kept his eyes straight ahead, focused on the road.

X

Later that morning, as they reached the gates of Fort Leonard Wood, Katherine drew a tight breath. It was time to pay attention.

Soon enough she saw the drab uniforms of the GI's standing in formation or marching on the side streets that fell away from the main road. But she was watching for a different group of men.

The hospital sat close to the front of the post, and they were there before she realized it. In the parking lot, John swung his car into the spots reserved for officers around the side of the building.

They walked toward the entrance together, but Katherine's attention was elsewhere. John watched as his sister intently scanned the people that passed on the busy sidewalk, scouring the faces for one man in particular.

The smell of antiseptic washed over them as they entered the hospital. The place was silent; other than an occasional moan or cough, most patients lay quietly in their beds. Only a few were able to turn and look at the visitors who passed.

A dozen steps down the hall, a hulking nurse in white looked up from her desk. Ellen suddenly turned shy, clinging close to her daddy's leg.

"We're here to see a patient," said John as they approached the desk. The nurse was an older woman, whose disposition had deteriorated with age judging by the sour look on her face.

"Who?" she demanded.

"Haertling. Otto Haertling," said Katherine.

The woman scowled.

"We don't have anyone by that name."

"He's a German," said John, "a POW."

The woman behind the desk frowned at them again, then muttering to herself, flipped through a clipboard full of names.

"Is there a problem, ma'am?" John leaned forward. "I'm John Lorberg, commander of the POW branch camp at Augusta. He was one of my charges."

She looked at the captain's rank on his collar and the crossed pistols of the military police that went with it.

"Hmmph," she huffed at him from her clipboard. "He's in 12A, but that's a secure ward. Normally no visitors allowed." She glanced up just in time to see them already headed down the hall.

"Sir?" she called after them. "Sir!"

"We'll just show ourselves there," called Lorberg over his shoulder as he rounded the corner into another hallway, hearing her protests growing fainter behind him.

Following the signs, John led Katherine and Ellen to 12A. A private sat just outside the door with a carbine across his lap. He leaned back in his chair, his cap pulled down over his eyes. His head was tilted back, his mouth hung open, and he snored softly as they approached.

Lorberg went to the man and stood quietly next to him. He winked at Ellen and Katherine.

"Everything secure?" hollered Lorberg in a loud voice.

"Sir!" shouted the private, jumping from his chair to stand at attention. The chair tipped backwards and clattered to the floor. The man tried to regain some semblance of coherence and military bearing, starting with his cap, which perched crookedly on his head.

"Stand at ease," chuckled Lorberg. "It's okay. We're just going to go in for a minute and see one of the Germans."

The GI relaxed just a bit, and John nodded to him encouragingly. The man responded, still embarrassed but smiling faintly. He finally fixed his hat and picked up his chair, but never took his eyes off of Captain Lorberg.

"Can you tell me where Otto Haertling is?" asked Lorberg, gesturing to the door behind him.

"Don't know, sir," said the private. "I just sit out here. Don't get much interaction with the prisoners, even to know their names. As long as there are eleven in there, I'm good."

"We'll just go in and find him," said John. He nodded at the private, and led Ellen and Katherine through the doorway into the prisoners' ward.

"Wow, it's dark in here," murmured Katherine as they entered. Thick shades blocked the afternoon sunlight that had flooded the other wards. Only a little leaked in around the edges, enough to faintly illuminate the room. They could see a dozen beds standing before them, six on a side. All were occupied except the last one on the right.

John led them slowly down the middle aisle, and they scanned the beds on either side. Where the faces were visible, they knew right away that they hadn't found Otto. For the other beds, John picked up the clipboard that hung on the foot, squinting in the darkness to read the name of the man that laid there. As the number of beds grew fewer, they wondered if the whole trip had been futile. Finally, as John read the name on the clipboard hanging on the next to last one, he saw those familiar eyes twinkling from behind the bandages that wrapped his face.

"Ellen!" came the muffled call as Otto recognized his little visitor. He tried to sit upright, but didn't quite make it before the girl jumped on him with a smile on her face that lit the whole room, and the painful "oof" she knocked from him was a happy sound for all.

"He looks pretty bad, but really, he'll be fine," said a doctor, who stepped in behind them. "Just needs some time to recover."

John and Katherine watched as Ellen joyfully reconnected with Otto, the two going on with each other as if no time had passed at all.

"Otto's going to be okay," said Ellen, beaming broadly as she looked to her father. He smiled as his daughter turned back to her friend, telling him all about the long drive and what had happened at the farm since he left. John turned and walked a couple of steps down the way. He wouldn't rush Ellen, seeing her delight at being with her friend.

Katherine came and stood next to him.

"She's really happy," Katherine said, glancing at John. "Wish I felt the same way." It had been a foolish dream, a needle-in-the-haystack kind of hunt. From the first minute they had arrived at Fort Leonard Wood, she had watched intently for Stefan and his familiar form among the groups of POWs. Of course she had seen nothing.

"How foolish I was," she thought, disgusted again for allowing herself to be so vulnerable. "Did I think that I'd just see him standing there? That I could walk right up to him and start talking?"

Katherine turned from John as a familiar lump rose in her throat. She tried to swallow it but the tears welled in her eyes. Soon it would be time to go. Desperation set in as she realized that she would likely never see Stefan again.

An orderly entered and began stripping the linens from the last empty bed, replacing them with fresh sheets.

Katherine closed her eyes and tried to block the thoughts but they still came. It was all her fault. She had a man who loved her and she blew it. Whether through stupidity or simple misfortune, she had missed her chance. And she would regret it forever.

Low voices interrupted her thoughts and she opened her eyes. Another orderly wheeled a gurney with a patient toward them, to the bed that had just been made.

"Excuse us, ma'am," said the orderly. She stepped aside, the wheels of the bed creaking faintly as it rolled past on the smooth linoleum. Like the other patients in the ward, the man in the bed was silent and still. Bandages wrapped his head and his face was turned the other way.

They rolled the cart next to the empty bed and carefully guided him in. John moved to talk to the orderlies while Katherine turned her attention back to the little girl.

Perched on the edge of the bed, Ellen still talked to Otto, telling him about the latest adventures of her dollies, but his responses didn't come so fast now. The visit had been a great pleasure for him, but he was still very weak and all the excitement had sapped his strength.

Away from the others, John spoke softly to the orderlies. "What's with this guy?" he asked, nodding to the still man in the bed.

"Just got out of surgery, sir," said the orderly before wheeling the gurney out of the room. "Bad head injury."

John picked up the folder of medical records that hung from the clipboard at the foot of the man's bed and looked for the name of the patient.

"I'll be damned," said Lorberg. He tucked the file back into its holder and glanced at his sister. She stood nearby watching Ellen, the same mournful look on her face that she had carried for the past week. He knew what he had to do.

"Katherine," he said, calling her over. As she approached, he leaned in closely and gestured to the still form in the bed. "It's Stefan."

Katherine's heart leapt in her chest. She rushed to the bed and knelt alongside, taking Stefan's cool hands into her own and leaned in close to him. Yes, it was him but his face was frightfully swollen and bruised. His eyes were closed and he breathed so lightly and slowly that his chest barely moved.

"Stefan," she whispered, her lips close to his battered cheek, speaking so softly that she could barely hear herself. She thought his eyelids might have fluttered for just a second but then he was still again.

"Stefan," she said again, this time a bit louder and Stefan opened his eyes.

"Katherine?" He tried to focus on her face, wondering if he was dreaming.

"Oh Stefan," she cried, wrapping her arms around him. Her warm tears against his cheek convinced him that she was really there and not just an apparition dancing through his pain-wracked brain.

"Katherine, what happened . . . ?" Stefan's voice trailed.

"Oh Stefan, I'm so sorry," she wept. "I misunderstood and then didn't believe you. It's all my fault. I thought I would never see you again."

"I don't know what you're talking about," whispered Stefan, only faintly remembering his confusion at her earlier distance and anger. "But that's not important. There's only one thing that is. . . do you still love me?"

"Oh God, yes, Stefan. I'll always love you." She looked at him, holding her breath, waiting for his response.

"And I love you, too," he said. He fought to stay with her but his eyes grew heavy again as he faded from consciousness.

She smiled, and for a moment watched him resting, unable to believe that she was with him again. Then John cleared his throat loudly, trying to get her attention. The doctor had reentered the ward and was flipping through a sheaf of papers as he came towards them. Katherine stood quickly, and smoothed her skirt, wiping her cheeks with the back of her hands.

"You know this prisoner, Captain?" asked the doctor, stopping at the foot of the bed.

"Yes, I do. He was at the branch camp at Augusta," replied John.

"He was in pretty bad shape when he came in," said the doctor. "Somebody beat the hell out of him." John flushed slightly. "But we fixed him up good. With some rest and therapy, he should come out just fine."

The doctor bent over Stefan's bed and checked his pupils with a flashlight. He put his head to Stefan's chest to listen to him breathe. Satisfied, the doctor turned and left the ward.

Stefan's eyes closed again after the doctor's check and he slept. While John went to Otto's bed to retrieve his daughter, Katherine leaned over Stefan again, and kissed him softly on the lips.

"Good-bye darling," she whispered to him, smiling as the tears came again to her eyes. "I'll see you soon."

She stood and stared at him for a moment more, then turned and followed her brother and Ellen from the hospital ward and back into the afternoon sunshine.

Chapter 56

On the drive home, the happiness Katherine felt at being reunited with her love ended abruptly once John turned on the radio.

"We interrupt this broadcast with an important news flash," came the announcer's tinny voice, crackling over the airwaves. "Nazi Germany has surrendered to the Allies. Members of the German military are laying down their weapons as U. S. and Russian forces announce that they've taken Berlin."

"Yes!" shouted John, pumping his fist so hard he nearly punched a hole in the cloth lining of the car's roof. "Yes!"

"Oh, John," said Katherine, her eyes filling with tears. She tilted her head toward her lap, and covered her face with her hands. Stefan would be sent back home. Just when it seemed that things might finally be good again, forces outside her control were tearing it apart.

"What?" said John, glancing over at her. "Kat, no. No. You can't be sad about this. The war is over - that great news. It means I'll be coming home. It means Michael's coming home, too."

"I know John, it's just . . ." her voice trailed off as she looked out the window.

John glanced in the rear-view mirror at Ellen who sat in the back seat quietly engrossed in a book. She was happy now that she had rejoined her friend Otto and saw with her own eyes that he was okay. And soon the sadness she would feel at Otto's leaving would vanish, recollections of their many happy days together taking its place.

John glanced at his sister again before turning them back to the road. He sighed and set his jaw. This matter with his sister and the German would have to be dealt with. Unlike Otto and Ellen, it wasn't just going to fade away, sliding into sweet memory as the days went on.

"Kat, what are you going to do?" John looked at her square on. "He has to go back to Germany, you know."

Katherine stared out the windshield. She knew that their secret was a secret no more, but it was still difficult to talk with her brother. It was obvious that he knew, but she couldn't get a handle on how he felt about it.

"I never intended for there to be anything between us." She looked sideways at John, trying to gauge his reaction. "But it all happened before I even knew it."

"Kat, it is what it is. I don't blame you, and I don't hold it against you. Could you have had better timing on this? Yes. Could you have picked someone who was not a German? Yes. But Biermann seems to be a decent guy and I know you deserve to have someone. And Lord knows we can't predict where Cupid's going to shoot those stupid arrows."

He paused, looked again at his sister. "I think I have an idea," he said carefully. "But it has to involve Dad."

"What?" she said. "We can't!"

"We must," said John, "if we have any hopes of keeping Stefan here. This is what we do . . ."

John spent the rest of the trip explaining to Katherine his idea. It was a long shot, she knew—but Katherine desperately wanted the plan to succeed and was willing to risk whatever it took to try.

✕

After dinner that night, it was time to try out their plan.

"Dad, can we speak to you in the living room, please," asked John.

Any sort of staged meeting automatically made him suspicious, and he frowned at them skeptically.

"What is it you want?" he said.

"Dad," said Katherine, "I'll get right to the point. The POWs who worked here are getting ready to leave Fort Leonard Wood. The grapes are at a crucial time. If there is any hope of saving the vineyard, we've got to find a way to keep that one German here to see the project through to the finish."

"We need you to use your connections to get him to stay back at Fort Leonard Wood," said John. "If you can get that done, I think I can have him detailed out to this farm."

Walter said nothing for a long time, just looked slowly from one to the other.

"Is this really about the grapes?" he asked, reaching into his shirt pocket. With deliberate motion, extracted Stefan's letter to Maria and laid it on the table next to him, smoothing out the wrinkles in the crumpled pages with his fingertips. Gus had brought it to him after he caught Katherine's emotional reaction to the message it carried.

"You and this German have something going on."

It was both a statement and question, and Walter looked at Katherine with eyebrows raised, seeing his daughter now as the woman she had become.

"Oh, dad, it's true," said Katherine, her chin starting to quiver. This was not going as they had planned. "I didn't mean for anything to happen."

"Katherine, for God's sake, he's a German."

"That doesn't make him some sort of savage," she said. "He's a professor back home, and only here now because he got drafted. In fact, he's the one who found out that they were stealing from us and reported it."

"What she's saying is true, dad," vouched John.

"Well," said Walter slowly, looking at his daughter, "I respect Katherine and her judgment. She has shown many times in running this farm that she's a good judge of character. She doesn't make a decision without considering things carefully."

He paused again, choosing his words carefully.

"This is a difficult situation, but Katherine, if you really feel that way about this man," said Walter finally, "who am I to go against that?"

Katherine sighed with relief. John smiled.

"There is a practical problem we still face however," he said. "They've made it real clear that the Germans have to go back home when the war is done. We can't just keep him here when all the rest are getting shipped back to Europe."

Katherine knew this, of course, but it seemed as if each step of this drama had taken a new turn at tearing her insides out.

"But Kat," continued her father, "you've been putting too much of your life into this farm. If this is meant to be, you'll be together with him again soon enough, and I'll help with that any way I can."

With that, Walt stood and went back to his office to see if he could figure out some way to make it work.

Chapter 57

With the war finished, the Germans began to depart Fort Leonard Wood almost immediately. Katherine didn't see Stefan again. When the doctor declared him stable enough to travel, he was gone from Missouri.

Month by month, she tried to get a handle on life at the farm as she sank herself again in the business. She was hopeful that she'd hear from Stefan again, but wondered about his health. And Katherine still worried that it had all been a farce. Back in Germany, might he find himself again with this Maria? She had been through too much to let herself completely trust that love was still on her side.

One day that fall, six months after the Germans had gone, the sound of a car drew Katherine's eyes to the end of the lane. It was her father, returning from a trip to town. He stopped at the mailbox at the end of the lane and then drove slowly to the house. She sat in the rocking chair on the front porch, golden sunlight all around.

John was there too, released from the army and home again with his little girl, who sat next to him on the porch swing. The farm's operations were expanding, and he had waded happily again into managing its extensive operations. He drank a glass of iced tea while the little girl read. Walter parked his car around the side of the house, and joined them on the porch.

"Katherine, you've got a letter," said Walter Lorberg, as he climbed the steps. She leaped out of the chair, and he handed her a colorful airmail envelope from Germany. As she hoped, it was from Stefan, postmarked four weeks earlier.

"Dear Katherine," it read in his neat script, black ink following closely along the narrow lines of the onionskin paper.

"I hope this note finds you well. I miss you and love you. I've remained in the hospital, but my recovery is going well and I expect to be released soon."

"This is an exciting letter to write with lots of great news, and so I'll get right to the point. Despite the restriction on immigration to the U.S., your father's influence appears to be coming through again. Because of his connections in Washington, I'm going to be able to come back to the States on a special visa sponsored by the Department of Agriculture."

She paused to look at her father, who watched her intently, then returned her attention to the letter.

"Apparently with my university credentials and experience, he's got me certified as an expert on grape growing, and I will be coming to advise farmers in the Midwest. It's all happening very fast, and if it all falls in place like it seems, I may be there very soon. In fact, I might even beat this letter to the U.S."

Katherine lowered the paper, her heart beating quickly as the emotions poured over her. She closed her eyes and covered them with her hand as she tried to take it all in.

Suddenly she heard a second set of footsteps on the porch. Opening her eyes, Katherine looked to see Stefan standing before her.

"Oh, yes, Katherine," said her father, "I didn't tell you I picked up someone else in town."

"Stefan," shouted Katherine, and she ran to him and threw her arms around him.

He embraced her tightly for a few moments, but then stopped, gently pushing her back so he could go to one knee in front of her.

"I brought you something," he said. "I have wanted to give you this since the day we met."

She looked at him with surprise and puzzlement. Taking her hand, Stefan opened his fingers slowly to expose a delicate silver ring. It had a finely etched series of intertwined grapevines that circled the ring.

"My dear Katherine," he said as he slipped it on to her finger, "will you marry me?"

"Yes," she said. "Yes."

The family watched as Stefan rose to his feet and pulled Katherine to him. The two joined in a tight embrace, together once more.

Afterword and Acknowledgements

My Enemy, My Love was an outgrowth of the non-fiction book I wrote called *The Enemy Among Us: POWs in Missouri during WWII*. That book, first published in 2003, is a history of the 15,000 German and Italian soldiers held as prisoners in two dozen camps in Missouri between 1942 and 1946. The idea for this story, however, has been around for awhile. Even going back to the very first time I learned of these stateside prisoners, I wondered about what might have taken place among people brought together unexpectedly by the war. The prisoners were in a setting which often offered a great deal of freedom as they worked on farms and factories in small towns across the state, and often with very little supervision.

My first exposure to the existence of German POWs in the United States during WWII came as a young army officer at Camp Bullis, Texas, outside of San Antonio. One warm October day as we took a break from a training exercise, I sat down on a concrete cistern cover to rest for a minute in the shade. I happened to look down and there etched in the concrete next to me were the words *"Built by the German soldiers, 1945."*

I was astounded at this. German soldiers, our enemy, there in Texas during the war itself? This seemed almost incomprehensible and I wanted to find out more. Later, black and white photos in the engineer museum at Fort Leonard Wood of German soldiers working on farms in the countryside outside the post renewed that fascination with the prisoners of war, and in particular, the 15,000 German and Italian soldiers held in Missouri. Ultimately this carried me down the path that lead to the 2003 publication of *The Enemy Among Us*, for which I received the Governor's Award for the Humanities.

This story was inspired by the multiple accounts of romance – some real, some only longed-for – that sprang up between POWs and local people, told to me in the course of my research by those who knew the prisoners firsthand.

These stories include a German who borrowed a little girl's bike to pedal off at night to visit his lover, but who gave himself away when he parked the bike just once in a different spot upon his return. And there are more. A hole in a fence and a path through a field marking the way to a woman's house whose husband worked away at night. Always forbidden and risky, these love stories happened nonetheless; yet another validation of that age-old truth that no one can be safe when Cupid starts shooting those arrows.

I owe many people thanks and acknowledgement for their assistance with this book. Dagmar Ford and Alice Jensen allowed use of the Paul Markl artwork, and I am sincerely grateful to both of them for that as his sketches add much to the book. Kate Huffman did the cover design and layout, and John F.D. Taff provided editing and proofreading services.

I am also indebted to those who offered feedback on the manuscript at various points of its evolution including Stacey Theobald Bray, Jennifer Corcoran, Haley Morrison, and Lynne Marvin. Tricia Mosser Offutt has been wonderful to me throughout all my work on the POW story. She was the editor at Missouri Life magazine who gave me the assignment to first write about it; provided wonderful feedback on *The Enemy Among Us*; and since then has read several drafts of this manuscript as I have worked on it. Marlies Mayer and Björn Dupré helped with the German expressions, and Hans Fischer, a friend and former POW held in the U.S., recounted experiences that inspired some scenes in this novel.

My parents, Leonard and Janet Fiedler and father-in-law, Rich Holtmann, also gave helpful advice, and my wife Shelly, of course, has been wonderfully supportive and patient all along. Many others helped along the way, and to those who were not mentioned, please know you have my sincere appreciation nonetheless.

Finally I want to remember my friend Kevin Wade (1963-2008), who was an encouragement to me in this and many other things. To him along with my children, Aaron and Lauren, this book is dedicated.

David Fiedler
September 2011

About Paul Markl

This book contains several pieces created by Paul Markl, a German prisoner
of war in the Missouri from 1944 through 1946. He was a gifted artist who
created a remarkable collection during his time in the American POW camps.
Markl frequently gave his work to others or bartered it for chocolate, cigarettes
or other desirables, a common and legitimate second economy that existed in
every POW camp. His pieces ended up with fellow prisoners or the Americans
around him, the military personnel or civilian workers at the camp. Viggo
Jensen was one of these. An older man with a family, Jensen was assigned
stateside duty as an MP with the German prisoners after being drafted. He
and Markl spent time together at a number of camps like the ones in this
book as they worked in locations around the Midwest following the need for
agricultural labor. After the war, Jensen came home with several Markl pieces,
some of which appear in this book. Additionally, Markl often dedicated pieces
specifically to prisoners he considered his friends. They marveled at the way he
captured the images and feelings from their own lives in the camp, and recalled
with great pride their association with Markl. These men saved Markl's work,
and took the sketches and paintings home with them after the war.

That Markl's work has survived for more than sixty years is a testament
to the accuracy with which he captured camp life with his sketches, and to the
strength of the bonds he formed with his fellow soldiers in the camps, Germans
and Americans alike.

About the author

 David Fiedler graduated from Washington University in St. Louis with majors in German and Political Science, and served eight years as an officer in the U.S. Army Reserve. He is the author of four books to date, including the award-winning history of Missouri's WWII prisoner-of-war camps called *The Enemy Among Us: POWs in Missouri During World War II*.

Photo by William Goetz

Praise for *The Enemy Among Us:*

"POWs in Missouri? With orchestras, theaters, and libraries? Who knew? Thanks to David Fiedler for making this almost untold connection between World War II and the Midwest!"
– Charles Brennan, KMOX Radio, St. Louis

"David Fiedler provides us with a fascinating look at a seldom-examined facet of World War II and, in the process, gives us a fascinating look at ourselves during those times."
– General John W. Vessey, Former Chairman, Joint Chiefs of Staff

"David Fiedler's book not only lays out the facts of the camps, their dates, numbers of prisoners and what the men did but also, more tellingly, recounts the stories from the human angle. These prisoners of war worked in the corn and cotton fields, swam in local pools an impacted the lives of the people in the towns where they were held."
– From nomination endorsement, Governor's Award for the Humanities

"A POW study about Missouri is long overdue."
– Dr. Arnold Krammer, author of *Nazi Prisoners of War in America*

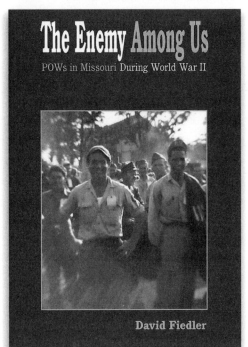

"Fiedler's work is a fascinating discussion of the POW situation in Missouri during World War II... He maintains a balanced view of the prisoners and their captors, and presents both sides of an uncomfortable situation with grace and style."
– Paul Springer, PhD, Texas A&M University

www.mopows.com

CONTACT AND ORDERING INFORMATION

Books may be ordered at http://www.mopows.com, or by using this page

PLEASE SEND

_____ copies of *The Enemy Among Us:*
POWs in Missouri During World War II @ $29.95
Hardcover, 460 pages with 110 maps, photos and illustrations.
Non-fiction.

_____ copies of *My Enemy, My Love* @ $16.95
Paperback, 272 pages, including illustrations. Fiction

Best value – both books $37.95

_____ Total amount owed

Shipping and taxes included for all domestic U.S. orders.
Prices subject to change without notice.

YOUR INFORMATION:

NAME: _____

ADDRESS: _____

ADDRESS2: _____

CITY, STATE, ZIP: _____

PHONE: _____

EMAIL: _____

SEND PAYMENT TO:

ENEMY
10709 Roxanna Drive
Saint Louis MO 63128-1621

For information on arranging a speaking engagement, bulk orders or other special
arrangements, please call (314) 956-7353, or email MoPOWs@aol.com.